This was exactly what he wanted to avoid!

When Karl walked through the doorway to his apartment at eleven o'clock on Friday, he found Vivian sitting on a dining chair in the entryway, reading *What To Expect When You're Expecting*. He should have known it had been too much to hope that he could dodge her for eight months.

"Good evening, Karl." She rested the book on her lap and looked up at him. "Have you been avoiding me?"

It sounded cowardly when she put it like that. He stared at the curve of her bottom lip over her pointed chin. soft over sharp, and he had to stop himself from running his thumb over the bow. He didn't have to be drunk to be susceptible to the arcs of her face, but he needed to remember that she was only temporary. The baby was permanent, but Vivian was fleeting.

"I work a lot." It came out like a defense.

"Well, you're home now and I'm still up so we can finally talk."

Dear Reader,

Jo Beverley has a post on the blog *Word Wenches* where she talks about the marriage-of-convenience trope, calling it "vows before love." This trope appeals to Beverley because the vulnerability of the heroine required for the story shows her strengths to the fullest effect. (Beverley compares this to a thriller where the hero starts out trapped.) To me, this is Vivian in a nutshell. When the book opens, there is little more in her life she can lose, and we see her battle her fears, weakness and, occasionally, her husband to become a fuller, stronger person.

Karl has a different journey to take. If you've read the other two books in the Milek series (*Reservations for Two,* February 2013, and *The First Move,* April 2013), then you know Karl is a bit uptight and a serial dater. Finding the perfect match for him was hard; my laptop is full of first chapters where Karl meets a heroine who is great—but not for him. It took me several tries before I realized Karl needs someone to challenge his preconceived notions about himself and the world, without shaking him loose from his core. Love stories work best when we have to push ourselves to be worthy of our beloved.

If you're interested in Vivian's background and family in the novel, I recommend Iris Chang's *The Chinese in America: A Narrative History.*

Enjoy!

Jennifer Lohmann

JENNIFER LOHMANN

—

A Promise for the Baby

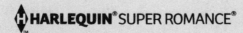

HARLEQUIN® SUPER ROMANCE®

Recycling programs
for this product may
not exist in your area.

ISBN-13: 978-0-373-60822-5

A PROMISE FOR THE BABY

Printed in U.S.A.

ABOUT THE AUTHOR

Jennifer Lohmann is a Rocky Mountain girl at heart, having grown up in southern Idaho and Salt Lake City. After graduating with a degree in economics from the University of Chicago, she moved to Shanghai to teach English. Back in the United States, she earned a master's in library science and now works as a public librarian. She was the Romance Writers of America librarian of the year in 2010. She lives in the Southeast with a dog, five chickens, four cats and a husband who gamely eats everything she cooks.

Books by Jennifer Lohmann

HARLEQUIN SUPERROMANCE

1834—RESERVATIONS FOR TWO
1844—THE FIRST MOVE

Other titles by this author available in ebook format.

To big brothers everywhere, especially mine.

CHAPTER ONE

VIVIAN SAT ON an uncomfortable chair in the starkly decorated lobby of her husband's apartment building and waited for Karl to come home from work. She'd been waiting for hours, her feet propped up by a couple of suitcases, garnering suspicious looks, but the doorman hadn't kicked her out yet. He'd tried, but she had a marriage certificate that said she was Karl Milek's wife. Unwilling to throw her out onto the street, he'd also been unwilling to let her into Karl's apartment.

She was pretty sure he was regretting both decisions. At least Xìnyùn, her father's blue parrot, had stopped talking an hour ago. His chipper conversation wasn't welcome in this modern building and his brightness was an unwanted distraction in the white-and-black interior.

Every time someone came through the rotating doors, the February winds whistled and Xìnyùn responded with his own tune, dancing up and down the rainbow ladder in his cage. Not a single person who'd walked past had smiled at Xìnyùn's antics. Her husband lived in a building as cold as his hands.

She had called his office five times, but "he is in a meeting," they said. "We will pass on the message," they said. She didn't tell them she was his wife. With divorce terms agreed upon, he probably hadn't told his coworkers about his Vegas mistake. He'd probably figured—as she had—that their secret would keep until the divorce was finalized, and then it wouldn't matter anymore. They'd be divorced and have moved on with their lives. But now she needed him, and she needed him to be her husband. Outing him to his coworkers seemed a poor way to gain his cooperation.

What happens in Vegas stays in Vegas.

She was supposed to have stayed in Vegas.

The energy in the lobby flared when her husband walked through the door. He was the cold, stiff man she remembered from their morning after, and he didn't seem to be any warmer with all of his clothes on—and *not* hungover. Maybe he didn't notice the freezing temperatures outside. He wore a forest-green scarf wrapped around his neck and a tan wool coat as though they were for show, so the people around him wouldn't wonder at his ability to walk through snow naked and not get frostbite. No hat covered his brown hair. His hazel eyes were more attractive when not bloodshot, but glasses didn't soften the sharp planes of his face. She had assumed his face only looked hard when angry—but he didn't have a reason to be angry. Yet.

She needed Karl to be the man whose eyes had been mostly brown when he'd offered to buy her a drink, but had turned a lush green when she'd brushed her hand against his as she reached for that drink. The man who'd noticed her shiver and tucked her tightly against him as they walked out of the hotel, even though they had both known she wasn't cold. The man who had made her laugh when she felt as if nothing in her life could ever be funny again.

Perhaps that man had been an illusion and as fake as the Luxor pyramid, given flesh only by the carnival lights of Las Vegas. That she was even sitting here in the lobby of this apartment building was evidence that she wasn't as immune to Las Vegas magic as she thought she'd been.

The doorman scurried over to her husband, his arms out in supplication and face creased in apology. Tingles shot down her spine when Karl looked over at her. He showed no hurry as he walked across the lobby to her, his face as blank as she remembered.

"You were the woman calling my office today," he said in greeting.

"Hello to you, too." They hadn't planned on seeing each other again, but there was no reason not to be civil. In theory, theirs was an amicable divorce. "Can we talk somewhere private?"

His eyes took in the pile of suitcases and the

birdcage sitting next to them. He didn't nod or say a word, just picked up the birdcage and a suitcase and walked toward the elevator. Vivian scrambled to her feet, slung her purse over her shoulder, picked up two more suitcases and hurried to follow him, the heels of her boots clicking on the marble floor.

On the elevator ride up to his apartment, Vivian opened her mouth a couple times to speak, but Karl silenced her with a raise of his eyebrow. "You wanted private. We can at least wait until we are in my apartment."

She closed her eyes and nodded. She'd waited for hours; another couple of minutes wasn't going to kill her.

In his apartment, she put down her suitcases in the entryway and followed him to the couch, taking the birdcage with her. Dark wood floors made his apartment more welcoming than the lobby, though his furniture looked to be just as uncomfortable. The only sign of softness amidst the leather, glass, steel and stone was a plush rug in the living room. He didn't even have any curtains to soften the floor-to-ceiling windows. She sat on the couch. He sat in one of the armchairs and looked at her expectantly.

If she was waiting for a greeting of some kind, apparently she would be disappointed.

"I'm sorry to drop in on you like this," she said,

gesturing to the luggage near the door. "I didn't feel I had any choice."

"Were the terms of our divorce not sufficient?" His elbows rested on the arms of the chair and he'd laced his fingers together in a bridge over the chest of his charcoal-gray suit. Anyone looking in on the scene through the windows would see Karl's cocked head and casual pose and imagine they were discussing some local curiosity. Vivian imagined that he must have soon-to-be ex-wives drop in on him as a regular occurrence if he managed to remain so self-possessed about the whole thing.

His absolute composure was the reason she'd answered "sure" when he'd gestured to the doors of the chapel, a half smile on his face, and asked, "Shall we?" She had *wanted* to be a part of his stability then; it was unfair of her to be irritated by it now. And what if she also wanted the passion they'd shared? Well, that had gotten her into this mess in the first place.

"Yes. I mean, no, they were fine. But I don't want a divorce right now."

If she'd shocked him, his only reaction was to lean back in the chair and lift his left foot to rest on his knee. She was glad he hadn't sat on the couch next to her. She felt crowded enough by him without having to make room for his knees and elbows— *and* his infinite placidity, which took up far more space than any single lack of reaction should.

Xìnyùn said, "I fold." At least the parrot showed a reaction.

"I'm pregnant and I want to keep the baby."

"Hɪᴛ ᴍᴇ," ᴛʜᴇ bird squeaked.

Karl looked at the blue bird dirtying his coffee table and wondered what was more ridiculous, his one-night stand/wife telling him she was pregnant or the bird asking to be punched.

If this was his punishment for indulging his emotions with liquor, he would pour every ounce of booze in the apartment down the toilet and shatter the wineglasses. Unfortunately, humoring his impulses was unlikely to allow time to flow backward until he walked into his apartment building and passed through the lobby up to his apartment without a wife—pregnant wife—in the way.

"Are you sure you're pregnant?" Three weeks ago—his birthday—he'd sat at a hotel bar and gulped down whiskey every time he remembered he was older than his father ever had been or would be, only without a wife or child. Now he had both, and he didn't want either of them. "Are you sure it's mine?"

"Yes, I'm sure. About both questions. I don't make a habit of sex with strangers." A series of rapid blinks over her light brown eyes—barely a shade darker than her skin—were evidence of her nerves, but she didn't shrink away from him. She was on a mission and determined to see it through.

"I don't know anything about you other than you *did* once have sex with a stranger." And her maiden name was Yap. He'd learned that from the marriage certificate he'd found under some tiger lilies on a table in his hotel suite.

"I wasn't the only one in that room."

No, but he wished to God the man in the hotel room had been someone other than himself. His office was in the middle of a sole-source contract investigation; he didn't have time for whatever she needed from him. "If the only thing you know about me is that I also did once have sex with a stranger, then I assure you, if you are pregnant with my child, I can change the terms of the divorce. You'll get sufficient child support."

"No argument about my keeping the baby?"

He swallowed his irritation. The night they'd stumbled around Las Vegas now seemed like a mirage, and if he concentrated on his memories, the images wavered before disappearing completely. The alcohol and the lights had made every smile the secret smile of a lover, and when she'd slipped her hand into his, he'd felt as though they'd shared souls. *Also the alcohol talking.* The alcohol and being surrounded by the constant—fake—sounds of people winning had turned him into a man charming enough to pick up a woman in a bar.

Vivian would soon learn that the man who had made jokes and removed the sadness from her eyes didn't exist outside of that night in Vegas.

But she'd taken a chance coming here. She couldn't know for certain that he'd meant what he said when he'd spoken about the responsibility a man had to his family. Or that he would never argue about an abortion with a woman, because her body was her body and his faith was his faith.

That night she had also talked about the importance of family—had argued with him when he had referred to a "man's responsibility to his family." Every member of a family, she'd said, had responsibility for keeping the unit whole. She'd squeezed his thigh when she'd said that, probably more to make her point than out of any sexual advance, though he hadn't had the wits about him to care either way.

Were the opinions she'd expressed about family a product of the night—as his sudden charm had been—or were they as heartfelt as his words, alcohol or no alcohol? It didn't matter. She was pregnant and he'd learn about her dedication to family soon enough.

"I respect your choice, though you don't need to be here in Chicago for me to send you child support."

She drew back in surprise, covering her jeans and still-flat stomach with a hand. "You wouldn't want contact with our baby?"

He thought about the tiny infant she would give birth to. With its small fingernails and fat face not yet grown into Vivian's pointed chin. Food poisoning. Croup. The shattered glass of a car accident ripping a dimpled face to pieces. Better not to see the child at all. Better to get them both out of his apartment and back to Las Vegas.

"I would want to know you cared for it." Him? Her? When could you find out the sex of the baby? What was he supposed to call it until then?

She folded her other hand over her stomach. There was a baby under there. "I need health insurance."

"You said you had a job." Back in his hotel room, when he'd been sober, and the harsh lights of the hotel bathroom had ripped the dream away, he'd accused her of marrying a stranger for money. She'd told him to keep his damn money and that maybe there was room for it wherever he stored his ego. She'd said she had a job and didn't need to have sex in exchange for handouts.

"I lost it." She kept her hands on her stomach, the twisting of her fingers another sign of her nerves. "I will find another—I was hoping to find one in Chicago—but until then, I need health insurance. The baby needs health insurance. I have no other place to go."

Karl did some quick math in his head. They still

had four days to get Vivian and the baby on his health insurance. "I'll need the marriage certificate."

"Just like that?"

"Double," the bird squeaked, then whistled.

"Do you want health insurance?" At one time in the distant past, he'd thought he understood women. Exposure had cured him of such idiotic thinking.

"Yes, but, you didn't say so much as 'hi' to me downstairs. You accuse me of trying to sell you a pig in a poke, insinuating I'm some kind of slut who bangs tourists for fun, but when I say I need health insurance for a baby you don't believe is yours, you say 'sure'?"

"Even if that baby isn't mine, you should have insurance while you're pregnant. And you *are* my wife. If the baby is mine, I can provide it with health insurance and child support. If it's not mine, I can provide it with health insurance until you are able to provide for it yourself. I won't force a fetus to get less care than I can provide because I don't trust its mother."

"I can get a DNA test done while pregnant, as early as the ninth week."

"Where are you staying?"

She turned her head to look out the windows of his apartment, the first time she'd not been willing to meet his eyes since he had walked into the lobby of his building. "I was hoping to stay here."

"You don't have another place to go?"

She faced him again, the pertness of her chin softened by her full, pale pink lips. How had he not remembered the lushness of her lips? "I have ten dollars, three suitcases and a parrot to my name."

"Family?"

"They're not available."

When he'd considered her presence punishment for his behavior, he'd lacked the imagination to envision how the situation could get worse. If mother and child needed medical care, they also needed a roof over their heads. Not to mention the little bird she called a parrot. Chicago had enough wild parakeets without him adding to the population.

"What did you do in Las Vegas?"

"I wasn't a prostitute."

Any twinge of guilt he'd felt over accusing her of that the morning he'd woken up married to a stranger had long since vanished. Three weeks ago he'd hurled accusations at her, but he hadn't asked what she actually did. He wasn't going to ask more than once now. If he was silent long enough, she would share. She needed a place to stay and didn't know him well enough to know he'd offer her a bed regardless.

She blinked first. "I was a table dealer. Craps, blackjack, roulette."

God, how much had he had to drink to take her up to his room? At least she wasn't a stripper.

"At Middle Kingdom?" His assistant had booked

him a room at the Chinese-themed resort instead of the conference hotel. Greta had thought it would be good for him to have a minivacation—her words. But he'd ignored the brochures about the Hoover Dam and Grand Canyon she'd tucked into his work papers in favor of overpriced hotel whiskey. If he'd listened to Greta, he would've come back with a couple of postcards instead of a wife.

Though postcards wouldn't have looked nearly as pretty sitting on his couch in a pink cable-knit sweater and cowboy boots.

Thoughts like that had prompted him to engage Vivian in conversation, to fall under the spell of her mysterious smile and be hypnotized by the rise and fall of her breasts when she breathed. If all he'd done was invite her up to his room, the night in Las Vegas would make more sense, but he'd been thinking about marriage and families, and in his drunken haze had decided he wanted to wake up with her warm skin pressed against his for the rest of his life.

Reality had intruded the next morning and, almost a month later, was sitting on his couch.

"And you're not working there anymore because…"

"My supervisor disagreed with a decision I made."

"Was I your decision?" She wouldn't have been

the first woman unfairly fired because of sex, and she wouldn't be the last.

She turned her head to look out the windows again. An effective nonanswer, which he let go for now. She was—the fetus was—his responsibility for another eight months. He'd get his answer eventually.

"I have a guest bedroom. You can sleep there for now."

She closed her eyes, the light pink of her eye shadow sparkling in the lamplight, and exhaled. The wool of her sweater must be stiffer than it looked, because even though she went boneless with relief, she didn't sink into the back of the couch. "Thank you."

"Have you eaten dinner?"

"I'm fine."

He took that as a no and didn't ask how long it had been since she'd eaten. The worry lines at the corners of her eyes said it had been too long. "What do you like?"

"I'm fine," she said again, as though hoping if she said it enough times he would believe her. Or maybe she hoped to believe it herself.

Karl stood and walked over to the small table in his entryway. He riffled through the menus in the drawer until he found the one he was looking for, then he handed it to Vivian. "Pick out what you want."

She looked up at him, one thin black eyebrow raised. "Chinese?"

He ignored the uncomfortable reference. "They have the fastest delivery."

"Buddha's vegetable delight. Brown rice, please."

"Soup? Egg rolls?"

Her stomach growled, betraying the casual look on her face and making a lie of her insistence of being "fine." How long had those ten dollars been all she had to her name? Had she had no savings? All things he could learn tomorrow, after she'd eaten and had a good night's sleep. He called in her order and his, adding enough extra food to give them leftovers for days. He didn't know if she could cook, and he sure as hell didn't. If not for takeout, the baby might starve.

"Let's get your bags put in the guest room."

FOR ALL ITS personality, the guest room might have been in a hotel. There was less glass and more wood than in the living room, but that was because the single piece of furniture in the room was a large, wooden platform bed with a built-in nightstand. The bedspread wasn't white or black, so Karl must at least know color existed, but the geometric pattern and primary colors didn't invite Vivian to snuggle. Still no curtains. What did this man have against curtains?

"There's a dresser in the closet."

"Thank you." *Thank you for acknowledging I might be here longer than just tonight.* "Is there something I can put Xìnyùn's cage on?"

"Who?"

"The parrot's name is Xìnyùn. It means luck in Chinese."

He eyed the cage sitting on the floor. Xìnyùn eyed him back nervously. "Are you sure it doesn't mean bad luck?"

She picked the cage up off the floor and opened the closet doors to find the dresser to set the cage on. Parakeets didn't like humans to loom over them and Karl loomed as naturally as most people breathed.

"Double," Xìnyùn whistled in approval.

She was pregnant, unemployed and homeless. Her father had fallen off the face of the planet and taken her life savings with him. Xìnyùn, at least, was happy to be off the floor. "At this point, I'm not sure of anything."

He nodded, left the room for a moment and returned with a small table. "Here's a table for the bird." He had his hand on the doorknob, about to leave the room, when he turned back to face her, his eyes in shadow and his expression unreadable. "How did you get to Chicago?"

"I drove." As her gas gauge edged toward empty and the ten dollars felt lighter and lighter in her pocket, she'd turned the dial on her radio until she found a country music station and Carrie Underwood singing "Jesus, Take the Wheel." She hadn't run out of gas, even if she had coasted into Chicago on wishes and a prayer.

"Where's your car?"

She described where it was parked.

"Give me your keys and I'll move it into the garage. I'll leave money for dinner with the doorman and bring it up when I return." Without so much as a goodbye, he closed the door, leaving her alone with the skyline.

Inviting or not, all she wanted to do was curl up on the bed and sleep until the nightmare of her life was over and she woke up single, employed and not pregnant. Impossibilities. Time didn't travel backward.

She picked up one suitcase and hefted it over to the closet, which—except for the dresser and some hangers—was completely empty. Karl didn't accumulate crap. Or, if he did, he didn't store it in the closet of his guest bedroom. The room gave her nothing to judge her husband by, other than that his decorating sense was as cold as his hands and as lacking in expression as his face.

No, she was being unfair. She opened a small drawer and shoved underwear in. He'd invited her—a near stranger, no matter that the marriage certificate said otherwise—to stay in his home. He was moving her car and buying her dinner. And the morning she'd woken up naked in a hotel room with him calling her Vivian Milek and asking her if she was a prostitute, he'd handed her a cup of coffee and gotten her a robe.

Maybe he wasn't as unfeeling as his language and his composure made him seem.

She tossed some hangers on the bed and unpacked the rest of her clothes. When she was finished, she turned back to the other suitcase on the floor. Even if she'd wanted to unpack her mementoes, there wasn't a flat surface in the room to hold them. She shoved the last suitcase, without bothering to open it, into the closet and shut the door on her past.

Too melodramatic, Vivian. You just don't want it to look like you're moving in.

CHAPTER TWO

KARL RETURNED TO the apartment later than he'd planned. Her little convertible had been easy enough to find. It'd been parked exactly where she'd said it would be and the Nevada plates gave away that it was hers. So had the pile of fast food containers on the floor of the passenger side. The blankets and pillows in the backseat had been a surprise. As had the empty gas tank. He'd thrown the trash away when he'd filled up her tank. The blankets and pillows he'd left in the backseat, though he'd left them folded rather than in a heap.

Riding up the elevator with bags of Chinese food and a growing sense of unease, he prepared to face his wife.

Vivian had set the table he never used with the place mats, white cotton napkins and flatware he also never used. Jessica, his ex-wife, had bought them. She hadn't taken them with her when they'd divorced. Neither had she taken the apartment nor the BMW. All were status symbols he was certain she'd considered more important than their marriage, but not important enough to possess after the divorce was final. An indication, he'd felt when he'd signed the divorce papers, of the low regard in which she had held their marriage.

Time allowed him to be more generous with his reflections. Marriage to him hadn't given Jessica anything she'd really wanted, so why keep the trappings? Leaving the flatware, china and linens in the apartment with her ex-husband, she was free to start fresh.

He wondered if Vivian had been married before. Did she have an apartment, friends or a book club? Why had she estranged herself from her life to drive halfway across the country in search of an unknown husband? After setting the bags of food on the counter, he looked around the room for her. He could learn the answers to his questions later. Eventually, people always told him the information he wanted.

Just as he determined that the living room was empty, he noticed Vivian leaning against the rail on his terrace, looking north over the skyline of Chicago. With the room lit up against the dark night sky, Karl could only make out contours of her slim body. When he turned off the lights in the living room, her form gained substance. She reached up with her arm, pulling her hair off her neck and over her shoulder, exposing skin to the cold.

The night they'd spent together existed in a dream world, but his memories of the morning after were clear and sharp. He remembered waking up to find her sleeping, her black hair spread across the pillow and her neck exposed. He remembered looking at the knobs of her spine as they trailed from her nape down her back and under the covers. How kissable those knobs had looked. But then he'd gotten out of the bed to make coffee, found the marriage certificate and any thought of kissing her neck was gone.

Stepping outside into the cold pushed away those memories. They were married, she was in Chicago, and kissing the slim line of her neck had never been further away from possible. "Do you have a winter coat?"

She was standing outside in jeans, her sweater and pink argyle socks. "I'm not cold."

Even in the hazy moonlight he could see goose bumps dotting her neck, but she didn't shiver or tuck her hands around her body for warmth.

"I bought the apartment for this view," he said, folding his arms on the railing of the terrace and leaning forward to look out over the city with her.

"What are the names of some of the buildings?"

He pointed out the Aon Center and Smurfit-Stone Building. "If you're still here in the summer, maybe you can go on an architecture boat tour. Or they have walking tours year-round."

"You don't have curtains."

"No." Removing the curtains was one of the few changes he'd made when Jessica had moved out.

"Not even in your bedroom?"

"I value openness."

"You should come west."

"I've been to Vegas." He slid closer to her on the terrace. Not so close that their arms touched, but close enough to feel her presence. She still smelled like jasmine.

"Not Vegas. Vegas is the flashy west. I mean southern Idaho, where you can see for miles in every direction and there's nothing but sky and canyons."

"Is that where you're from?"

"I graduated high school in Jackpot, Nevada. It's right across the border."

He'd married a blackjack dealer from a town called Jackpot. The world had an unfortunate sense of humor. "It would've been a shorter drive from Vegas to Jackpot."

She turned her head to the side to look at him, the corners of her mouth turned up in a mysterious smile. "Shorter, yes, but there's nothing for me in Jackpot. Plus, it would be wrong not to let you know you're going to be a father."

"A phone call would've sufficed."

"Would you want to learn that you're going to be a father with a phone call from a stranger?" She didn't slip again and admit to not being able to go home, as she had when they'd been talking in the living room.

He didn't have an answer to that question. If asked this morning, he would've said yes. Now, standing next to Vivian on his terrace, looking at the lights sparkle across Grant Park and smelling her jasmine perfume, he wasn't so sure. Her neck was even more kissable up close.

"Dinner's getting cold." He pushed off the railing and walked back into the apartment, not looking to see if she followed.

KARL WASN'T MUCH for words, Vivian thought, as she picked up the plates after dinner. They were strangers, sure, but they were *married* strangers who were having a child together. Even after they finalized the divorce, they would still have a child to raise together. The least they could do during the next eight months was to get to know each other.

But based on his terse responses over dinner, he didn't agree. She heaped the utensils on the stacked plates and took them into the kitchen. When she turned, he had followed with the cups and trash.

"I'll get those." She took the glasses from his hand and loaded them into the dishwasher. "Don't worry about the plates," she said when he started rinsing them. "Go sit down. I'll clean up."

"I'm not letting you stay here so you can clean up after me." He didn't stop rinsing the plates, but did let her load them into the dishwasher. He had rolled up his shirtsleeves before turning on the water, and light brown hair dusted his forearms.

She blinked, uncomfortable after catching herself staring at his arms. The plates clinked against one another as she used a little too much force to close the dishwasher.

"I know, but..." She didn't want to finish that statement.

"But?"

But I'm here because we had a one-night stand and I got pregnant, and we were drunk when we got married and I now need help and you're giving it to me and I don't know how long I'll need the help and I don't know how long you'll offer the help and I wish you'd let me clean up after dinner. Her insecurities nearly pushed her down as they flooded over her, but all she said was, "I'm happy to help out."

He nodded before grabbing a sponge and leaving to wipe down the table. He wasn't nodding because he knew she was happy to help out. She could feel in his intense hazel eyes that he knew what she had left unsaid. He knew she would act as maid in a poor attempt to make up for invading his life. He knew and he still went to clean the table.

She knew very little about her husband. Their night together had been his last day in Vegas, and their conversation over breakfast had been about the details of a divorce. The next day she'd received a phone call from a lawyer saying he represented Karl Milek and they would pursue a divorce according to Nevada laws. When could she come by his office? Did she have her own lawyer? No? Did she need time to find one?

Like all things in Nevada, getting out of the trappings of your sins was far more complicated than getting into them.

Karl's efficiency had intrigued her enough that she'd done an internet search on him. After reading newspaper articles, exploring his office's website and watching snippets of televised news stories, she'd felt as though she had a sense of who this man was. But now she realized every movement he made, everything he said, was carefully constructed to give the illusion of revelation without actually revealing anything. Not that any of that had been important to her at the time.

Then she'd gone home to an apartment emptied of anything of value and a note containing an apology from her father folded on the kitchen counter. When she had checked her bank account she'd found every penny she had carefully saved was gone. Then she had missed her period, and by that point it had been too late for Plan B. She hadn't even had enough money for an abortion, if she had decided to go that route, anyway. Then she had been fired, and suddenly the most important thing in the world was that her husband seemed to be the kind of person who fixed problems.

Their marriage had been a problem, and he was going to fix that. Now her pregnancy was the problem, and his magical fix had smoothed away the practical, immediate problems of that, too. She didn't want to have to rely on him, but she couldn't predict what help she would need after the baby was born—or what he would be willing to provide.

Once the activity of cleaning up after dinner was done, they were left with nothing to do but face each other and feel awkward. At least, Vivian felt awkward. She had the sense that Karl could have a fox eating out his stomach under his shirt and his face wouldn't reveal any pain. How drunk had he been to indulge himself in a feeling as human as lust? What else had been going on in his life that he'd allowed himself to get that drunk?

"Well—" she clapped her hands together "—I'm beat." She was no such thing. Wired and punchy would be a more accurate description of how she felt right now. "Do you have a book I could read before I fall asleep?"

"I thought you said you were beat."

She opened her mouth to respond but he'd already left the kitchen. He returned with *Mr. Midshipman Hornblower,* as well as *Gerard Manley Hopkins: The Major Works* and a military history of World War I.

"A selection," he said, holding them out to her. Not a muscle had changed in his bland expression, but Vivian was pretty sure he was amused with himself for his offerings.

"Thank you." She'd hoped for a mystery or thriller, but lying in bed with one of these books would help her fall right to sleep. "I'm sure I'll learn something."

KARL WOKE EARLY the next morning to a dark, silent apartment. Not even the ridiculous bird was making any noise. He pulled his boxers on and went into the kitchen to make coffee. When he didn't hear any noise in his guest bedroom after the coffee grinder whirled, he cracked the door open to check on his guest. She was lying on her side, facing the door, the Keegan book on World War I flopped over her hand. The down comforter covered any rise and fall of her chest and he was about to check her pulse when she snorted and twitched before settling down again. Vivian wasn't dead, and she hadn't run off.

It looked like she'd made it halfway through the book before finally falling asleep. Despite its appearance, the Keegan book was unlikely to bore someone to sleep. He eased the door shut and went to get himself a cup of coffee. In the kitchen, he found a travel mug for Vivian to keep her coffee warm and poured her a cup, as well. Last night, before bed, he'd read a little about pregnancy—he was glad he'd had decaf in the freezer—and he remembered how grateful she'd been when he brought her coffee that one time in their Vegas hotel room. But when he went back into the guest bedroom to put the coffee on the nightstand, she still didn't stir.

When he had awoken in the hotel room a month ago to find himself married, he'd assumed her deathlike sleep had been due to alcohol. She hadn't seemed hungover—God knew he'd been too bleary-eyed and angry to notice if she had been—but she'd slept until he'd yelled her name and shaken her awake. This morning she seemed on course to do much the same. The bird stirred in its cage behind a cover, but Karl ignored it. Even if the bird was awake, he had no idea what to do with it unless it also wanted a cup of coffee.

It. The bird had a name. Luck, only not luck. Whatever was Chinese for luck. He still didn't know if the bird was male or female.

And the bird was probably easier than a baby. Not that he hadn't planned on having children. He had. One day. He'd just expected a little warning and time to read every baby book the Harold Washington Library had on its shelves before hearing the words, "I'm pregnant."

He turned his attention back to the mother of his child. Though he believed she was telling the truth about who the father was, he'd still insist on a DNA test. He believed her, but he wasn't stupid.

Yet looking at her sleeping, the test felt like a formality. The mother of his child slept on her side and snorted in her sleep.

Karl was surprised how much her sleeping in his guest bed pleased him. He thought he'd been pleased when his divorce lawyer had confirmed she didn't protest the divorce or the terms. That feeling was nothing like the warmth in his heart at seeing the contrast of her black hair against the primary colors of the duvet cover.

Before he left for the gym and office—both to work and to investigate his wife—Karl checked his laptop to make sure she wouldn't find anything personal on it, and then he wrote her a note.

VIVIAN WOKE UP to sunlight, though the west-facing room wasn't as bright as she'd expected with the lack of curtains. The gray clouds pressed as heavily on Chicago today as they had yesterday. The travel mug on the nightstand next to a note that said "decaf" was full of lukewarm, black coffee, which she drank anyway. At the sound of the mug hitting the table, Xìnyùn started shuffling his feet and whistling, "Deal, deal, deal." When he finally squeaked out, "Deal, goddammit," Vivian swung her feet out of bed to face the day and her father's parrot.

In the kitchen she found a laptop and another note. Karl's first two suggestions seemed reasonable, the third she was going to ignore completely. After showering and eating a small breakfast of leftover egg roll and cold, hard rice topped with honey, she opened the laptop and prepared to look for a job. A résumé was something she'd always planned to create, once she finally graduated from college. Middle Kingdom had only required a desperately prepared job application when it had opened in grandeur before the big economic downturn.

Her job history was easy enough to write, but what name should she put at the top? There were riverboat casinos around Chicago, but they would call Vegas and learn Vivian Yap was unemployable. Yet, as Vivian Milek, she didn't have ID.

When Karl got home, Vivian had prepared a draft of her résumé and notes of jobs to apply for— none of them at a casino. She was also ready with her arguments about the third point on his note. "You are not going to buy me a winter coat."

"Do you have a winter coat?" He unloaded takeout containers of Middle Eastern food on the counter without turning to face her.

"No."

"Do you have money to buy a winter coat?"

He knew the answer. Did he have to make her admit to it? "No."

"It is February in Chicago. I can buy you a winter coat or you can sit in my apartment until spring. If you're lucky, spring will come early this year." He handed her two plates, as tranquil as if they were talking about the weather and not how increasingly indebted to him she was.

Of course, they *were* talking about the weather. Next time she married a stranger, she was going to pick one from Florida or San Diego—someplace that didn't require a winter coat.

She took the plates and flatware to the table, her back stiff with the worry of what accepting a winter coat from a stranger implied. "I feel like Julia Roberts in *Pretty Woman,* and I don't like it."

"Are you a prostitute?"

The hair on the back of her neck prickled. The other thing she was going to keep in mind the next time she married a stranger was to pick a man who didn't feel the need to ask her if she was a prostitute more than once. "The first time you asked me that question was one too many times." In case he didn't get the point, she let the plates drop to the table with a clang.

He waited until he'd filled his plate with hummus and tabbouleh before responding. "Stop implying I'm a john and I'll stop wondering if you're a prostitute."

"I don't want you to spend money on me."

"Vivian," he said, setting his fork on his plate without making a clink like she would have. "A winter coat won't cost me anything near your health insurance and child support. Take the damn coat."

"I wasn't—"

"The only one in the hotel room, I know. We share equal responsibility for everything that happened. But you are the only one without a winter coat. Unless you count the baby."

She didn't miss that he'd used the word *baby* this time. *Baby* and not *fetus*. He chose his words carefully enough for it to be deliberate.

"Pregnant women aren't supposed to allow themselves to get overly hot." Arguing with him was stupid. She needed a winter coat. She knew she needed a winter coat. She just didn't want him to buy one for her.

"Then we'll get you a jacket, as well."

"It gets cold in Las Vegas, you know."

"The low there yesterday was forty-four. Today's high in Chicago will be thirty-two. Do you want to continue arguing about this?"

"No."

"You're a poor liar."

Vivian was too irritated to talk to him for the rest of the meal.

KARL HAILED A cab to take them to Macy's. The department store was close enough that he'd normally walk, but the cherry-red fleece Vivian came out of the guest room wearing wouldn't keep her warm for a mere walk across the street. Fortunately, she didn't argue about the coat once they were in the store, even when he bought her two—a dressy coat to wear to interviews and a casual coat to wear with jeans. Neither did she argue when he suggested she wear the casual coat over her fleece for the walk back home.

"What's that?"

Karl's gaze followed her pointing finger to the looming red building with green owls perched on the corners.

"The library."

"Can we go in and get some books?"

"Didn't like the ones I picked out for you last night?"

She rolled her eyes, and he suppressed a smile. "For someone who was, quote, 'beat' you read almost half the book."

"I've always enjoyed history." She stopped at the doors. "I don't know anything about being pregnant, and I'd like to at least know what questions to ask the doctor."

After seeing three people he knew at Macy's, Karl was pleasantly surprised not to run in to anyone he knew while looking through pregnancy books. He hadn't yet figured out how to inform people that he was married and expecting a child. Or, more accurately, he hadn't figured out how to deal with the constant questions that would follow

"I'm married and expecting a child" and still manage to get work done.

They had checked out several pregnancy books and Vivian was browsing the popular library when Karl heard his name. He turned to find his brother-in-law, Miles, and Miles's daughter, Sarah, standing there.

"A little light reading?" Miles nodded his head to the book Karl had slipped into the department store bag—apparently too slowly, because Miles had seen what it was.

"Enjoying a trip downtown?" Karl ignored the question and gesture. With Sarah around, Miles wouldn't press.

"We went to the Art Institute and then lunch," Sarah explained. She either hadn't seen the book or didn't recognize it on sight.

"Go pick out some movies for us to watch tonight," Miles told his daughter.

Stupid of Karl to think Miles would let this slide.

"You could just tell me to get lost," Sarah said.

"Get lost."

"I'm going to pick out something you'll hate," Sarah said with a flounce.

Miles waited until she was out of earshot before gesturing to the bag again. "The cover of that book hasn't changed that much since my ex bought a copy seventeen years ago."

Karl wasn't in the habit of lying. When he didn't

want to admit to anything, he just didn't acknowledge the conversation. "Is Renia working at a wedding today? Mom said her photography business has been in high demand for weddings lately."

"Don't think I'm not going to tell your sister about this."

Just what he needed—his family to know about Vivian and the baby before he was ready to tell them. "The book is for research."

Miles laughed loudly enough for the staff to stare at him. "You're a lawyer. Your research books are leather bound and cause seismic events when dropped." He at least had the forethought to look around before asking, "Who'd you get pregnant?"

"Karl," Vivian said from behind him, "I'll need your library card to check out."

Miles didn't bother to hide that he was peeking over Karl's shoulder to find the source of the voice. "I'm definitely telling your sister about this."

Karl shifted his body to include Vivian in the conversation. He couldn't dodge this forever. "Vivian, meet Miles. He's my brother-in-law. His daughter, Sarah, is over there. Miles, meet Vivian, my wife."

"Nice to meet you, Miles."

Relieved when Miles was too shocked to even offer his hand in greeting, Karl put his hand on Vivian's back and led her to the checkout.

CHAPTER THREE

KARL AVOIDED VIVIAN for the rest of the weekend. He made sure there was food in the house for her to eat, left his laptop out for her to use and otherwise stayed away.

Back at the library, when he'd put his hand on Vivian's back, he let himself imagine their connection was more than just her pregnancy. In that moment, the certainty about Vivian he'd felt in Las Vegas had broken through reality, and the enjoyment he'd gotten from leading her away from Miles scared him. He hadn't enjoyed silencing Miles— he'd enjoyed feeling Vivian's shoulder blades shift when he put his hand on her coat.

Hopefully she'd find a job soon and move out.

Given the fight she'd put up over the stupid winter coat, he didn't think she'd welcome being set up in her own apartment like some kept woman. But if she had a job, she might not turn down an offer of help to finance her own place.

Of course, if she were actually a kept woman, he would be able to sweep her hair aside and kiss the nape of her neck....

At work on Monday, Greta came into his office with some paperwork and his plans to keep Vivian a secret from his employees died.

"Does your mother know you're married?" She used the papers to gesture to the marriage license sitting in plain sight on his desk.

Karl looked from the benefits application on his computer to his overly maternal assistant. She was one of the few people who could outwait his ploy of ignoring a question, but he held out his hand for the papers and tried anyway.

She folded them against her chest. "When did you get married?"

"The papers, Greta." His hand stayed outstretched in supplication.

"You can't not tell me. What do I do if she calls?"

"She won't call." Or not again. Vivian had health insurance and a roof over her head. What more could she want right now?

"So you *are* married. No one in the office is going to believe this." The papers crinkled in her hands as she clenched her fists in excitement.

"No one in the office is going to know."

"Was she the woman calling the office on Friday?"

He waggled his fingers at her and she finally gave him the papers, along with a gust of cigarette fumes that had been lingering on her clothing.

"She *was*—oh, and I was so short with her."

Greta didn't leave the office. She'd handed over the paperwork, but she remained standing with her eyebrows raised at him, hoping for more information.

Despite a tendency to mother, Greta was a great legal assistant. She'd been working in the city's inspector general's office longer than anyone else in the building, and Karl was fairly certain that she'd be working here long after his tenure was up. He threw her a bone. "I met her in Las Vegas. But," he added, before she had a chance to beam and I-told-you-so, "don't think you can take credit or tell anyone about this."

"No more information?" The quickness with which her eyebrows collapsed amplified the ridiculousness of this entire situation.

"No."

"You should still tell your mother."

"What makes you think I haven't?"

"You don't lie outright, so if you won't tell me that you have told her, I can only assume you haven't. She'll want to know." Having said her piece, Greta left his office.

Since he hadn't gotten a phone call from his mother, it would seem Miles and Renia hadn't told her yet, either. Maybe he could put off telling his mother for another eight months and present her with a daughter-in-law and a grandchild at the same time. She might be so overwhelmed at the grandchild that she'd overlook the surprise daughter-in-law.

"You're married?"

Karl looked up from his computer again to see the director of investigations staring at him from the doorway. Malcolm's dark black skin and intense golden eyes made people feel as though he was a panther eyeing their suitability for dinner. Malcolm enjoyed the effect, multiplying it by wearing only dark colors.

"Did Greta tell you?"

"No." Malcolm smiled. "You should learn to keep your door closed. Your assistant has a voice like a bassoon. Everyone on this floor probably knows by now."

"Yes, Malcolm. I'm married. I'd not planned to tell anyone."

"Did you really think you could keep information like that a secret?"

Yes, he had thought he could keep this a secret, but apparently he'd been delusional. If Vivian had stayed in Las Vegas, they could have gotten the divorce and no one would have been the wiser. However, with her pregnant and in Chicago, he was going to have to tell people. Putting it off would only make the inevitable more painful— yet he was still thinking about postponing the inevitable.

"How did you meet the lovely new Mrs. Milek?

You're always working. Even when everyone thinks you're relaxing, you're working." Malcolm stroked his chin, a parody of the thoughtful investigator. "What kind of woman was able to slip through those defenses?"

"I'm not going to answer any of your questions, so you might as well stop wasting the city of Chicago's time."

Malcolm's grin widened. "It's funny how you think you can keep information a secret from me."

"Listen, Malcolm, if you're so curious about my wife, then why don't you just investigate her yourself—just as long as you don't do it on work time."

"Hah! And how much of the information I learn about the new Mrs. Milek do you want me to share when I'm done?"

"None." It wasn't a lie. Karl intended to find out everything he needed to know about Vivian before Malcolm could ferret it out.

"Apparently you don't think it counts as lying if you're also lying to yourself." With a salute, Malcolm left.

Karl could still hear Malcolm chuckling as he walked down the hall. Karl turned back to his computer, clicked on a browser. The cursor hovered over the search box. In a moment of uncharacteristic indecision, he closed the browser window and opened up work files, determined to put Vivian out of his mind for now.

Vivian picked up the note Karl had left her on Friday morning, balled it up and threw it to Xìnyùn, who lobbed it into a small glass she'd appropriated for the game. Since Karl had disappeared last Saturday after they returned from the library, Vivian and Xìnyùn had gotten very good at basketball. Her husband seemed to think communicating through notes was an appropriate way to manage a marriage.

Even if theirs had been a hasty, drunk marriage better left in Vegas, they couldn't hope to raise a child together communicating only through notes.

Dear Karl,
Jelly Bean flipped me off this morning. Apparently you said it was a "salute." Be careful what you say to a four-year-old.
Thank you for your concern,
Vivian

Of course that was ridiculous. Karl would be at work too much to teach Jelly Bean—the name Vivian had taken to calling the baby growing inside her—how to flip someone the bird.

Dear Karl,
Jelly Bean returns from visitation having forgotten how to talk, but has become a surpris-

ingly good correspondent. His teachers are
worried.
Talk, dammit!
Vivian

She needed things from him. Humiliating though
it was, she needed a place to live and health insurance. And she had also needed to get out of
Las Vegas. Karl had given her those things with
a poof of his magic fix-it sense. But an apartment
and health insurance—and food, and a laptop so
she could search for jobs, and a transit card and
gas to get her around Chicago and to interviews—
only solved her physical problems, not to mention
that they made her feel increasingly dependent and
trapped.

Maybe she didn't *need* someone to talk to, but
she *wanted* someone to talk to. Jelly Bean was
still abstract; she couldn't feel the baby yet, but
she could feel her body changing and she wanted to
talk with someone about it. When she told Xìnyùn
everything she ate tasted like metal, he only whistled. And she couldn't face her Las Vegas friends—
not yet anyway. Not until she found new bearings.

Chicago was a big city, with people who might be
her friends, eventually. But right now she was alone
and the one person she knew was hiding from her.

Plus, she had things she needed to discuss with
him. Such as whether or not she was officially on

his health insurance yet and could go to the doctor. And did he want to go with her? She didn't expect him to be an equal partner in her pregnancy—they were married, but they weren't intimate—she just wanted…

Hell, she didn't even know what she wanted.

She wanted to be able to stay awake past nine at night and catch him when he came home so she could eat dinner with him, rather than leaving his food on the stove. Maybe have a conversation with an animal that wasn't a bird. Play a game other than solitaire. Measure Karl's head for the hat she was making him as a gift rather than just guessing his size.

Vivian put Xìnyùn back in his cage, packed up her purse and headed out the door with a list of potential employers to visit. Her solution to her current situation was to get a job. A job would give her money. Money would give her the freedom to get her own apartment. There was always the possibility she'd make friends with someone she worked with.

Besides, being unemployed was not something she could handle for long, if only because getting up in the morning and going to a job had been a part of her daily routine for so long. She'd been working since it was legal for her to do so. It had been the only way to make sure she had money to save for college and find a life that didn't involve moving in the middle of the night.

Fat lot of good it had done her. Her father had taken her life savings and disappeared into the darkness, leaving her to do much the same.

She shook her father out of her head. He had no place in Chicago. He wouldn't think to find her here and if he couldn't find her, he couldn't ask her for more money. All the money she got from a job would go to providing for her and Jelly Bean. And she'd start to get some of her self-worth back. With a job would come the knowledge that she wasn't a leech on Karl's silent kindness. And maybe the hope that she could pay him back, somehow.

WHEN KARL WALKED through the doorway to his apartment at eleven o'clock on Friday night to find Vivian had pulled a dining chair into the entryway and was reading *What to Expect When You're Expecting,* he knew it had been too much to hope that he could dodge her for eight months.

"Good evening, Karl." She rested the book on her lap and looked up at him. "Have you been avoiding me?"

It sounded cowardly when she put it like that. He stared at the curve of her lips above her pointed chin—soft over sharp—and he had to stop himself from running his thumb over the bow. He didn't have to be drunk to be susceptible to the arcs of her face, but he needed to remember that she was only temporary. The baby was permanent, but Vivian fleeting.

"I work a lot." It came out like a defense.

"Well, you're home now, and I'm still up, so we can talk."

He beat her to picking up her chair to carry it back to the dining table. As he passed the bar area of the kitchen, someone whistled at him. The bird was climbing around on a miniature jungle gym. Xìnyùn whistled again, a high-pitched, squeaky wolf whistle. The bird was on his kitchen counter. And whistling at him. He stopped to look at the bird, who hopped in response.

Vivian made kissy noises—at the bird, not at him. "Xìnyùn always did prefer men."

Karl shook his head and continued carrying the chair to the dining room table. "Why is he out of his cage?" That wasn't the question he wanted answered. "Why do you have a bird that prefers men?"

That still wasn't the right question—the one that had been niggling at him. He wanted to know why she was here in Chicago. The growing fetus and health insurance didn't seem enough of a reason for a stranger to be living in his apartment. But he didn't ask those, because he was too caught up watching Vivian bend over and encourage the bird to hop onto her finger.

"Luck, be a lady tonight," the bird squeaked. At

least, that's what Karl thought the bird said. It might have been a whistle.

He sat in a chair at his table in the apartment that used to be his escape from the chaos of life.

"Xìnyùn's out of his cage because he needs the exercise and mental stimulation. Parrots are smart and need regular challenges to their intelligence. In answer to your second question, I have a parrot that prefers men to women because he's not my parrot."

"Are you going to be hunted down by someone whose parrot you stole?" What did he know about her other than that she claimed to be pregnant and was living in his apartment? And that he liked the curve of her lips and length of her neck.

She laughed, but a haunted look accompanied the noise. "Xìnyùn's my father's bird."

"Where's your father and why doesn't he have the bird?"

"Um…" She looked at the window.

"There's probably bird shit on my kitchen counter. You can at least tell me where your father is."

She looked back at him. "I'll clean up Xìnyùn's mess. I've been cleaning it all week."

Of course. He hadn't been home all week. The bird could've been dancing on his pillow for all he knew.

"And my father said he couldn't keep the bird right now. I came home from work one day to find Xìnyùn in my apartment, along with a note."

She said all that while looking at him, but then she looked out the window. There was more to the story of her father. "But I wanted to talk to you about our child."

She sat at the table across from him, and the bird hopped down her arm, landing on the belly of the pregnant woman on the cover of the book.

"Should you be around a bird while pregnant?" He really should know more about pregnancy than that Vivian shouldn't have caffeine or alcohol.

"It's fine. I wear gloves when I clean up after him and wash my hands often, but that's one of the things I wanted to talk with you about. I need to find a doctor."

"Are you sick?"

She pulled her chin back into her neck and gave him a funny look. "I'm pregnant."

Karl's throat tried to choke him and he coughed. "This is all new to me."

"It's new to me, too. I've not had much more time to get used to the idea than you have." She patted his hand like he was a child. Her hand was warm. "I need to start having regular checkups for myself and the baby. Would you like to go with me to the first visit?" When he turned his hand palm up, she grasped it and squeezed. "Maybe it will help this all be real to you."

It's not as though he hadn't imagined having a pregnant wife before. When he'd believed their marriage to be happy, he'd roll over in bed to look at Jessica and wonder what their children would look like. But with Jessica everything would've been planned. There would have been a calendar tracking when she was fertile, the *best* OB-GYN practice in Chicago already chosen and she would have picked out the crib she wanted before they even stopped using birth control. Jessica organized everything.

And he would've been a better partner to Jessica. Despite their arguments, Jessica wouldn't have questioned whether he would be around to discuss the pregnancy. She would have assumed.

Vivian was a stranger, but legally she was his wife and—until he knew for certain otherwise—she was carrying their child. He should be no less a partner to Vivian just because she and the baby were inconvenient. Pregnancy was hardly convenient for Vivian, either. Whatever had driven her out of Vegas, she'd had a life there.

He squeezed her hand in return. "Yes. I would like to go to the first prenatal visit. I'm not sure I can make all of them, but I'll make the ones I can, so long as you want me to."

"I dropped in on your doorstep with no warning and you've taken me in. You've been great, considering. Really."

"You're a bad liar." She looked out the window, but he saw the lie in the way her nostrils curled. "I didn't kick a pregnant woman out on the streets, which means I'm not a jerk. It doesn't make me great. We don't know each other now, but that doesn't mean we can't eventually become friends. Friendship would be a better place to start than many people having a baby together."

"Friends." She turned her head back to face him. She was wearing the same pink sweater she'd worn when she'd first arrived. At the time he'd been too overwhelmed by the situation to concentrate on anything other than small details of her features and the haze of his memories. Looking at her now, face-to-face and with his mind open to his changing circumstances, he could see how pretty she was. Simple and without fuss, like a sunrise over the lake. "I'd like that."

Neither of them noticed they were still holding hands until the bird climbed from the cover of the book to stand on Vivian's middle finger and whistle.

She blushed and eased her hand out from his grip, the bird still carefully balanced on her finger. "I need to go to bed. This is past my pregnancy bedtime. I'll clean up Xìnyùn's mess in the morning."

"Don't worry about it," he said to her back as she slumped off to the bedroom. Cleaning up after a parrot would give him something to think about, other than his suddenly empty hand.

CHAPTER FOUR

"I'M SORRY, DAD...."

Karl eased the front door closed, not wanting to disturb Vivian's conversation, and if he was being honest with himself, because he wanted to hear what she had to say to her father. She was in her bedroom, but the door was open so she couldn't have an expectation of privacy.

That she probably still expected him to be out getting their breakfast made that argument a bit specious—a technicality he was willing to ignore to learn more about his mysterious bride. Vivian wasn't forthcoming with information.

"...but I'm not going to tell you anything about what's happened to me if you're not going to tell me where you are."

Interesting. Not knowing her father's whereabouts was very different than his being unavailable.

"You always say it's important, Dad, but me telling you that I'm fine is all you need to know right now."

He slipped his shoes off and walked to the door

of the guest bedroom in his socks, indecision an unfamiliar and uncomfortable feeling.

"No, nothing much in my life has changed since I last saw you." The sarcasm in her voice cut through the door and Karl was certain her father was bleeding on the other end of the call, though it sounded as though her dad didn't know why she was being so cutting. Hell, Karl didn't know why she was being so cutting.

When had she last seen her father? She'd said he wasn't available—a bit of an overstatement—but did he even know she was pregnant? That she'd lost her job? Based on the present conversation, Karl was willing to bet the answer to all those questions was no. For all her dad knew, Vivian was still in Vegas, dealing, single and with an empty uterus.

Vivian sighed. "Yes, you're my father and you care about my well-being, but maybe you can see how that doesn't mean very much to me right now."

Clearly she didn't want her father to know about the upheaval in her life, but why? Was she lying about the pregnancy? He shook the second question from his head. She would be a fool to lie about a pregnancy and invite him to the doctor's office. He pulled his hand back from knocking at the door. It was unethical to eavesdrop and he now had more questions than answers—a punishment the Greek gods could have devised.

"I've been in Sin City for sixteen years and you

were never so interested in my well-being before."
One short thunk came from the room. "I will continue to take care of myself, and it will be easier without wondering if you'll show up on my doorstep."

Her words stopped his attempt to be courteous and find something else to listen to. However occasionally constricted Karl felt at having his entire family live in the same city, he couldn't imagine fearing their appearance on his stoop. Or worse, believing them to be more of a hindrance than help if he got in trouble.

"Dad, that was a fun time, but I'm too old to be looking for the next adventure."

The desperation in her voice echoed the strain on her face from the night she'd shown up in his lobby. It had been that strain that had convinced him she was pregnant and that she believed it was his baby. Both of their lives would be a lot easier if he'd never bought her that drink.

Realizing he wasn't going to learn any more about his wife, Karl walked to the kitchen, setting the newspapers and the bag of bagels on the counter. He was putting out plates when she came out of her room.

"Oh." She stopped short at the sight of him, blinking. "I didn't hear the front door."

He turned his back to her and poured two cups of

coffee. "I know." When he turned back to face her, she hadn't moved. "Sit down. Have some breakfast."

She clasped her hands together, twisting them. "How much did you hear?"

"Enough to know you don't know where your father is and that you've not told him you lost your job. Or that you're pregnant. Why?"

A quick, frightened glance at the bedroom door gave away her thoughts.

"Is there a reason the fact of your father's ignorance might induce me to kick you out of the apartment?"

"No." Her hands fell to her sides and she inched to the breakfast bar. She gave him one more cautious look before sitting down. "I have good reasons for not telling my father about losing my job."

He pushed a cup of coffee to her. "And for not telling him that you're pregnant."

"That, too." She wrapped her hands around the mug, but didn't drink any coffee. Karl waited. "I'm not going to tell you what those reasons are right now, no matter how silent you are."

His laughter surprised them both. "The tactic loses some of its effectiveness when you put it so baldly." That he was continuing to help her didn't disturb him—she was pregnant and he didn't believe in punishing a child for the sins of the mother, whatever the sins she was hiding might be—but how little he cared about her secret scared the hell out of him. Her attractiveness wasn't enough to justify his feelings. He liked her, simple as that. "At least tell me that you're not keeping a secret from me because you did something illegal."

"I didn't do anything illegal." The matter-of-factness with which she said those words left a myriad of other secretive possibilities undenied.

"Does the secret have to do with why you were fired?"

"I don't want my dad to know I'm pregnant because I don't want him to have extra incentive to come looking for me." Topic of conversation seemingly changed with the vague answer, she reached for a bagel, but Karl wasn't satisfied.

"Because?"

Vivian put the bagel on the plate with a sigh. "Because he's trouble, and I'm too old to go on thinking it's fun."

"Shouldn't it be a parent's prerogative to know if they're going to be a grandparent?"

"Have you told your parents about me yet?" she asked.

"Parent. My dad died when I was sixteen."

"I knew that. I'm sorry."

"The people responsible for his death are the ones who should be sorry. You didn't have anything to do with it."

"But I'm not the only one keeping secrets from one of the baby's grandparents." She looked out the window before reaching for the tub of cream cheese. "My dad is better off not knowing." Scrutinizing her bagel as she smeared it with cream cheese, she continued, "He wouldn't care that much anyway."

Interesting. She had the same tells when she was lying to herself as she did when lying to other people.

He took his time choosing his bagel and spreading it with cream cheese, enjoying her wary looks as she tore small bites off hers and chewed them slowly. If she didn't want to continue worrying about what would happen if he knew her secrets, she should spill them and get the pain over with.

His coffee was barely hot as he washed his breakfast down before changing the subject. "Speaking of a parent's prerogative and whether or not she knows about you, my mom planned a family dinner for tomorrow."

VIVIAN COUGHED, BUT managed to choke down her mouthful. *Couldn't he have waited until after I'd swallowed before laying that on me?*

"Am I invited?" Did she want to be invited? She didn't want to be a dirty secret locked up in a basement somewhere, but meeting Karl's family had seemed less scary when it was an abstract idea. Or when bumping into his brother-in-law at the library without the chance to escape or the opportunity to worry about it beforehand.

"We're married and you're carrying my child. I think that makes you family. Or do you plan to hide from my family like you're hiding from yours?"

How nicely Karl evaded the fact that he'd been hiding her, as well. "Hiding from my family is an exaggeration. My father could probably find me if he tried."

His shoulders fell, but he didn't sigh in exasperation at her. Since she was exasperated herself, this was a bit of a surprise. "There are aspects of your life you don't want to tell me right now," he said. "That's fine. Not great, but we're strangers in a rough situation and I'm trying to be understanding. But don't outright lie to me."

"Fine." She put down her bagel and looked him straight in the eye. "It's not an exaggeration, and I'm hoping he doesn't try, but not for the same reasons you're keeping me from your family, I'm sure." What she had to say next would be harder to admit to, but she wanted him to understand, even if she couldn't tell him everything. "My dad's fun, but he's not responsible. I need responsible."

"Did he do something illegal?" His voice expressed simple curiosity, but there had to be more behind the question. Vivian didn't believe Karl ever asked anything out of simple curiosity.

"What's your time frame?" She pushed her half-eaten bagel away, no longer hungry.

"It's not a trick question, Vivian. He either did or he didn't."

"Maybe it's easy for you, but you're a lawyer and you spend your time looking for evildoers. This is my father we're talking about. He's lazy and looking to make a quick buck involving the least amount of work. Combine that with Las Vegas…" She shrugged. "There are a million things he could have done that are *wrong* without being illegal."

And that was just Las Vegas. If she assumed that every time they had moved in the middle of the night it had been because her father was escaping the law…

Of course, on a few occasions he might have been escaping his partners in crime, not the authorities.

"You should tell your father the truth."

"No." The word came out more forcefully than she had meant it to, causing Xìnyùn to whistle from the next room. "When I'm settled, I'll tell him. Until then…" An offensive tactic seemed to be a better idea right now. "What are you going to tell your family about me?"

He took a sip of his coffee and grimaced. It was cold, which was probably why she hadn't touched hers. "At dinner will be my mom, my sister Tilly and her boyfriend, and my sister Renia and her husband, Miles. You met Miles at the library. I don't know if his daughter, Sarah, will be there."

"I'll get you another cup of coffee," she said, reaching out for his mug.

His hand was cool when it grabbed her wrist. "Don't. If I want another cup I'll get it myself."

"I'm just trying to be nice." *I'm still in your apartment, eating your food, without a job. And now we have this secret hanging between us.*

"When you're offering just to be nice, I'll let you get me a cup of coffee. Until then, you're doing it because you feel beholden to me and I'm not interested." He let go of her hand and she missed the cool touch of his palm on her skin.

Which was nuts. They weren't a *couple;* they were a couple of people stuck having a baby together. She would get a job and her own insurance, they would agree on divorce terms and child support and she would never feel his touch again. He was a domineering pain in the ass, anyway. *Because you feel beholden.* Assuming jerk.

But because he was right, she asked her question again. "What are you going to tell your family about me?"

"The truth."

"That we met while drunk, had sex and woke up married?"

The corner of his mouth kicked up in a smile, marking this morning as the first time she'd heard him laugh much less give any indication he *could* smile outside of Las Vegas. And she couldn't help notice that his hazel eyes twinkled when he smiled. "An edited version of the truth."

"Could you—" how to ask this question without sounding like she was trying to hide even more "—not tell them about the baby?"

The corners of his mouth fell as his smile turned suspicious. As he should be, Vivian thought, only not with regard to the baby. "Any particular reason to keep it a secret?"

"I'd always heard it was bad luck to tell anyone before the third month."

"Miles knows—or at least guesses. He saw the book."

"Just between us for now. Okay?"

KARL DIDN'T USUALLY lie to his mom, but he knew how to keep something from her. He'd hidden his impending divorce from her almost until Jessica had served him with the petition. It wasn't something he liked doing—his mom had been angry about the secret of the divorce for months—but he made it a habit not to answer questions people didn't ask. It hadn't occurred to his mother to ask if he was getting a divorce. However...

"Is she pregnant?" his mom asked in a whisper as she handed him a platter of sauerkraut pierogies to take to the dining room.

"Why do you ask?" If he could avoid answering the question, he wouldn't have to lie to his mother. He didn't *want* to. But he understood Vivian's reluctance to share the news—though his reasons were different. The fewer people who knew about the pregnancy, the fewer people who would insist on showing him adorable baby booties and maybe the fewer chances he'd have to think of all the horrible ways children die. As long as only he and Vivian knew about the baby, he could ignore the risk childhood posed to a child whenever he wasn't around his wife. Or so he told himself.

His mom grabbed the waistband of his pants, preventing him from walking out of the kitchen. He sighed in response. *Some days, you are still five years old to your mother.* "You married a woman I've never met. What am I supposed to think?"

"Mom, even if she were pregnant—and I'm not saying she is—I wouldn't tell you until she was three months along. It's bad luck." At least Vivian had been kind enough to give him something to tell his mother while he lied to her.

"What do you know about this woman you've married? Where's she from? What's her family like? How do you know if you have anything in common with her?"

He removed his mother's grip on his pants and turned to face her, surprised when her expression held fear. "We're here for family dinner. You can ask her all the questions you want. Get to know her. You'll probably like her."

I do. More than the curve of her lips and line of her neck. He could relax in Vivian's calm presence. She had a quiet, efficient manner and he found himself watching her move about the apartment instead of enjoying his view of the Chicago skyline. He had even changed the chair he sat in while in the living room so he could watch her knit or play solitaire.

"She's just—" his mom halted "—different, and I'm not sure she belongs."

Of all the things he expected to come out of his mother's mouth… "Are you saying you don't like Vivian because she's not from Chicago, not Catholic—" at least, he didn't think she was "—or not white?"

"I just think marriages work better when the couple shares a common background."

He set the pierogies on the counter in exasperation. "You complain about Tilly and Dan not even planning a wedding yet—"

"'I'm building my business' isn't a reason not to get married," she interrupted.

"*And* you're a devout Catholic wishing your sister could marry her longtime *female* partner."

"She's my favorite sister. Their relationship has lasted longer than most marriages I know."

"Vivian and I have done what Aunt Maria and

Josie can't do and what Tilly and Dan haven't cared to do. Be happy about that."

"I just wish I knew her."

"No, you wish you'd had the chance to approve of her before I married her." *Like you approved of Jessica because the two of you wanted the same things out of me, and they weren't what I was willing to give. The marriage you approved of led to divorce. And Jessica and I had* a lot *in common.*

He picked the pierogies up off the counter and headed through the living room to the dining room and the rest of his family.

In the dining room, Vivian was laughing at the anecdote of Dan panning Tilly's restaurant and then picking her up at the Taste of Chicago, each unaware that she was the chef to whose restaurant he'd given a bad review. Instead of being an uncomfortable story, Tilly's lively hand gestures and gift with words made it one of their best party stories. Karl slipped into the chair next to his wife with the odd feeling that the family table was finally complete. Until tonight, hearing Vivian chuckle at Dan's tales of the ribbing his friends had given him over the review, Karl hadn't known something had been missing.

THE CAR RIDE home was uncomfortable. Vivian's enjoyable chat with Karl's sisters had come to a screeching halt when his mom had entered the dining room with roast pork and twenty questions. Vivian had smiled and tried to remain pleasant, while avoiding the questions she thought were none of the woman's business—and inappropriate to be asked at a get-to-know-you dinner.

"Everyone seemed very nice," Vivian remarked to the passenger-side window and cars they were passing. By everyone, she meant Karl's sisters, his brother-in-law and Dan. She hadn't expected someone as straitlaced as Karl to have a sister with wild blue hair, and his other sister, Renia, while reserved, had an undercurrent of real warmth.

Qualifying her statement seemed rude, and she could be polite to Karl, who had watched the interaction between her and his mother with interest but hadn't done anything to interfere. Just because she came from mysterious people and a state that Easterners couldn't distinguish from Iowa, didn't mean she didn't know how to be polite.

"Did you enjoy the food?"

"Yes. It's the first time I've ever had pierogies. Probably the first time I've ever had Polish food that wasn't kielbasa from the grocery store." The only thing the sausage they'd eaten for dinner had in common with the vacuum-wrapped oval from the meat case was the name. Then there had been the cucumbers in a light sour cream dressing. "It was all delicious."

"No Polish blood in you?" His question was

lightly asked, but she'd been asked that question about ten different ways over the past two hours.

"I didn't realize you were also obsessed with my ancestry." Being offended warred with her fear of losing the little stability she had managed to grasp.

And she'd thought better of him.

"Of all my mom's questions that you avoided answering, that's the one I care least about. Tell me why you got fired and why you're hiding from your dad, and I won't bat an eye when you tell me that your grandparents are from Jupiter."

"Is that why you didn't stop your mom from combining dinner with a security clearance interview?"

He didn't sigh, but she could feel the frustration come off his body in waves at her remark. "Vivian," he said finally, "I haven't known you very long, but you don't strike me as the type of person who wants a man to rescue her just so he can prove he's not neutered. You were holding your own. If you had needed to be saved, I would have done so."

"What do you call me living in your apartment, eating your food and using the transit cards you leave on the table?" Suddenly she needed the parameters of their relationship defined. If he didn't see her as helpless and dependent, how did he see her?

"Providing you with a helping hand isn't the same as a rescue. If I were rescuing you, I'd have done this whole thing differently."

"How?"

"I'd have a suit of armor and horse," he said with the same flat tone with which he said everything else.

Something between a snicker and a sigh escaped her mouth. She hadn't told his mother anything about her heritage because she was offended that it seemed to matter. When Karl said he didn't care, she believed him.

Besides, if she offered him some answers, perhaps she'd win a reprieve from the questions about her father and why she was fired. She didn't know that much about "her people" anyway. Her father had a habit of alienating people, even family. Maybe *especially* family.

"The last name and most of the blood on my father's side is Chinese, but there's some Mexican and Sicilian in there, too, I think. There were lots of different ethnic groups working on the railroads, fighting forest fires and mining out west. My mom's a hundred percent Chinese, though." She let the silence consume the oxygen in the car and extinguish her fear. "Would your mom like me more if I had Polish blood?"

She didn't *want* to care what his mother thought, but this was his baby, too, and that woman was the baby's grandmother. If the baby's grandmother couldn't get past her nonwhite skin, well...well, she'd figure out something. She always had.

"It would give her something to hang on to until she got to know you better. Being Catholic would work just as well." Her leather seat creaked as she turned from the window to look at her husband, but the darkness swallowed his expression—if he had one.

She turned back to the window, disappointed in his answer and disappointed in herself for caring. "The Mexican and Sicilian parts are probably Catholic."

She started when his hand rested on her knee and squeezed. She'd touched him once or twice, but he'd steadfastly avoided initiating any contact with her since putting his hand on her back as they'd left the library that day. She'd noticed that he watched her when they were in the apartment together— whether out of suspicion, curiosity or some other emotion she didn't know and his expression didn't reveal—but he never touched her.

"It's not about you. My mom is mad at me for marrying someone she doesn't know and didn't get a chance to approve of, first. Since I am otherwise the golden child, she's not used to feeling disappointed in me and her disapproval is landing on you. She'll get over it, and you shouldn't feel that you need to put up with it. If she continues, I'll tell her to knock it off. Or you can opt out of future family dinners. Attendance isn't a requirement for my help."

If she hadn't been staring so intently at his expression, she wouldn't have noticed the slight lift of his mouth when he said "golden child." As it was, she wasn't sure she believed her own eyes. She ticked off her memories on her fingers, a laugh, two smiles and a touch all in the span of a couple days.

But the hint of a smile disappeared as quickly as it had come when he continued talking. "I don't know if that helps. I've never been—"

"Anything but the perfect man all mothers dream their beloved daughter will marry?"

He laughed. If she wasn't careful, she might have to take off her socks to keep track of the number of times she got a reaction out of him. "I was going to say 'on the receiving end of a mother's interrogation,' but we can let your statement stand."

"How your mother feels about me doesn't matter in the long run, I guess. I'll get a job, get my own health insurance. We'll have a baby and get a divorce. You'll be free to marry a Polish Catholic girl your mom has known since birth."

Karl didn't respond. But neither did he remove his hand from her knee until it was time to get off the freeway.

CHAPTER FIVE

VIVIAN WAS SHIFTING, trying to get comfortable in the waiting room chair and filling out yet another form with her medical history, when Karl came in.

"Hi," she said, surprised. She'd told him the time and date of her first doctor's appointment, and he'd said he'd come, but she'd expected some work emergency to conveniently detain him. Despite his touch of her knee on the way home from his mother's and his promise they would be friends, he'd been the same distant man of the previous week. And he still seemed to work all the time. "I didn't think you'd come."

"I'm sorry. Scheduling my own doctor's appointment made me late." He put a heavy hand on her head, smoothing down her hair before giving her neck a reassuring squeeze and sitting down. No, she wasn't being honest with herself. He hadn't been quite the same man. Instead of going straight to work after the gym, he'd come home and eaten breakfast with her yesterday and today. They'd talked about how her job search was going, and she'd reminded him of today's appointment.

And yesterday, instead of getting home from work after she'd gone to bed, he'd come home and taken her out to dinner. As she'd taken a bite of her stuffed mushrooms and peered at the pictures on the wall of the steakhouse that seemed to be a Chicago institution, Karl had turned into a different man.

No fewer than ten people, not including the gruff waitstaff, came to their table to say hello. Each time, he introduced her as his wife, accepted their congratulations, ignored their looks of surprise with ease and asked about their families. She'd started to wonder if the taciturn man she shared an apartment with had fallen into the twilight zone and been replaced by a politician. Then she'd noticed his gladhanding didn't extend to his eyes. He smiled, but the twinkle wasn't there. Her husband played Mr. Important out in public, but he didn't enjoy it.

The man next to her in the waiting room, silent, steady and *present,* was the natural Karl.

"What are all the forms for?"

"Everything." She handed the clipboard to him, embarrassed to be sharing her complete medical history with a man she barely knew. But he was going to learn more about her as soon as they got into the doctor's office so why hide it now? Jelly Bean was his baby, too. "Family medical history. Vitamins I take. Past illnesses. My doctor in Vegas hasn't sent over all my records yet, but I think they'd make me fill everything out, anyway."

"You missed information here."

She looked at the space he was pointing to. "I don't remember how old I was when I had my first period."

Karl's head jerked and he started to blush. "I guess, I didn't, I mean…"

This time she put the supportive hand on his knee. "It's okay. We have one night of sex and now my menstrual cycle has become important to both of us." She chuckled because her other option was to cry. "When we leave this office, I probably won't have any secrets left."

"Why'd you come to me instead of finding your father?"

Of course, she couldn't blame him for asking the question—she'd practically invited it—but still Vivian tried to pull her hand off his knee. He stopped her, placing his hand on top of hers and keeping it there. She could feel his touch all the way down to her toes.

"I thought I should tell you about the child in person," she said. It was the same stupid reason she always gave him.

"So, still some secrets." Someday, she knew, he wasn't going to let it slide.

"Yes." And she would keep those secrets as long as she could. He needed to know about her health and her body because the child growing inside her was his as well as hers. He didn't need to know how she'd waited until the last minute to decide not to sell her integrity, and how the fates had punished her anyway.

"You said you wanted me here. I can go back to my office if you need the privacy."

"No. We're a team on this—" *if on nothing else* "—and I'd like a friend."

IN THE SMALL exam room, Karl turned his back to give Vivian privacy while she changed into the hospital gown. He cracked the door once she had changed, then took a seat in a chair while she sat on the examination table, swinging her feet in the air. The false intimacy of the exam room, combined with the very real consequences of their night of sexual intimacy, made for an awkward situation.

"Oh, the father is here," the doctor said as she walked into the room. "This is a pleasant surprise."

Karl had felt discomfited enough as the only man in the waiting room without the doctor commenting on his presence in that chipper voice people use to inform their dogs a walk is coming. But the woman didn't seem to notice his discomfort—or she didn't care—and the visit wasn't about him, anyway.

"Considering how many times I hear people say 'we're pregnant,' I almost never see the father." His head jerked up when the doctor sat and patted them both on the knees. She looked old enough to be his grandmother, but he hadn't expected her to treat them like children. "Good." Pat. "This should be a partnership." Pat. "And I expect this means both of you will be abstaining from coffee, alcohol, soft cheese and lunch meats." Pat. "It's not fair for the mother to bear those burdens alone."

He knew about the coffee and alcohol. He hadn't known about the cheese. How much feta had been in the Middle Eastern food he'd brought home? Had Vivian picked it out? Had she eaten it? Was it even a soft cheese? Karl glanced at her and she lifted her eyebrows in what he expected was supposed to be reassurance, but he still felt as if he was swimming through a bizarre dream the consistency of gelatin and the color of black coffee—with grounds trapped beside him in the jelly.

"So." The doctor clapped her hands. "I imagine you have lots of questions…"

How had offering a drink to an attractive woman at a hotel bar in Las Vegas led to him sitting in an exam room with a stranger in a hospital gown?

"…let me tell you what's going to happen at this exam, and you can ask all the questions you want when we're done."

Now was probably not the best time to ask *that* question—or to ask when he was going to wake up. Although, he cocked his head to the side and caught sight of Vivian's pink toenails as they swayed in and out of his vision, the dream didn't really seem terrible. Still bizarre, but not definitively bad.

"The last thing we'll do is an internal ultrasound. It's early yet, so you won't see much, but we might get to listen to the heartbeat."

"The fetus has a heartbeat?" Karl asked, and immediately felt stupid.

"If the date of your last period is right, the fetus *may* have a detectible heartbeat. Don't worry, Dad." The doctor patted his knee again. "People ask questions when they're scared and sometimes they're silly questions. Babies are scary and they're also wonderful. Stick with your beautiful wife, here, and you'll be fine."

Vivian's legs had stopped swinging and her lips had pursed as though she might cry. Or—he re-evaluated the brightness of her eyes—burst into laughter. He wasn't the only one who found this scene ridiculous.

The exam was reinforcing all the many things he didn't know about his wife. He'd seen the stranger he'd married in a hospital gown, knew she couldn't remember the age at which she had her first period and knew she'd been exposed to a lot of secondhand smoke on her job. He didn't know why Vivian had lost her job, why her father was missing or why she wouldn't tell him about her pregnancy. Until she told the doctor, he hadn't realized she spent most of her days walking around the city when she wasn't applying for jobs and cleaning up after the stupid bird.

These were the repercussions of having a child with a stranger. These strange half intimacies of hearing her describe how regular her menstruation had been—*really, did such details matter now that she was actually pregnant?*—but not knowing if she'd ever gone to college defined their relationship.

Vivian and the doctor were talking about genetic testing, but Karl only heard half of it. This wasn't how he'd planned to have a baby. When he'd sat at the hotel bar knocking back whiskey and waiting to die because being older than his father was inconceivable, he'd thought back on what he'd accomplished in his life.

And he'd come up short, which had probably been the alcohol and his thirty-ninth birthday talking. He had a job that was more than just important to him, it was important to the city of Chicago. He was *the* independent watchdog for the taxpayer and that didn't mean he was looking out *only* for their money.

The worst effects of corruption and fraud weren't wasted dollars, but wasted lives. Two dead Milek men on the side of the highway and one dying Milek boy in the hospital were testimony to the devastation a bribe and a blind eye could leave.

He averted his eyes when Vivian started to scoot her butt to the edge of the exam table and put her feet in the stirruplike things. The doctor had a wand-ish instrument covered with a condom and lubricant. The woman who had just been patting his knee was now telling Vivian how the ultrasound would feel compared to a vaginal exam and he nearly leapt out of his chair and headed for the door.

His presence here was a mistake. Whatever was involved in an internal ultrasound was far, far too private for him to witness. They were strangers. He'd planned on having babies with Jessica, who would've known better than to ask him to come to the doctor's office to witness this. Jessica had wanted two children—preferably one boy and one girl. They were going to buy a house in Andersonville and he was going to have the beautiful wife, two perfectly behaved children and a meaningful job. And when his thirty-ninth birthday hit, he was going to compare his life to his father's and see that he'd lived up to all the man's expectations.

"Dad." The doctor's voice broke through the existential crisis he wouldn't admit he was having, even in confession, should the priest ask. "If you look on the monitor you can see the embryo. And your date for conception looks pretty spot-on with the embryo's growth."

The last, lingering nugget of doubt he'd had about Vivian's pregnancy burst when Karl looked up. On the screen was some pulsing gray matter and, in a flash of emptiness, a little thing that looked like a mouse standing up and dancing. Only it wasn't a mouse. It wasn't anywhere near the size of a mouse. It was his baby and the doctor was saying it was a quarter of an inch in size.

From somewhere in the room came the sound of a horse clopping. Vivian's wide smile made her cheeks pop like a chipmunk's, but he didn't know the source of the sound until the doctor said, "And this is your baby's heartbeat."

The blood pulsing in his ears took on the same rhythm of the horse galloping, the sound that the doctor was claiming was his baby. The baby he made with the beautiful woman lying back calmly on the exam table, looking at him as if she expected him to say something.

"Holy shit." His life was never going to be the same.

KARL WAS SILENT as he pushed the cart through the aisles of the grocery store. Normally, his quiet didn't bother Vivian, but there was quiet and then there was the silence that buzzed between them.

"Are you okay?" she asked for probably the tenth time since they'd left the doctor's office.

"Fine." He held the plastic bag full of apples high in the air, twisted it and tied the bag in a knot.

Already in the cart were bananas, oranges, clementines, grapefruit, grapes and strawberries that looked pretty but would probably be tasteless since it was only March. And that was just the fruit.

They also had sweet potatoes, kale, Swiss chard, carrots, cabbage and a rainbow of peppers. If a doctor sitting on Oprah's couch had ever called a plant a "superfood," Karl had put it in their cart. His previously empty fridge was likely to expire with the pressure of the extra work. At least she'd be able to make every recipe on the planet without having to go to the store again.

She weighed the bleak look that had been on Karl's face when their baby's heartbeat had filled the exam room and the fact that they were strangers and she was dependent on him. The bleak look won. She put a hand on his before he could bag some rocks masquerading as peaches.

"You are not fine. You nearly fainted at the doctor's." A muscle pulsed where his ear rounded into his jaw, but Vivian ignored the warning. "And your silence has a deathlike quality about it. We're partners in this. Friends, right?"

At the word *death* the twitch had stopped. Karl left the peaches on the display and moved on to the pears. When he'd bagged five pears, he turned his attention to her. "This is not how I expected to have a child."

He pushed the cart away from the produce, leaving her wishing she had a bag of potatoes she could bean him over the head with. She caught up to him in the bread aisle as he was reading nutritional information.

"This wasn't how I expected to have a child, either." All through adulthood, she'd held on to her dream of a perfect nuclear family, raising children in a house they would own into retirement, the memories made in the home impossible to distinguish from the stuff cluttering the shelves. When she'd decided she couldn't abort the baby, no matter how desperate her situation seemed, she'd surrendered that dream. Karl hadn't been offered the same choices she had, and he probably had completely different dreams.

She grabbed one of the loaves and added cinnamon-raisin bread to the cart, as well. "I suspect there's more to your reaction."

As they passed the fancy cheeses, Vivian added Gruyère to the cart.

"No cheese." Karl put it back in the cooler.

"No soft cheese." She put it back into the cart.

"Huh." He added a couple more cheeses to the pile, then crossed his arms on the cart handle and pushed his way along the aisle. She'd never seen a man look so uncomfortable while trying to look so relaxed, and again she had to hurry after him.

"Is the cheese for you?"

"No. You seem to like cheese."

"I can't eat all that. It'll go bad."

"You're supposed to eat more, and a variety of foods."

She put her hand on the front of the cart and

turned it before he could knock down a display of potato chips with his manic forward progress. "After the second trimester, I should eat an extra three hundred calories a day. That does not mean I get to gorge myself on cheese."

He sighed. "I'll help eat the cheese."

"And the fruit? And the bread? And whatever else you plan to buy me and Jelly Bean while we're in the store?"

"Jelly Bean?" *Finally,* she had his attention. "You call our baby Jelly Bean?"

"You call our baby the fetus."

"Apparently I should be calling it an embryo for another three or four weeks."

She sighed. "Can we talk about this possessed shopping trip and what happened in the doctor's office?"

"Not here."

"Fine." She navigated the cart past the dairy and around several displays until she'd dragged Karl and his cornucopia in front of the shoe polish and laces. "This is as empty as a grocery store gets. Spill."

He looked over his shoulder. She wanted to smack him, but she also needed him. No one could call her actions patient, but she *was* waiting. "Hearing the heartbeat was the first time this became real. Until then I expected to wake up. But it's not a dream and we're in this together. I want to make sure you have all you need."

The warmth in his voice glided above the soft hits that were playing over the loudspeakers. For the first time since she'd sat on her bathroom floor in Vegas looking at the third positive pregnancy test in a row, Vivian felt like something other than a problem. She'd come to Karl because he was the father and he was a fixer. But now...she and Jelly Bean might be something more than a speed bump in his perfectly ordered and sterile life.

His hand didn't feel cool to the touch when she grabbed on to it—a phantom warmth she attributed to the hope rising in her own chest. "We won't be left communicating with each other through notes about Jelly Bean's progress in school."

"What?" Karl hid his emotions most of the time, but puzzlement was clear on his face.

"I had visions of us as divorced parents exchanging notes through Jelly Bean's backpack."

"Oh." And then he laughed. "What a ridiculous thing to think. That's what text messages are for."

She laughed along with him, ignoring the looks they got from passing shoppers.

"Vivian." He lifted her hand to his lips and kissed it. "I may not have imagined this as how I was going to have children, but I'm finding I could do much worse."

"It's not much of a compliment, but I'll take it."

She lifted up onto her toes and kissed him once on the lips. Then she headed for the cereal aisle before he could read anything other than humor in her expression.

CHAPTER SIX

DINNER EATEN AND the dishes done, Vivian followed Karl around the bar and into the living room. She sat at one end of the couch and picked up her knitting. He sat on the other end of the couch and picked up his book. It was progress. Only a week ago, he'd never been home while she was still awake. Only a couple of days ago, he was sitting in the armchair rather than sharing the couch. They were getting to know each other and, slowly, coming to trust each other.

Sometime in the near future, Karl might even tell her about his day as they sat down to dinner. She might talk about the jobs she was applying for. They might have a relationship outside of the shared parentage of their child.

The rich green wool slid through her fingers. The hat's shape was slowly emerging out of the yarn and she could begin to picture it on Karl's head. He needed something more than the righteous fire burning within him to keep his ears warm.

With a child on the way, she should probably be knitting baby blankets and little sweaters, but she wanted to give Karl something that didn't originate in his own largesse. The yarn was one of the few possessions she'd brought to Chicago that wasn't a necessity. The wool was soft, and she had needed something comforting with her.

The metal of her needles clicked. The pages of Karl's book rustled. If, on the other side of the city, someone with a telescope was scanning windows, they would see what appeared to be an old married couple so comfortable with each other they didn't need to talk—not two strangers with no idea what to say to each other.

"What book are you reading?" Vivian was struck by the sudden and silly fear that a stranger looking in the windows with a telescope knew what Karl was reading while she, sitting next to him, had no idea.

"Hmm?" Karl looked up and it took a moment for his eyes to focus on her across the cushions. "It's a collection of Herman Melville's short works. He wrote *Moby Dick*."

"I know who Melville is. I may not have graduated, but I've taken some college classes. I'm not stupid."

He turned his head back to the pages, giving her snippy comment all the attention it deserved.

"I'm sorry," she said. "You've never said or even implied I was stupid. I don't know why I reacted so poorly."

Only she did. The uncertainty of her existence and unwanted helplessness wore on her, coming out in bile when she was least prepared to stop it. Feeling close to, yet so distant from, the man on whom her life currently depended on was unsettling.

Which was no reason to be a bitch when all he'd done was answer her question.

He lifted his head and turned to her again, his face as expressionless as desert sand. "Not knowing who Melville is would only imply a deficit of education. It wouldn't say anything about your innate intelligence." Then, though there was no discernible change in his expression, his eyes softened. "I didn't know you went to college. What did you study?"

"Nothing." His expression hardened and he was turning his attention back to his book when she started talking again. "I didn't mean that to be snippy. Working full time meant I didn't have much time for school, and so I took what I wanted when it was available. It didn't amount to much of anything in particular."

She didn't tell him that the thought of finally graduating from college and facing job applications was terrifying. What if she'd spent all that time and money getting a degree and then still couldn't get a job other than dealing in casinos? So long as she never graduated, she never had to face losing the security of a job that offered health insurance and paid enough for her to keep an apartment and a car. She never had to leave the comfort of walking through the same doors for sixteen years and the security of knowing exactly who she was and what she was doing, even if she didn't like it.

It hadn't escaped Vivian that her father had been responsible for both destroying her chance at college after high school *and* destroying the life she'd built for herself once she'd realized "college student" wasn't something she could make work and still hope to eat. She could've handled the pregnancy on her own if she'd still had that job security.

"When did you learn to knit?" He was focused completely on her, the book on his lap closed, without even his finger to mark where he'd stopped.

Vivian admired Karl's ability to focus, although she was afraid she might come to crave it. When his hazel eyes fixed on her, her heart raced and her entire body warmed by ten degrees. Between pregnancy and being in the same room with Karl, she didn't need a winter coat.

"About ten years ago—when it seemed like everyone was learning how to knit. I've always liked activities that used my hands." Mostly she'd made dishcloths, which she'd had to donate to the thrift store before driving to Chicago because she couldn't justify taking them with her.

"Like card dealing?"

"The casino had automatic shufflers and the fancy shuffling techniques my father taught me would have been forbidden anyhow." Some of which made counting cards really easy and had been designed to facilitate cheating. But she'd always preferred the ones that looked fancy without being deceitful.

"Can you show me?"

"Card shuffling tricks or knitting?"

He appeared to take her question seriously, even though she'd meant it as a bit of a joke. "Card shuffling tricks."

"Really?" Karl had tried to hide his opinion of her previous career, but he hadn't been as successful as he probably thought.

"We're trying to be friends, right?"

Friendship had been a great idea in the doctor's office when she'd been lying back on the examination table feeling about as sexy as an ottoman. Now, sitting on the couch with him scooching closer to her, those intense eyes burning into her, friendship seemed a sure path to sex, and sex was a bad idea. They'd had sex as strangers and look where it had gotten them.

What's stopping you? The horse is already out; no use shutting the barn door now. Think of how his hazel eyes will burn when he explodes into you.

That was just the pregnancy talking. The books

had warned her that pregnancy made some women horny. It had to be the pregnancy. It couldn't be seeing the fine hairs on his strong, bare forearms and being reminded of why she'd broken her own rules and slept with a resort guest to begin with.

"Um, sure." She stood up quickly—to find a deck of cards, not to escape Karl and her own lustful thoughts.

When she returned, she had a new deck of cards and a plan. She sat in the chair Karl normally used and faced him across the coffee table. He gave her a knowing smile, as though what was bothering her was bothering him, too, but he didn't argue or ask her to sit next to him.

Friendship was a good idea. This wanting she was feeling would only lead to bad things. He had bought her two winter coats, was paying for her health insurance and providing her with a place to live because they were married, but they weren't married because they were in love. The child growing inside her wasn't an expression of their love. She'd been feeling vulnerable and he'd been talking about how important family was to him and she'd succumbed to a dream that didn't exist. They'd had hot, dirty, wonderful, random stranger sex, and now they couldn't stay strangers.

Sex would change the bargain. Sex would put them uncomfortably close to an exchange of pleasure for material goods, and that wasn't a bargain she was willing to make. In that moment she made a promise to herself. They would be partners when she was finally able to put her lips against one of his chiseled cheeks and lick her way to his collarbone and down his chest until she made his heartbeat pound and echo through her body. She would have a job and contribute something other than dinner to his day. She wouldn't be helpless anymore.

"What do you want to see?"

He shrugged. "Impress me."

She held the deck of cards in her left hand and gripped two corners with her right. Both thumb and ring finger two-thirds on the corner, one-third off, just as her dad had taught her. Then she lifted the deck of cards with her right hand nearly two feet from her left, angled her thumb and let the cards fall.

THE CARDS BARELY made a whisper as they cascaded into her left hand. When Karl had been in high school, there was a kid in his class who'd liked to show off his card tricks. The kid had bragged about his mastery of the cards, but when he'd done that trick, the cards had sounded like someone was rustling through a trash can and he'd had to brace his arm against his body in such a way that the cards shot into his gut, rather than flowing through the air.

"Wanna see it again?" she asked.

"Yes." At the bar that fateful night, he'd watched her long fingers wrap around her drink and wondered if he could let go of himself long enough to enjoy the company of a beautiful woman. She had smiled, a little shy and a little sad, and suddenly making her laugh had become more important than his own problems.

He paid attention to those hands again, now, watching exactly where she placed her fingers and how she bent the cards before releasing them. He wasn't any less impressed seeing her card trick the second time.

You were so focused on what her lips would feel like on your body that you didn't stop to think what effect those dexterous fingers could have. Her eyes were twinkling and the way her pink lips curved into a half smile when he looked from her fingers up to her face confirmed that he'd been right to focus on the power of those lips. The nimble fingers were an added bonus.

"You weren't expecting to be impressed," she said.

"No. I've never seen cards shuffled that way so well." He realized that compliment sounded hollow when Vivian's eyes narrowed. "I couldn't do it and I'm not foolish enough *not* to credit expertise when I see it, even if I don't fully understand it."

Her lips twitched and she started shuffling the deck. "What card do you want?"

"What?"

"Before you continue to damn me with faint praise—"

The well-deserved dry tone of her voice made him smile. Not many people were willing to poke at him, and a perverse part of him was attracted to those who dared.

"—I have another trick for you. Name a card."

"Three of diamonds."

She dealt them each five cards. "The top card in your pile is the three of diamonds."

When he turned the card over, he was staring at the three of diamonds. "Five of clubs," he said, not willing to believe what he saw.

She blinked, then dealt out another ten cards and looked up at him, one brow raised. He turned over his top card.

"Ten of hearts."

"It's the third card from the bottom on the table."

He riffled through the cards to find the card he'd asked for, right where she'd said it was.

"Impressed yet?"

"Yes." And a little appalled. These were not an honest person's tricks. "Where did you learn to do this?"

"I've been shuffling cards since I could hold a

deck. Some of the tricks my dad taught me are just for flourish. Others are made to look innocent and win money."

"You play solitaire. How do you not win every time?"

"If you're not gambling, cheating takes all the fun out of it. And I don't like gambling."

"But you worked at a casino."

She shrugged. "At the time, I needed any job I could get and I got a job at Middle Kingdom."

"And you kept it because…"

"How I feel about gambling doesn't pay the bills."

"And your college classes…"

"Didn't get me anything other than an appreciation of Melville," she said dryly.

He laughed. They were going about this relationship backward, with marriage and pregnancy first and the get-to-know-you later. Done the normal way, he probably wouldn't have looked past her job to bother getting to know her. And he would've missed out on the sly sense of humor he was growing to really appreciate.

And those fingers.

She was shuffling the cards again. A nervous habit.

"Can you teach me?"

"To deal exactly the card you want? No."

"To do the first card trick. The bit of flourish."

He didn't know why he was doing this, other than

that he liked being near her and wanted to keep her talking.

"Probably."

He patted the seat next to him on the couch. When she raised an eyebrow at him, he politely asked if he could sit next to her.

I shouldn't do this, he thought as he scooted closer to her. But she smelled like jasmine and suddenly he didn't care if she had secrets, so long as her thigh was pressed against his.

"This would be easier if I had some room to maneuver." She smiled up at him and her eyes colored to warm amber. Her pupils had gotten larger and her gaze softer.

"Probably," he said. If she evidenced any resistance at all, he would pull back and learn a card trick he'd never use. Instead, her mouth opened and the tip of her tongue ran along her bottom lip. Karl stayed where he was.

We shouldn't do this. They were strangers forced to live in an apartment together because they were having a baby. The intimacy he'd felt sitting across the dining room table from her, cleaning up after dinner with her, her hands soapy and warm as she passed dishes to him, sharing a couch—that was all a lie. They were still strangers.

He took the deck of cards from her hands, reaching blindly for the table and not caring when the cards tumbled onto the floor.

"I thought you wanted to learn a card trick."

He took her breathy voice as further confirmation that she was as affected by him as he was by her.

"You don't have to do this," he said. He leaned in until the fact that they weren't kissing was a technicality. The warm air she expelled from her nose spread across his face. "Nothing I give you has a price."

His heart pumped rationalizations in his ears. *You've already had sex with her. The damage is done. What do you have to gain by denying yourself the feeling of the delicate bones of her spine under your lips?*

When she leaned in to kiss him, he had his answer.

CHAPTER SEVEN

VIVIAN HAD ALWAYS known Karl must be warm inside, despite his cold hands. His face might be frozen, without expression, but his small kindnesses and sense of righteousness had hinted at a fire burning within. It was the only explanation for his lips inflaming her.

He took her bottom lip between his teeth and nibbled. She made a wanting noise deep in her throat. Her nipples were hard against her blouse—had been since they sat together on the couch—and she was wet with desire. Pregnancy hormones made the tingle of his hand as it ran up the length of her body linger. Pregnancy kept the memory of his nip at her ear fresh, long after he moved on to kiss her neck.

She either had to blame the pregnancy or take responsibility for getting up off the couch and straddling him. But she wanted him. Wanted him despite the fact that the secrets she kept could come back and destroy the little bit of security she'd managed to find in Chicago. Could ruin the trust that she and Karl had developed.

She didn't want to think about that now, with his hands strong against her back while his lips were soft on her neck. All she wanted to think about was that when she pressed her hands against his chest it was solid, and his heartbeat was powerful and real. She could worry about her secrets tomorrow.

The pressure of his hands on her back released. Karl pulled away from her and watched her face intently as he slowly unbuttoned her blouse. Though his expression didn't change, she could feel the pulse of his thighs as each undone button revealed more of her skin. He didn't make a sound until the front of her shirt hung open and he smoothed it off her shoulders with a sigh.

He pressed his lips against the crest of each breast and this time it was her thighs that tightened in response. Then he looked up at her and she didn't know how she could have ever thought those eyes were cold. "I wish the night that got us here was clearer in my memory."

Why did he have to talk? She didn't want to think about that night and the morning she'd woken up to his cold eyes. That night she'd been seeking solace and someone to take her mind off what her father had asked her to do—and she'd nearly done.

She was in Chicago because she would be burned by the consequences of what she *hadn't* done for the rest of her life.

He licked a line of skin along the edge of her bra

and she pressed her hips into him, to lose herself in the present. "I intend to take my time tonight," he murmured as he lifted her small breast closer to him and his tongue slipped under the fabric of her bra.

She moaned. Her body had wanted him since the first moment she'd seen him. In Las Vegas, she'd slid onto a bar stool next to him, felt the nip of his emotions radiating off his body and wanted to warm the chill of his eyes as she'd wanted him to cool her anger. She'd ordered a gin and tonic, instead, trying not to look at the sharp line of his profile.

She remembered the next gin and tonic, which Karl had bought her, and later the bottle of tequila he'd gotten for them to share. By the time they'd made it up to his room and noticed they didn't have any limes, neither of them had cared. She had wanted to forget how she had nearly allowed her father to sell her soul. What Karl had been trying to forget she hadn't known and hadn't cared.

"Why were you drinking?" Crystal decanters on a fancy bar cart by his dining table held whiskey and brandy, but she'd never seen him open one. He hadn't had so much as a beer since she'd arrived. "That night in Las Vegas, why were you drinking?"

He murmured a nonresponse as his tongue curled around her nipple, her head falling back in pleasure.

When his fingers started working on the button of her jeans, she put her hand down to stop them.

"Does it matter?" He spoke to her skin as he pressed butterfly kisses around her collarbone. His fingers burrowed themselves between hers, a suggestion that she open herself up to him, and suddenly the reason he had been drinking mattered more than the aching between her legs.

"Yes." She lifted herself up and off him so she sat on the couch again. She'd lived with him for two weeks and she knew no more about him than what she'd read in the Chicago papers.

"Do you have to know tonight?" His voice was rough with desire and, she was certain, frustration.

He didn't look at her, but she could see the throb of aggravation in his jawline. He reached out a hand to rest on her thigh, and her body pulsed in response. They were both going to be angry with her for stopping now, but she couldn't let the night go further.

Her questions had been a flash of sanity. Having sex with this man without thinking had gotten her into this helpless position to begin with. She couldn't get pregnant again, but she *could* lose what little independence and self-respect she had. He said this wasn't an exchange, but what if it became one?

"Yes."

He made an incoherent growl and pulled his hand away from her leg. When he turned to look at her,

the skin around his eyes was tight, but any other irritation had been smoothed out of his face. "We're
not going to do this tonight, are we?"

"No. I'm sorry," she offered. Now she was a
tease, as well as being the suspicious pregnant
woman who showed up unannounced on his doorstep. Better a tease than a woman who used sex
now for permanence later.

He pushed off the couch. "Not nearly as sorry as
I am." His butt was now directly at her eye level,
and she could imagine its hard muscles under her
hands when her nails clung to him. She wanted to
feel the strength of him between her thighs. It was
her own fault for stopping.

"Make some coffee while I shower." His "please"
was an afterthought.

"Coffee?"

"I want you, Vivian. If this—" he gestured to the
couch and her still gaping blouse "—won't happen
until you get your questions answered, I'll answer
your questions. All of them."

"Tonight?" God, she sounded stupid, but of all
the reactions she'd expected, this hadn't been one
of them. Anger, maybe, so she could feel justified
in denying herself pleasure. As it was, with her
breasts exposed to the world through the floor-to-
ceiling windows, she just felt awkward.

When he looked at her, Vivian felt stripped to
the bone. "Yes, tonight." He ran his hand over his

face—as if he was a normal man who actually felt emotions like exasperation rather than the wax figure she preferred to imagine him to be. "I don't know what it says about me that I can't think of a single thing to ask you in return. When I get back from the shower…"

He looked from the door to his bedroom and back to her. "I keep thinking of the baby as a Trojan horse, delivered to ruin my life in a form I can't resist. But maybe you are my Helen, and my fate is to be brought down by a beautiful woman, instead. Even worse, I can't make myself care."

She flinched from the disgust in his voice, even though it was self-directed, because he might be right. She'd left her secrets and her troubles back in Las Vegas, and she was only in his life until she could get back on her feet. She buttoned her shirt, still feeling unprotected. If she didn't get a job soon, Karl would wonder why she wasn't applying for any of the dealer jobs at nearby casinos. She could fob off his questions with "I want a change" for only so long.

Maybe she shouldn't have let her fears get in the way of sex. She could've kept his brain clouded with desire, and he wouldn't have realized he had questions about her still unanswered.

Who would've thought she'd rather play the siren than Helen of Troy?

Water started in his bathroom. She swung her

legs over the side of the couch and got up to make the coffee before she could think any longer about the sanity of coming to Chicago. She was pregnant, broke and blacklisted in Las Vegas. Along with everything else, Karl provided her with time to find a new job in a new city with a married last name.

He might not see the baby as anything other than the ruin of his life, but he wasn't the one who had to pee every time he blinked, so what the hell did he have to complain about?

CHAPTER EIGHT

VIVIAN WAS SITTING on the couch, wrapped in flannel pajamas and a blanket, when Karl stepped from his bedroom into the living room. Her face glowed in the light of the full moon coming in through the windows.

"I made coffee." She didn't look up.

"Why did you turn the lights off?"

"I keep hoping I'm asleep."

At least he wasn't the only one upset with how the evening had turned out. He walked into the kitchen and poured himself a cup. "Would you like some?"

"No." She sounded like someone had kicked her in the stomach, though he didn't know what she had to be upset about. The night may not have gone the way she wanted, but she wasn't the one jerking off in the shower because he had questions that could have waited until morning. "It will just keep me up."

"It's decaf." A stupid, mundane conversation for them to be having when he wanted her in his bed, naked and willing, not wrapped up like a nun and worried about getting enough sleep.

He'd never been the type of heel to be mad at a woman who changed her mind about sex. Of course, he'd never been kissing a woman's breasts when she hopped away from him and said, "I have a question first." Vivian was full of surprises—most of them unpleasant.

And he still wanted her. He wanted her in his bed, and he wanted her on his couch, and he was willing to live with the stupid bird hopping on his dining table if it meant she was around when he got home from work.

If they weren't having this tedious conversation about caffeine, he'd be letting his anger get the better of him or trying to seduce her. Maybe both.

But soon she would get a job and find an apartment. They would agree to divorce and visitation terms, and he wouldn't be constantly surrounded by the scent of jasmine anymore. His life would return to normal.

He looked up from pouring his coffee to see Vivian sweep her hair off her neck. Until the moment she packed her bags, he would have to get used to a new normal of sexual frustration and bird shit.

He sat in the same armchair he'd sat in when she'd first arrived at his apartment with her bags, bird and baby. He hadn't wanted to sit next to her that day for fear she'd be real. Now he knew she was real and was afraid he would reach for her if he sat next to her. And he wanted to look at her. She was pleasant to look at.

"Well?" Her head jerked up in surprise at his words. "Despite having lived in my apartment for two weeks, you want to know more about me now."

"Um…" She looked out the window and he wondered if the questions were just a ruse to cover up another reason she didn't want to have sex. The woman could really bring out the worst, most suspicious thoughts in him. "Why were you in the bar that night?"

"I'll answer your questions if you'll answer mine." The shower hadn't been as pleasurable as the woman sitting across from him would have been, but it had cleared his mind.

Her shoulders dropped in resignation, but she didn't look surprised. "Why were you in the bar that night?" she repeated.

"It was my birthday. I was celebrating."

She blinked. "That's it?"

He sighed. It was the truth, but it wasn't the whole truth. "I turned thirty-nine years old that night. My father was thirty-eight when he died and I still can't believe I'm older than he will ever be. You're in this apartment because I'm not enough of a louse to turn a pregnant woman out onto the streets. But the only reason I'm not a louse is because I measure my actions against what my dad would think. And he's dead."

"I'm sorry."

The dark made it easier to be honest. "My father always wanted me to get married and have a big family. When I bought you the first drink, I was thinking about how I was divorced with no kids." By the time he'd bought the bottle of tequila, he hadn't been thinking of his father or kids at all. His father would definitely have been disappointed in what happened that night, especially the misguided attempt to solve his problems with marriage to a stranger because she was good-looking and he didn't feel maudlin when she smiled.

"Am I a Trojan horse or a blessing in disguise?"

"The jury's still out." Karl didn't apologize for his earlier comment. He'd meant every word. "Why were *you* at the bar that night?"

"I work—worked—at the hotel."

He supposed her flippant answer was his reward for being honest. "You weren't in the habit of having a drink after work." She cocked her head at him again and he gave into her curiosity. "I wasn't so drunk I didn't notice how surprised the bartender was to see you there."

"You are two completely different men. At home, you barely say a word and act like you don't know how to use the muscles in your face. Out in public, you shake hands and smile at people." She pursed her lips, and he waited to see what she would say next. "Of course, even out in public, if someone asks a question you don't like, nothing in the movement of your face gives away a smidgen of answer. I fell into the trap of thinking you're two different people, when really the public face is just a mask over the private, listening and watching one."

"You're not the first to have made that mistake."

"You say that like it's a damnation of the entire city of Chicago. How many people have been in your apartment long enough to notice the private man behind the very sincere fake smile?"

His ex-wife, but it had taken her years to realize that the Karl who shook hands with strangers was the fake one. It wasn't until Jessica asked for a divorce that Karl realized she'd been mistaken. His first marriage had been full of misunderstood beliefs and poorly conceived, even if sincere, attempts to fix the missteps. This second marriage was still unbelievable.

"You assume it's a fake smile. But I'm very sincere." He had a duty to each and every citizen of Chicago.

"Why do you do it? The shaking hands and greeting people? You don't like it."

Jessica had never been perceptive enough to notice that. Thankfully, most other people weren't, either. "You still didn't answer my question, Vivian."

"Sure I did. I was there to get a drink." Despite

looking right at him as she talked, her voice lightened to a ridiculous pitch for anyone telling the truth. Still, she was becoming a better liar.

He ignored her evasion. If she was so determined to lie, the reason she was at the bar must be pretty damning, and there was probably evidence he could find if he dug deep enough. And he would. He just didn't want to—not quite yet.

Despite the lack of full satisfaction he'd gotten from his hand in the shower, and his unaccountable interest in the curve of her lips, he was glad she'd stopped their lovemaking. It was bad enough to *want* someone with deep secrets.

"I smile and shake hands with everyone I meet because I want the city of Chicago to know who I am. I want them to realize there is an independent city office dedicated to investigating and prosecuting corruption, fraud and waste. If they know or suspect something, I want them to pull out my business card and give my office a call. If they are taking money under the table so an inferior building passes inspection, I want them to know I'll find them and they'll go to prison."

Pressure was building up in his chest and he stopped before he exploded. In a world with starvation, war and disease, one city employee taking a bribe so a building passes inspection probably doesn't seem like a big deal, but government corruption prevented the Mexican government from being able to prosecute drug dealers. Government corruption nearly brought down Kabul Bank and made the United States's exit from Afghanistan more difficult. And in the city of Chicago, it was a big deal to the family that lost their lives when their house burned down because shoddy electrical work had passed inspection when money changed hands.

One small employee in a huge organization—what harm could it cause? After all, bribery was supposed to be a victimless crime.

He sank back into the depths of his chair. Among the forty thousand people who died in car accidents every year, three may not have seemed like so many, except to the five people left to mourn.

"I read on the internet about the death of your family," she said. "I'm sorry."

"It was over twenty years ago." Twenty-three years, but who was keeping track? Karl could recite the key dates in the scandal as if he had memorized them for a history test. Former Illinois Secretary of State George Ryan was elected governor in 1998. Twenty days later, two of his employees pled guilty to racketeering. On September 27, 1999, a trucking company official admitted to paying to fix licenses for his drivers, including the driver involved in the crash that killed Karl's family and one who was involved in the crash that killed six children in Wisconsin. It took Governor Ryan five months to apologize for corruption in the secretary of state office and it took until December 17, 2003, for Ryan to be indicted for taking payoffs. By that time, Karl was old enough to know justice was a slow and frustrating process.

He wanted Vivian to understand. This wasn't just about why his job was important, but also about who he was.

"Did you know that the inspector general for the state of Illinois at the time, a man named Dan Bauer, removed a briefcase full of cash and campaign fundraising receipts during a raid of a driver's license agency? He eventually pled guilty to obstruction of justice, but the raid happened almost a full year before the Willis children were killed. It was too late to save my family, but someone might have noticed in time to save the Willis children." Bauer had had a responsibility to those children— and everyone who drove on Illinois highways—and he'd failed on the job. His failures had cost lives.

Karl didn't notice Vivian had stood up until she returned with his coffee cup, full and steaming. "Thank you," he said.

They sat in silence for a while, the clock flashing on the coffeemaker in the kitchen, marking the time they were in each other's company. His anger cooled. Enjoying her company was too active a phrase for how he felt right now.

Content. He was content to have her in his apartment, even though they were in the living room and not in his bed. Content to feel her presence across the coffee table and know she would still smell faintly of jasmine if he sat next to her and gathered her into his arms.

If he was actively anything, he was being actively foolish for feeling this way while still not knowing her secrets.

She owed him an answer—a real one—to at least one of his questions. Karl picked something easy. "So, if—what was the phrase you used?—'the last name and most of the blood's Chinese,' how did you end up in some town in the middle-of-nowhere Nevada for high school?"

The moment she smiled at him, he knew it was a stupid question. Blame it on the decaf, the late hours, or the woman. He was smart enough to know immigrants lived everywhere in the United States, not just in big cities and ethnic communities like Chinatowns—or Archer Heights, where he had grown up, for that matter.

"You're making the same mistake most people make, assuming that someone with Chinese heritage has parents who came in the 1970s and studied engineering. The first Yaps came to the United States in 1852, to mine for gold."

Ah, his question had been even dumber than he'd realized.

"When the Yap men had enough money, they brought over women from China to be their wives.

In times of poor fortune, or during the times immigration from China was banned, they married within the United States, if they could find a Chinese wife. In 1910, a Yap ended up in Idaho to fight the great wildfire and found love, but not with a Chinese woman. Because she was white, and intermarriages were illegal, I don't think he married the Sicilian woman he took to Nevada with him. But my dad remembers his grandmother's strange Sicilian-Chinese stir-fry. I have a Mexican grandmother, too, also on my dad's side. They were able to marry because my grandfather argued Mexican wasn't Caucasian."

She smiled at him as if he was a child being taught a lesson, and he deserved it. He'd learned in history classes about the Chinese workers on the railroads and the Chinese Exclusion Act; he'd just never come face-to-face with the actual history of it.

"The Yaps may have been in the United States longer than the Mileks," she said.

He chuckled. "The Mileks, yes, but please try not to compare notes with my mother, lest you get the great history of the Poles in the United States from her. It's much like the lecture you just gave me, only hers starts with Casimir Pulaski and the Revolutionary War. She conveniently forgets that Casimir Pulaski had no children and the only evidence of relation is a coincidence of dates, locations and last names."

"They say men marry women like their mothers."

This time his laugh was full and hearty, all residual anger gone in the enjoyment of being teased by a beautiful woman. "Next time my mother asks why I married you, I'll be sure to tell her that you remind me of her."

"Just what every mother *and* daughter-in-law wants to hear."

He lifted his hands in mock innocence. "Don't blame me. You said it first."

Vivian's mouth opened to respond, but whatever she was going to say ended in a great yawn, which she tried to cover with her hands.

"It's late. We should go to bed." He still had questions for her, but she would be here in the morning.

"I'm sorry about tonight," she said behind another yawn.

"Don't be too sorry, or I'll think you've changed your mind." He wanted her to change her mind.

She shook her head. "I kept telling myself I'm already pregnant and the horse is out of the barn, but it's not enough to make up for me being here and dependent on you."

They'd had much the same thoughts, only he'd let the heat of passion overwhelm practicality. Vivian had occupied nearly all of his thoughts since she'd arrived, and it would've been a relief to know how accurate his imagination was. Then he could come up with new fantasies.

"My reassurance that your housing and health care didn't come with a cost wasn't enough?" He knew it wasn't enough. It wouldn't have been enough for him and he respected her more for it.

"When I have a job of my own, and my own apartment, then that will be enough."

"Why haven't you applied for one of the jobs at the casinos?" They'd talked about the jobs she'd applied for and what she was interested in doing. Not once had she mentioned applying for a riverboat casino position.

"I've worked in casinos since I was eighteen, and I grew up around them. I'd like to try something new."

Ah, there was the guilty look, he thought, when she turned toward the window, but he was suddenly too worn out by emotion to pursue it. Like his other questions, this one could wait until morning.

CHAPTER NINE

"DAD, I'M ASKING you again, where is my money?" Vivian heard herself shriek the words and quickly lowered her voice before she woke up Karl.

"It's not my fault," her father pleaded. Nothing was ever his fault. "How was I supposed to leave Las Vegas with no money?"

"How was I supposed to *live* in Las Vegas with no money, especially after you got me fired?" She shared responsibility for getting fired, but blaming her father seemed fair since he wouldn't take responsibility for anything else.

"You've managed before. You're resourceful."

"Resourceful?" Of course that's how he would see her. Good ol' Vivian. It's the first day of school in a new town, but she doesn't need her dad to help her register for classes. There's no food in the house, but he needs to meet with the guys because "it's gonna be big." She'll figure it out because she's resourceful. Go ahead, gamble away the college fund she worked and scrimped to save. She'll get to college anyway, because she always manages.

Apparently she hadn't managed well enough.

She'd registered for school and gotten them groceries, but she'd never made college happen. A random series of college courses taken when she had the money didn't make a college degree. All it made was a table dealer who'd read Homer and taken calculus.

All her dreams of college and getting a good, respectable job—developed out of the scares of years spent in a world that hoped for one big score to fix all problems—lost in a card game.

Marriage and pregnancy had gotten her out of Las Vegas, but not in the way she had wanted. She hadn't *earned* her way into this beautiful apartment through hard work, and neither had she *loved* her way here with the man of her dreams. She'd *slept* her way into this apartment, and the truth of it broke her heart. But she couldn't leave, because outside of this apartment was a quicksand world of unstable housing and unemployment. She hadn't loved Las Vegas, but at least she'd been on stable ground there.

"Yeah. I heard you were fired and aren't even in Vegas anymore. You must have figured something out, though."

"I could be in a homeless shelter somewhere, or out on the street begging for money. What do you know?" *What do you care?*

"But you're not. I know you're not because you're…"

"Resourceful. I know. You've said it before."

"I've almost got all the money to pay these guys back. Then I only need one more big hit to pay you back. I'll pay all of it back to you, Vivy, I swear." *I swear this is a sure thing. By next year, you won't even need financial aid to help with college. We'll pay your way through any school you want.*

"Are you going to get me back my money the same way you lost all of yours and got me in this situation to begin with?"

"The next time…"

The next score. Over the next big mountain. Around the next corner. "Get a job and earn money the hard way, like the rest of us do, Dad. You know what, if you get a job, I won't even charge you interest on the money you owe me."

"Ah, Vivy, you wouldn't charge me interest. I'm your father. Even if you are frustrated with me now, we'll have a fun road trip from wherever you are back to Vegas and you'll remember how much you love your old man." Even on the other end of the phone she could see the laugh lines at the corners of his eyes and his wide smile. When he smiled like this, old women stopped him on the street to pinch his cheeks, and he had such a look of innocence that he could walk out of Fort Knox with bars of gold in his hands.

She had tears in her eyes, but she wasn't fooled. "Emphasis on old."

"Don't be that way."

"Dad, I want my money back." *I want my life back.*

"My plan's going to work this time, Vivy. I swear it. I can win. I won you that bird, remember. That bird has to be worth something. Most parakeets can't talk, and Xìnyùn's a regular conversationalist."

Yeah, if gambling phrases were all I wanted to talk about.

Of all the apps that were available for smartphones, the one Vivian wanted most right now would enable her to reach through the phone and shake sense into her father. She probably couldn't shake hard enough.

They said their goodbyes and hung up, which was good because Vivian didn't think she could keep calm much longer.

When she looked up and saw Karl standing next to her in the kitchen, she nearly dropped her phone in the sink. "Did it ever occur to you that eavesdropping on conversations is rude?"

"No." He didn't even look ashamed of himself for listening in. His face had the unfeeling, immovable look of suspicious-Karl. Last night's open, honest laughing-Karl was gone.

"How much of that conversation did you hear?"

"Enough to know you're resourceful and that your father took your money."

"Oh." Thirst rushed her and she got herself a glass of water. And then another. She pressed the third against her head, hoping to cool her nerves. Karl waited.

He didn't speak until she'd drunk the third glass of water. "I'd like to hear the story from you."

Vivian thought about lying. Though she hadn't been forthcoming with everything she hadn't lied to Karl yet, and she didn't want to start. Until she got a job, he was all that stood between her and that homeless shelter she'd hung over her father's head. She could tell most of the story honestly.

"My father hopes that around the next corner will be a golden ticket to wealth. He bet more than he had at a private poker game." She couldn't tell this story while staring at him staring at her. She needed something to distract her from her own foolishness. Since the coffee was already made, she got out mixing bowls and started making pancakes.

"I don't even know why he was allowed into such a high-stakes game." Especially with the men he'd ended up playing with. They'd scared her in the short time she'd interacted with them. How her father managed to spend his free time with them...

When she shook her head at her own ignorance about what her father had been doing since she'd moved out of the house, flour from her measuring cup spilled onto the counter. To get something to wipe it up, she would have to turn around and face

Karl. She left it to clean up later. "No, I do know how he got into the game. When he wants something, my dad is nothing but charm and flattery." And that innocent smile.

"It's a rare person who's not susceptible to flattery." Karl was standing so close to her she could feel his breath on her neck.

"Yes, especially when it's in the form of an eager puppy." Her father was a small-time grifter, hoping to be big-time one day. And to big-time grifters, her dad was a mark, because he didn't have the smarts not to get in over his head. She took a step to the right, shifting the pancake-making operation with her. "Apparently he won for a while and got cocky. Then he started losing. So he kept betting bigger and bigger to win his money back, but it never happened. When he couldn't meet his obligations, he stole every penny I had. He'd been visiting me and I was stupid enough not to make it hard for him." All her security and the cushion she'd built up for sixteen years, gone in an instant.

God, this was embarrassing to admit. Since she'd left Jackpot, Vivian had tried to live a normal, stable life. Get to work on time. Save her money. Pay her bills. She'd thought she was safe from the chaos of her father because she only interacted with him when he said he needed money.

She dumped the milk and eggs into the flour mixture with a splash, adding to the mess on the counter. No wonder her dad had thought she would help him. She'd left Jackpot intent on leaving schemes behind, but she'd always given him money whenever he'd needed it. She'd gotten out; that was all she had been concerned about.

She started mixing. "Then he disappeared. I don't think that even everything I had was enough to cover his debts."

Karl put his hand on hers, stopping her furious beating. She looked down at the bowl. There were no lumps in the pancake mixture. They were over-mixed and would be tough.

"You were at the bar that night because of what your father did."

"Yes." The actual timeline was a little different than what Karl was assuming, but it was close enough.

"And your job?"

The frying pan banged when she set it on the stove, a great, satisfying sound that rang through the apartment and echoed in her ears. "My father's debts cost me that, too."

"Ah." Karl nodded as though he understood, but he didn't understand anything. Not her fear, not how close she had come to slipping and crashing into a hole deeper than the Grand Canyon. "If you hadn't been fired, would you have come to me for help?"

"No. I would've told you about the baby, but..."

"But you would've done it with a phone call rather than a cross-country drive."

"I was raised by a single parent. I could've made it work." Plus, she wouldn't have had a long drive with which to talk herself out of an abortion. And she would've had the money to pay for one, too. As life had actually happened, though, she'd driven to Chicago certain she would ask Karl for abortion money, but then spent the drive coming to the realization that she couldn't go through with one.

Objectively, she could see she was vulnerable both financially and emotionally. If a friend had been in her situation, she would suggest an abortion and then question the friend's judgment when she decided to have the baby anyway. But there was nothing objective about being faced with such a decision, and she couldn't say anything other than "I'm keeping my baby"—as if she was in a Madonna song.

She'd given herself trigger reactions. If Karl had said "I don't want a baby" or "How dare you bring this into my life?" or something else of the sort, she'd have mentioned abortion. He hadn't, and so *she* hadn't. It hadn't been the best way to decide to have a child, but Vivian was certain there were people who'd had children based on a fuzzier decision-making process. Even if she didn't know any.

She wasn't going to let herself think about the consequences of leaving a major life decision, such as having a child, in the hands of one man's reaction to the news. She'd been in an emotional chasm at the time. If she were being honest with herself, she hadn't fully climbed back out yet. She was on the edge of the canyon, teetering, and her life could go either way. Sometimes lifting herself over the edge and back onto solid ground seemed a sure way to lose her grip completely.

"And we can see how well that turned out," Karl said.

Pancake batter dripped onto the counter as she whipped around to face him. "I've done the best I could with what I have. When the longest *you've* ever lived in a place after your seventh birthday is two years, let me know how willing you would be to pack up and leave your life behind, no matter how less than ideal it is. Until then, shove off."

"Your mother?"

"She died in childbirth. And, yes," she added, turning back to the pancakes on the stove, "women still die in childbirth." The thought should scare her, but death seemed the least of her worries right now, especially since her baby would have a stable father and welcoming family. More than she'd started out with.

"Your father raised you."

"My mom's sister helped out for a while, but Aunt Kitty left when I was about seven. Not long after she left, we moved for the first time." They'd exchanged letters until Aunt Kitty couldn't keep up with their moves. When Vivian was in high school, she had mailed her aunt a letter that had been returned, marked undeliverable. And her one blood connection to her mother had disappeared from her life.

Vivian had thought about Aunt Kitty on and off over the years, but now was the first time she understood why her aunt had left.

She flipped a pancake too early and poorly; half of it ended up on the stove top. "My father should never have had children. But—" her childhood hadn't been all bad and she had to credit her father for that, too "—he loved me. I never doubted that. He made the moving seem fun and he protected me the best he knew how."

"If he showed up at my door tomorrow, what would you do?"

"I'd turn him away." She didn't have to look at Karl to know he didn't believe her. She sighed. "I'd let him in and make him dinner. He's my father." And she would remember how he'd turned the experience of buying her first maxi pads into a spy game so she forgot her embarrassment. How they'd started their time in each new house by searching for secret passages, though they'd never found one. And how he'd never laughed at her for believing a wardrobe could take her to Narnia.

Karl put his hand on her shoulder. Vivian supposed it was meant to be supportive, but it felt holier-than-thou. "Just because he's family, doesn't mean he shouldn't be subject to the same rules as the rest of us."

She swatted his hand away with the spatula. "It's easier to preach when you don't have to practice."

"How do you know I haven't practiced what I preach?"

"Because if you did, you'd at least have a little sympathy for how hard it would be to shut the door in my father's face." She set the spatula down on the counter, sick of this conversation. "I'm going to get dressed. You can finish the pancakes."

KARL DIDN'T SEEM to get any less suspicious as they cleaned up breakfast and he got ready to spend his Saturday at work, while Vivian got ready to do very little with her day.

With her hours upon hours of free time last week, she'd applied for thirty different jobs and was waiting until new positions were posted on Monday. And waiting for people to call her back—hopefully—and waiting for the proper amount of time to pass before she could call and check up on her applications. Or wait to hear nothing and decide it was time to rework her résumé. Into what, she didn't know.

Not to mention that she wanted a job before she started showing. Employers weren't supposed to refuse to hire a pregnant woman, but she had little faith that someone would give the woman who waddled into their office a fair shake. If she could only get hired, it would be much harder to fire her when her belly started to show.

As if she needed another worry on her shoulders.

Hearing the front door shut she got her tennis shoes out of the closet. Staying cooped up in Karl's apartment—even if the view was beautiful—was driving her crazy. So she'd gotten into a new habit lately. After Karl left for the day and Vivian had completed what few chores she had, she would put on her shoes and winter coat and take a walk around the city. Surrounded by public art and grand buildings, the sticky situation she found herself in seemed less important.

She slipped out of the apartment building before the doorman saw her. He was nicer to her these days, but his obsequiousness was just as insulting as his previous rudeness. She was nothing to him but Karl Milek's wife, when she only wished to be treated as a person.

Once she escaped the protection of the building's awning, snowflakes danced in the air before dying on her neck, and she took the time to readjust her scarf and hat. Whatever winter resilience she'd gained during her high school years in northern Nevada had been ruined by her years in Las Vegas. A couple of blocks and turns later and she was on Michigan Avenue, headed north and bent a little forward into the wind. Slush seeping through her tennis shoes sent chills up her spine. Even bundled in her Karl-bought winter coat, scarf and hat, she shivered.

Today she was hoping the snow and ice would freeze one problem in particular.

Keeping her pregnancy a secret wasn't just about superstition—it was also about shame. A little over a month ago she had been moderately successful with a job she didn't hate, a nice apartment and some security safeguarded in the bank.

Now, she was the woman who got married and pregnant while drunk, topping any scheme her father could have come up with—and it had been an accident. More damaging to her pride, she couldn't even claim to have quit her job to be at home with her child; she'd been fired. Even if Karl shared responsibility for the baby, he couldn't share how trapped she presently felt here in Chicago. His family would probably expect her to be happy about the baby growing inside her—when the only thing she could feel right now was terror. Holding on to the idea of a baby being real wasn't the same thing as being excited about the child.

Until she had a job—income of her own—she was vulnerable and the baby meant her vulnerability risked more than just her own life. And if Karl decided he didn't trust her anymore, or couldn't forgive the reason she'd been forced to leave Las Vegas, she and Jelly Bean would be out on the street.

Stopping in front of the Art Institute, she dug some cash out of her pocket—more of Karl's largesse—and bought herself a *Streetwise,* the Chicago weekly produced mostly by the homeless and formerly homeless. It wasn't a new issue, despite the claims of the man selling it, but she didn't care. When she gave the vendor a couple of bucks of someone else's money, it seemed like an investment against her own homelessness.

Only she had a home to go to, and especially with the baby, she was fully aware that she'd throw herself into whatever scheme her father was cooking up before she would live on the street. But the knowledge of a bed, welcoming or not, didn't make the feeling of being entangled by her mistakes any easier to shake.

Instead of walking to the river and watching the water flow under the DuSable Bridge, she stopped at the ice rink to watch a few intrepid families skate in the snow. In another life, with different choices made, she could have been a part of those families.

She brushed the snow off her coat, wishing her despondent mood was as easy to brush away. Karl wouldn't let her live on the streets. No matter how he felt about her, Jelly Bean was his responsibility and he took care of his own as naturally as he breathed.

But overly responsible Karl and her under-responsible father didn't have to be her only family. Aunt Kitty was probably still alive, and maybe Vivian could find her. Having another relative in the world might make being alone in Chicago a little less scary.

"WHERE HAVE YOU BEEN?" Karl asked when she walked through the door, before she had a chance to remove her shoes.

"Out." She unwound the scarf and set it, dripping, on the table in the entry, refusing to acknowledge Karl as she walked past him into her bedroom to get Xìnyùn.

Of course he followed her into the bedroom. He wasn't a man used to being ignored. "Where is it that you had to go?"

"If you had cared before, you might know the answer to that question." She said her words in a sweet, singsong voice so she didn't scare the bird. The saccharine tone probably had the added benefit of irritating Karl. Xìnyùn hopped onto her finger, whistling his approval—probably his approval at Karl's presence as much as getting out of his cage.

"I've asked, and you said you didn't have a job." He looked more confused than irritated, which wasn't the effect she'd wanted at all. But she hadn't wanted to be interrogated when she got home, either.

"Out walking, Karl. Remember, I go out walking. Like Xìnyùn—" she put the bird on his shoulder, ignoring the possible damage to the fine cotton of his shirt by the bird's nails "—I need to get out of my cage."

Karl looked at the bird hopping back and forth on his shoulder, then back to Vivian. "Shit, Vivian, you're right, and I'm sorry. It's even worse because I promised myself I would be a better partner, and I told you I would be a better friend. Then, this morning, I left for work and didn't think of you past the moment I stepped out the front door."

The truth of his statement made her feel colder than all the ice and slush of Chicago winters ever could. "Of course you didn't. Why should you? If you're lucky, the only change Jelly Bean will bring to your life is a roommate for a couple months and money out of your pocketbook for eighteen years. Maybe through college. A steep price for you, but sometimes it feels like a life sentence for me."

Vivian wanted to be happy about the baby. She wanted to be one of those glowing expectant mothers accepting pastel-wrapped gifts at an office baby shower. But her friends were in Las Vegas, where she could never get a job again, and she was in Chicago, dependent on a man she barely knew. Self-pity consumed her, even as she reminded herself that children had been brought into the world in worse situations. Hollow praise, indeed.

"Hit me," Xìnyùn whistled.

This time the look Karl gave the bird was full of amused irritation. "Does he know what to say to make your point strike an artery, or is he just lucky?"

She went to the kitchen for a glass of water, not bothering to answer. He didn't deserve one. He deserved more than her scarf dripping on his expensive furniture, but right now she didn't have the energy for anything other than a drink.

After Karl slipped onto one of the bar stools, Xìnyùn hopped down his arm to the counter and over to his miniature gym. If the tension in the room bothered the little bird, he didn't show it.

"You're right, of course." Vivian and Xìnyùn both looked up in surprise when Karl's voice broke the silence. "I can come up with a million excuses for my behavior, but I don't accept excuses from the people around me and I shouldn't accept them from myself. I keep thinking my world should return to normal, but the truth is you are a life-altering event. The sooner I act like it, the better off we both will be."

She eyed him over the rim of her water glass as she lowered it.

"If I were you, I wouldn't believe me either," Karl said.

"Hit me," the bird said and Karl laughed. He had a surprisingly hearty laugh that she expected didn't get much use.

"I swear that bird knows what he's doing. No matter how much you claim he prefers men, I think he only prefers to put men in their place." He chuckled. "And if I can be put in my place by a tiny parrot who whistles as much as speaks, I deserve all the criticism he can dish out."

Vivian's irritation deflated. "This isn't about punishing you or you changing your life, but this apartment could become a trap for me, if I let it. Not getting a job could become a trap for me. Even Jelly Bean could become a trap for me. But I won't let that happen." She blinked back tears. She wasn't a crier. She had *never* been a crier—she was a doer. This was the pregnancy crying.

She didn't see him hop off his stool and come around to give her a hug. The cotton of his crisp white shirt was cool on her cheek, but his arms were warm around her shoulders and she didn't want to think too hard about why he was giving her a hug. Karl did what a person in any situation was *supposed to do,* and right now that meant hug his crying wife. She wanted comfort and would take what she could get. It's not as though she had a lot of options.

"I'm scared." His arms swallowed her words, but not fast enough that he didn't hear them.

"I'm scared, too. This wasn't how either of us imagined marriage or pregnancy. We don't have to be scared alone."

Her tears had dampened his dress shirt through to his undershirt, so that the fabric adhered to his chest where she pressed against him and nodded. When she pulled away and looked up at him, his face had softened. "I still don't understand why you can't tell your father what happened. Make him face the consequences of his actions."

"I can't. Not yet."

"Why?"

"Because he'll only make the situation worse."

CHAPTER TEN

TRUE TO HIS promise to be a better partner and friend, Karl came home after the gym to eat breakfast with Vivian. She made congee—the one food her father had known how to cook—and they sat at the table with their rice porridge and coffee. Xìnyùn made a morning of it by climbing on his gym and showing off for Karl, whistling and ringing his bell. Karl ate his breakfast as if the noise was the calming sound of waves hitting the beach, instead of an attention-hungry parrot. Only when he was done eating and had washed his bowl did Karl pay Xìnyùn any mind. Karl got out a small wad of paper and a cup, and played basketball with the little bird until he had to leave for work.

Vivian wondered if Karl would manage to be so patient with a four-year-old who had made a drum set out of pots and pans.

All told, Karl was probably only home for forty-five minutes between the gym and work. But it was forty-five minutes during which Vivian wasn't reliant on a bird for conversation—a bird who'd learned to speak from a gambler. And it was forty-five minutes when Vivian wasn't facing the mess of her life alone. They had also arranged what time he would be home, even if he had to bring work home with him.

When the door shut behind him, Vivian didn't get out her shoes for another contemplative walk around Chicago. She decided that those walks had stopped being introspective and had become brooding. Instead, she got out the laptop, but not for another round of résumé edits and job applications. Vivian opened up her email and faced the messages from her friends. She'd let them sit unread for too long.

They all knew why she'd been fired, but none of them knew the real reason she'd fled Las Vegas so quickly. She'd let her fear and her humiliation over the situation she'd found herself in stop her from letting them know she was okay.

Maybe Karl was the only support she had in Chicago, but he wasn't the only person she *knew*. Her friends could be supportive from Las Vegas, if she let them.

She didn't tell them all the details of her past couple weeks, but gave them a brief outline of where she was staying and that she was looking for work. She told her two closest friends about the pregnancy and trusted them to share the news—or not—with the others.

That hurdle jumped, Vivian opened another browser window and began the process of looking for her aunt. It felt wrong to hope Aunt Kitty had never married, so Vivian just hoped her aunt hadn't changed her name. The public librarian who answered Vivian's first call of the day suggested a few databases that might help her track down her aunt, including finding out if she might have gotten married.

Providence was on her side. The first database Vivian tried came up with one Katherine Chin in Reno. The clock showed it was noon there, which meant she couldn't use the time as an excuse not to call. She took a deep breath and dialed.

"Hello." The voice that answered rang some distant memory in Vivian's mind.

"Is Kitty Chin available?" Maybe this wasn't the right Katherine.

"Yes?"

Xìnyùn whistled, but Vivian didn't believe in luck. "Did you have a sister named Tina, who married a Victor Yap?"

"Who is this?" The woman's voice wasn't suspicious, more just full of wonder.

"Aunt Kitty, this is Vivian."

Silence reverberated through the line. Vivian's heart bounced up in her throat. Finally her aunt said, "My sister's Vivian?"

Vivian swallowed, but her heart still didn't leave her throat. She scrubbed at her eyes with the heel of her palm. "Yes."

"My darling child."

"I'm—" Vivian's voice stopped and she had to suck her breath in to say the rest of her sentence. "I'm sorry I didn't call earlier." Because she was. For all those years when her address had changed with regular irregularity, staying in contact with her aunt had been beyond her young knowledge. But when she was an adult in Las Vegas with the same apartment for years—Vivian really had no excuse for not tracking down her aunt over the past sixteen years.

"Where...where are you?" The amazement in her aunt's voice slowed her speech down such that Vivian heard the cadence of her childhood in each syllable.

"I'm in Chicago. I'm married. I'm going to have a baby in seven months." How do you sum up the past thirty years in one phone conversation? "I want my baby to know my family." *She* wanted to know her family. She and her father had been a unit until Vivian had left home. Now she only saw her father when he needed money. Jelly Bean would grow up knowing generations of Mileks and eating pierogies, but the child should know her mother had family, too.

"And your father?"

"He's…" Vivian didn't know what to say. "He's fine."

Over the phone came a soft murmur of understanding. "Do you know why I left?"

"No."

"I never liked your father. It's a terrible thing to say to a child, but it's true. Your mom swore he was a good man, be he always seemed unsatisfied with what he had." There was a loud intake of air and Vivian realized her aunt was trying not to cry. "Except for your mom. He loved Tina with all his heart, but the little anchor he had to reality died with her. It started small, but the writing was on the wall."

Her aunt Kitty sniffed and the next words came out in a shudder. "I wasn't able to get custody of you. I didn't think he'd fight so hard for you, but you were all either of us had left of Tina, and he wouldn't let you go. Eventually he said if I didn't give up the custody fight, he'd disappear with you into the night."

"And we moved, anyway." Vivian remembered her fear of their first move and how her father had made it into a make-believe game. In every move after that one, he'd come up with a ridiculous villain who was chasing them: monsters, aliens, pirates and once—when she was studying American history—the British were coming. Then, one move,

Vivian had to leave her first best friend. From that day forward she refused to play along.

"The truth is, Aunt Kitty, I don't know where my dad is." Vivian wiped her eyes.

An hour later, they had stopped crying, and Vivian had told her aunt everything.

"It really wasn't a bad childhood."

"You don't have to protect your father."

Vivian gave a snotty, wet giggle. "It wasn't a perfect childhood, but he did his best."

"I wish I could have been there for you."

"I wish you could have been there, for both of us." They sat in silence on the phone for several seconds before Vivian asked, "Did you marry? Do I have cousins?"

"I married, and when I divorced I changed my name back to Chin. You have two cousins, Conner is twenty. Carmen is eighteen. You should come visit over a holiday, when both of them are home."

Vivian thanked the fates that had led her aunt to change back to her maiden name so they could reconnect later in life. "I would love to meet my cousins and see you again. Maybe next Thanksgiving or Christmas. I can bring the baby."

"Hopefully, you can bring your husband, too."

A wish Vivian echoed. She respected and *liked* her husband. Marriages had been made on less, after all, and she had to admit that she hoped theirs might eventually be built on more. Karl's quiet righteousness wouldn't be easy to love, but it would be rewarding. And the woman he gave his heart to would never have to worry about his devotion.

They said their goodbyes and Vivian hung up the phone with a new sense of hope. Karl was not her only connection to stability in this world. Even if they were on the other side of the Rocky Mountains, she had friends and an aunt. Soon she would find a job and get an apartment. And whatever relationship she and Karl developed wouldn't be based on her feelings of dependency and helplessness.

The clouds must have broken because the computer screen became impossible to read for the glare. Vivian closed the laptop, put Xìnyùn back in his cage and headed out for a walk in the sun.

KARL GOT TO work on Tuesday morning having spent a pleasant Sunday and Monday with Vivian. Sunday, after he'd gone to Mass, he'd taken her to brunch and then to the Field Museum. As they had gone upstairs to look at the rocks and gems, Karl realized how much he felt as if he could be himself when around her. Actually himself. Not the silent, unfeeling lawyer or the smiling, hand-shaking politician, but himself. Someone who could guffaw at stupid jokes and be vulnerable without being weak. The person he'd been in Las Vegas when all he'd wanted to do was make Vivian smile.

Monday felt as if they were a regular married

couple expecting their first child. He came home to a home-cooked dinner, they talked about their days while eating, cleaned up, and then he worked while she knitted. Okay, so it felt a little like a regular married couple in a 1950s sitcom—separate beds included—but he wasn't going to turn his nose up at roast chicken, mashed potatoes and broccoli. Dinners like this every night couldn't last, but he would enjoy them while he got them.

Something about Vivian was lighter on Monday night. He didn't feel right saying a burden seemed to have lifted off of her soul—especially since she still had a twinge of secret about her person—but her skin looked less tight around her face, and her eyes were brighter. He wouldn't have thought contacting an aunt and emailing a couple of friends would be so rejuvenating, but then he'd never felt absolutely alone in the world as she had.

Their relationship was complicated. Until she found work of her own she was reliant on him, and he was surprised at how little that bothered him. Not that he wanted her to depend upon him, but when she'd first said she was pregnant and broke and unemployed, he'd felt as though someone had wrapped a noose around his neck, thrown it over a tree and at any moment would kick the horse out from under him.

The noose had disappeared without him noticing. He hadn't even realized it was gone until they were in the echoing silence of the only empty space in a busy museum and he could take deep, relaxing breaths. She'd smiled when he grabbed her wrist and they'd finished touring the museum holding hands.

It was a pleasant memory that had carried him through to today when he picked up the CD left on top of his desk. The law department must have sent someone over with it first thing Tuesday morning because it hadn't been here on Monday. He loaded the disc onto the computer and began searching for files. File after file was full of black where information had been redacted from the scanned documents.

He took a deep breath before he called for his assistant. The smell of cigarette smoke preceded her entrance into his office. "Did they send another disc, Greta? Perhaps one without half the information redacted?"

"There was a note on the disc."

He picked up the jewel case and found the note, which was nothing more than a sticky with the excuses of "attorney-client privilege" and "work papers" written on it.

"The bastard didn't even have the decency to type it," he muttered. The lawyer, Ken Jorgenson, was skirting the line of complying with his subpoena and blatantly ignoring legal courtesy.

"What was that?" Greta asked.

"Nothing. I'll need Kevin Jorgenson on the phone as soon as you can get him."

"The courier who dropped off the CD said Jorgenson left for his annual fishing vacation last night."

Coward. Jorgenson had known what he was doing and left some poor underling to deal with the angry phone calls.

"Track down whoever Jorgenson left behind to take the heat. It'll give me someone to refine my anger on. Schedule a meeting for after lunch."

"BAD DAY?"

Karl looked up from the computer, wincing when his neck protested the change in position. Malcolm leaned against the office door frame, his arms crossed and an amused smile on his face. Working for the FBI had given Malcolm a decidedly *off* sense of humor.

"You know it is." Between staring at the computer and trying to guess what the redacted words were, Karl had a headache to match the crick in his neck. "What law school Jorgenson went to that would give him the idea he could withhold this information from me by claiming attorney-client privilege is beyond me. Their accreditation should be revoked."

Malcolm's smile widened. "Do you want the good news or the bad news?"

"There's good news?"

"Sure. I found out why your wife was fired from her job in Vegas."

Karl didn't remember telling Malcolm that Vivian had been fired, and only Malcolm would think that was good news. Karl found himself in the awkward position of not wanting to know for fear he'd have to care. And, as ashamed as he was to admit it to himself, this was why he hadn't tried to find out the information on his own. "And the bad news?"

The smile was gone. "Your lovely wife—and I know she's lovely now because I've seen pictures—was fired because she cheated the casino out of money while dealing a table."

Karl set his pen down on his notepad and minimized the computer window. Vivian's secrets were worse than he'd suspected. "Explain."

"After you as good as told me not to bother probing, I knew I had to figure out where your wife came from." Malcolm could never pass a rock without turning it over. "If Middle Kingdom hadn't been so cagey about my inquiries, I probably would've left it alone. Given how closely they were holding on to their secrets, you should be impressed it took me less than two weeks to get the information and I didn't even have to go there in person."

Karl stared impassively at Malcolm, who laughed in response. "I've had hardened criminals try to intimidate me, Karl. You'd be better off trying your luck with Greta."

Karl sighed. Since when had everyone in his life become immune to his silent stare? "She'd only mother me in response."

"One of the new paralegals, then. Anyway, Vivian Milek, née Yap, was dealing roulette when an associate of her father's sat at the table. There were some serious chips on the table when Vivian shifted, blocking the view of the camera."

"And her father's associate took the casino to the cleaners, as it were."

For the first time, Malcolm looked unsure of his information. "That's the strange part. The associate didn't win that much. Probably the only reason anyone gave the video a second look was that someone else at the table made a fuss over the bet."

"So, she didn't cheat."

"The casino investigated. Her father owed the man thousands of dollars—"

The wheels turning in Karl's head clicked into place. Vivian hadn't gotten fired because her father gambled, but because she'd tried to help him get out of his hole.

"And the video is clear, especially when compared to every other video they have of your wife dealing. Successful or not, the man sat at her table because he expected her to help her cheat, and she knew that was her role."

"So these crimes are alleged. She'd be in prison otherwise."

"Alleged is lawyer-speak. As far as a government dick like me is concerned, she's either guilty or she's innocent. Middle Kingdom is pretty certain she's guilty. She's been added to their black book and is banned from walking into any casino in the state. She'd be lucky to find employment in Nevada, period. The casinos take cheating seriously—especially by an employee."

Karl leaned back in his chair, folded his arms and closed his eyes. Unwittingly, Malcolm had answered more than just the question of why Vivian got fired. Karl now knew why she'd been so desperate to get out of Nevada and why she wasn't looking for a job on a riverboat casino. Vivian was a hot potato no casino would ever touch again.

When he opened his eyes, Malcolm was looking at him with pity. "Are you sure she's pregnant with your kid? She's a fine-lookin' woman, and someone who would accept cheating as payback might accept more physical forms of payment."

"I'm sure she's pregnant."

CHAPTER ELEVEN

VIVIAN DIDN'T REALIZE someone else was in the apartment until Xìnyùn started to whistle. When she turned around, Karl was standing by the bar, still in his coat and scarf.

"I didn't hear you come in. You must have shut the front door just when I shut the oven on dinner. It won't be ready for another two hours. I didn't expect you home so soon." She knew she was rambling, but seeing Karl lifted her heart, especially after the past couple of days. Despite their talking about friendship and the night of near sex, Sunday at the museum had been the first day she'd really felt as if they could be friends and actually maintain a relationship through Jelly Bean's birth. Topped off by reconnecting with her aunt Kitty and the email correspondence with her friends, she was ready for whatever relationship she and Karl developed.

Especially relationships that involved hand holding. Or more near sex. Or actual sex.

"I'm not staying. I have to go back to work."

"Oh." He wasn't still wearing his coat and scarf because he'd wanted to see her before taking them off. He was still dressed for the outside because he was going back outside. "It's snowing."

A stupid, nervous thing to say. Of course he knew it was snowing. It had probably been snowing when he came in.

"I've lived in Chicago almost all my life. I don't mind the snow."

"I finished your hat yesterday." She rushed past him into the living room and dug the green-and-brown fisherman's cap out of her knitting bag. When she held it out to him, he just stared at it. "The color matches your eyes, and even though you seem impervious to the cold, I think you should hide your superhuman powers from the masses."

She smiled at him and he continued to stare at the hat. Her throat tightened. They had laughed at a similar joke at the museum. What had changed such that he wouldn't even take the stupid hat?

"If you're worried about the wool, it's really soft. I bought it on a whim a year ago, not sure what I would make with it and I couldn't sell it before coming."

"Vivian," he said, still not reaching out to touch the damn hat. "How do you cheat at roulette?"

Her legs buckled and her butt bumped against the edge of the couch on its way to the floor. "How did you find out?"

It's not like it had made the papers or anything. Middle Kingdom had promised her they'd keep the incident a secret, so long as she never tried to work at a casino again. When she'd asked what would happen if they were called for a reference, the men around the table had been silent. She'd been stupid enough to hope their silence had meant they'd at least not mention the cheating.

"I have former FBI agents working in my office. They get curious."

"I didn't do it. And they could never prove I did it, either."

"Which is why you're not awaiting trial, I assume. Cheating a casino is a felony."

Her heartbeat pounding in her ears meant she had to stare at his mouth to know what he was saying. "They couldn't even prove I intended to do anything."

"Why don't you tell me what actually happened, rather than what they could or couldn't prove."

Why wouldn't he sit down? This conversation would be easier if he wasn't looming over her.

"I agreed to the scheme. I wouldn't have, but I didn't have enough money to cover everything my father lost, and, well, Frank liked the idea of having a dealer in his pocket so he was cutting my dad a deal. Everything was going according to plan. Frank and his stooge sat at the table and we played some normal rounds. When the appointed time came, I moved to block the camera, like I was supposed to. Only when I moved back, I didn't let the extra chips stay."

"How does the cheat work?"

She sighed. "It's called past posting. You place your bets and, when the marker lands, you place a late bet. The dealer calls you on the late bet, but if you're good, what the dealer doesn't see is that you slipped extra chips under a winning bet at the same time you pull the late one. If you have a team, the person trying to place the late bet puts the extra chips under his partner's bet. It's less suspicious that way."

"And your role?"

"With the 360-degree cameras, past posting is pretty hard to pull off. All I had to do was move my body such that I blocked the camera. I did, and then I changed my mind. When I moved my body again, I removed the extra chips. Frank saw and would've kept his mouth shut, but his stooge balked and we got caught."

"That's why you were at the bar the night we met."

"Yes. I didn't lie on Saturday. I just let you assume the wrong order."

"You lied by omission."

She wanted to reach out and strike something. Karl was the obvious target, but she'd break her hand before she cracked his granite facade. "I hoped you wouldn't find out."

"The classic hope of every criminal."

"Why are you coming after me?" She gripped the edge of the coffee table, desperate for something to keep her stable when the floor was crumbling beneath her. "Why don't you go after Frank and his stooge criminals? They threatened me when I got off work that night, so that I was afraid to go home."

"Why don't you call your father a thief for stealing all your money?"

"Because he's my father." The rug she sat on absorbed her voice; she could barely even hear herself. "But, yes, he's also a thief. When I came home from the hotel the next morning, after I'd spent the night with you, everything of value I owned was gone. Even when I missed my period, I thought I would be okay. I had a job, an apartment and benefits. And I figured you would probably provide some money for the child."

She looked up, because she wasn't, and would never be, a coward. "But then they fired me and told me never to look for employment in Nevada again. They offered me a severance package if I could tell them where my father and Frank were, but I didn't know."

"Do you not want to be found because you're afraid of what Frank will do to you?"

"No. He threatened me, but I asked around. Frank's been cheating casinos for years and has never gotten caught, but he's also never done anything violent."

"So, why are you hiding?"

"I'm afraid my father will ask me for money." It was the story of her adult life—and would have been the story of her childhood, had she had money as a kid.

"You don't have any."

"But you do."

He raised an eyebrow, the first sign of movement in his face since he'd confronted her. "You would steal from me for your father?"

"I'd like to say no, but…after Aunt Kitty left, it was just my dad and me. His schemes and plans always sounded like a game. 'Vivian,' he'd say, 'this week's winnings are going into your college fund.' He knew I wanted to settle down somewhere, get a real job and live a real life."

"And you believed him about the college fund?" He sounded so skeptical that Vivian wondered if he'd ever believed a family member's lies because he *wanted* to, even if his heart knew the truth.

"I had the money I'd earned working. It was enough for four years at UNLV, plus a little extra. I did well on my SATs. I had good grades, even if they were from four different high schools. I was going to make it. And then one day he came home and told me my college fund—the fund that I'd saved—was gone. He'd invested it all in a no-fail scheme. My future was gone before I had one."

"And still you let your father talk you into cheating at roulette." His voice was cold. Not distant, but as icy as the wind cascading down the Chicago streets and freezing her to the bone.

"I changed my mind," she pleaded. She'd changed her mind because cheating meant submitting to the life her father lived. She wanted to stay in Las Vegas, where she had a job, apartment and security. She didn't want to wander again, living off schemes. *This one's gonna hit it big, Vivy, and then we'll be living!* "Frank gave me this look, and I knew if I gave in this once, he'd use it against me again and again until he owned me." She dropped her head between her knees. Being punished for something she hadn't done wasn't fair.

"Is the baby really mine?"

"What?" Anger burned in her stomach at his question, melting the ice of his tone.

"I know you're pregnant. You couldn't fake the doctor appointment, but is the baby mine? Or are we married because you knew you would need someone, and I looked like a chump with money?"

She ignored her own anger and pleaded, rather than yelled. "I know what you must think of me...."

"No," he drew the word out and it echoed through the apartment. "I don't think you have any idea how I feel about you right now."

"But I haven't lied to you. I didn't tell you the full truth, but when I told you something, I didn't lie."

"Mother of my child or not, I have no sympathy for cheaters or liars."

"But I didn't…" She stopped begging when she realized Karl's face hadn't softened. "Are you going to kick me out?" *God, what a position to be in. To not be able to fight back for fear of being homeless while pregnant.*

Karl closed his eyes briefly. "I have to go back to work and figure out how to nail someone who thought they could use city money to enrich a friend's pocketbook. I'll think about what to do with you while I'm working."

She'd rather he decide what to do with her while he was looking at kittens and puppies frolicking in a meadow. "It's not the same, Karl," she murmured. "I changed my mind."

"Pack. By the time I get home, I'll have someplace else for you to go. Mine or not, you're still pregnant, and I'm not going to kick you to the street without a roof over your head. It just can't be my roof anymore."

He turned toward the front door, then seemed to think better of it. "As soon as that baby is born, we're getting a divorce. I'll provide you with money for the baby, but you had better be able to provide me with a detailed accounting of every penny you spend so I know it was all put toward the baby."

Without sitting down, without even unbuttoning his coat, Karl left her sitting on the floor holding tight to the hat she'd knit him.

SHE DIDN'T KNOW how long she stayed on the floor. By the time she unfolded herself, every muscle in her body was stiff. The apartment smelled like pot roast. Like a home with people who sat around a table together and talked about their days. The pot roast was a liar. She turned the oven off, but left the pot roast in so it could continue to cook in the cooling oven until Karl got home. Then she went into her room to pack.

Resourceful. She shoved her clothes into her suitcase, leaving one of her winter coats in the closet. Practicality beat out pride, so she took the cheaper of the coats Karl had bought for her.

You'll manage, Vivian, you always do. She yanked the bags filled with her personal items out of the closet. She'd planned on unpacking them tomorrow—good thing she hadn't grown too comfortable. Her father had gotten her ejected from the only permanent home she'd ever known, and now his specter managed to get her kicked out of her temporary home, as well, just as she'd begun to feel settled.

You always land on your feet. Just like your mother. Except her mother was dead.

She hadn't seen Aunt Kitty in two decades, but

her aunt was still family and family looked out for one another. Even if neither of them had any Irish blood in them, St. Patrick's Day counted as a holiday, right? By the time Vivian drove from Chicago to Reno, it would nearly be time to don the green shamrocks. When Aunt Kitty expressed surprise at seeing her, Vivian could just make vague references to the upcoming holiday.

Or she could throw herself into her aunt's arms and cry.

The fact that Reno was still Nevada and jobs would be hard to find in casino-land was a problem she would have the entire drive to think up a solution to. Anything was better than seeing Karl and his expressionless face again.

Vivian didn't think she could stand Karl's cold gaze, not after she knew what he looked like when warmth filled his eyes.

She left Xìnyùn in his cage on the kitchen counter. If Aunt Kitty wouldn't take her in, Vivian wanted to limit the number of dependents she had.

The odious doorman must have had a sixth sense about her, because he was waiting in the garage for an elevator when she stepped off with her bags.

He raised an eyebrow. "May I help you with your bags, Mrs. Milek? It is Mrs. Milek, right?"

Humiliation flooded her face, but she blinked it away. She didn't owe this man an explanation. She didn't owe him anything. "I can get it, thanks."

And she would carry her own bags, even if her back was killing her. Feeling his smirk on her shoulders for the walk from the elevators to her car would hurt worse than her back, anyway.

She realized she had forgotten to leave Karl a note—and that she'd embarked on a foolish mission—at the same moment she was able to see through the snow long enough to realize she'd gotten on the wrong highway.

Despite their long and comfortable phone conversation, she'd still not seen her aunt since she was a child. Showing up on Aunt Kitty's doorstep with an unborn child for which her aunt bore no responsibility was hardly the way to further a pleasant family relationship. Jelly Bean was a responsibility she and Karl shared; they would share the bond even if neither of them wanted anything to do with each other. Not to mention that her aunt lived in Reno. Vivian might be able to say, "I'll think about how I'll get a job in Nevada later," while in an apartment in Chicago. But that laissez-faire attitude would desert her the moment she crossed the Nevada–Utah border.

No matter how cold Karl's eyes had looked as he'd informed her she no longer had any secrets, she couldn't be the type of person to hurl herself off into the distance with no plan.

Her more immediate problem was that she'd left her keys in the apartment, which she had meant to do so that she couldn't convince herself her behavior was stupid and return to Karl's. She'd been so driven by her shame and anger that she'd purposely made it impossible for herself to retreat without anyone noticing she'd been reckless. If she wanted back in the apartment, she'd have to ask the odious doorman to let her in.

Or sit in the apartment lobby with all her bags again—another humiliating option.

She had flicked on her blinker to get on the highway headed in the correct direction when she noticed the light glowing on the name of her current highway through the dark—Stevenson Expressway.

Mrs. Milek, the Mrs. Milek who deserved the title, lived off the Stevenson. Karl had taken Vivian near here for the family dinner. Mrs. Milek didn't like her, would probably be happy the marriage was going to fail, but she would also probably give Vivian a place to sit until Karl got off work and announced what he planned to do with her. Mrs. Milek's open suspicion was preferable to the doorman's smarmy obsequiousness. At least Mrs. Milek was honest.

Moving from one mostly white western town to another mostly white western town had taught Vivian that she preferred the children who were hostile to the ones who asked, oh-so-politely, if her dad was the cook at the Chinese restaurant—every western town, no matter how small, had one. Then they snickered, "I didn't know Chinese people did anything but work in restaurants," to their friends while pretending they thought she wasn't listening. Only they hadn't said "Chinese people."

Vivian didn't like thinking about either of those two types of kids because it did a disservice to the vast majority of her classmates for whom she was only ever "the new girl" and who never got to know her because she always moved before she stopped being the new girl. For whatever reason, her father had managed to keep himself out of trouble for her last two years of high school, and she'd actually made the leap from "the new girl" to "Vivian." Even after he gambled away her college fund, they'd stayed in Jackpot so she could graduate from high school with friends.

After a couple wrong turns and one minor skid, Vivian found the house she was looking for. The lights in the living room were on, and the television flickered through the curtains. She sat in the car trying to convince herself that driving from Chicago to Reno was a good idea, then shook the nonsense out of her head and marched to the front door. When no one answered the bell, Vivian knocked. Still no one answered. It felt as though somebody was in the house, and a car was even in the driveway. Vivian looked at the clock on her phone, then pounded on the door. When no one answered after two minutes, she tried the knob. The front door was locked, so she went around to the side entrance.

"Mrs. Milek?" she called through the door as she eased it open. "Mrs. Milek, are you here?"

Canned laughter floated through the doorway between the living room and the kitchen. She followed the laughter, hoping to find Mrs. Milek engrossed in the television or on the phone with one of her children and simply ignoring the door.

The first thing she saw was a pool of coffee seeping into newish beige carpeting. Then she saw a coffee mug. The sound of vomiting rolled from the hall into the living room.

"Mrs. Milek?" Vivian eased her way down the hall—not wanting to leave her mother-in-law if she was sick, though not willing to burst in on the woman while she was vomiting. "Are you okay? Mrs. Milek?"

"Who's out there?" The question came out in a huff.

"It's Vivian, Karl's wife." Vivian risked Mrs. Milek's privacy to look in the bathroom. Her mother-in-law sat on a rug in front of the toilet, wiping her mouth with one hand and holding her back with the other. Vivian swallowed her first question—the answer to "are you okay?" was clearly "no." Instead she asked, "Can I help?"

"It's just the flu." Mrs. Milek's breath caught on the next words, like she'd been running a marathon rather than sitting on the floor. "A little rest and I'll be fine."

Middle Kingdom had been adamant that every employee learn to recognize the signs of a heart attack and be able to provide bystander CPR or administer a defibrillator shock if needed. Nausea, back pain and shortness of breath were all signs of a heart attack. "Do you have chest pains?"

"No," Mrs. Milek wheezed. "Not any longer. It's just the flu."

"Mrs. Milek, I think you're having a heart attack. I'm going to call 911."

"It's just—" the woman wheezed "—the flu."

"If I'm wrong, they'll send you home. If I'm right, you need paramedics."

When Mrs. Milek turned back to the toilet and lost any ability she had to argue, Vivian called 911. After Mrs. Milek was loaded in the ambulance, Vivian grabbed her mother-in-law's purse and dug out the house keys. She locked the door, then tried to call Karl at work. After leaving an anxious voice mail on some number in the inspector general's office that she hoped would get to Karl, she got in her car and drove to the hospital.

CHAPTER TWELVE

KARL KNEW THE apartment was empty the moment he walked through the door. Despite the bird hopping from side to side in his cage—on the kitchen counter!—and whistling a greeting, his once-peaceful apartment felt devoid of life. He hung his coat and scarf in the closet, then grabbed a towel to dry the snow off his head.

"Vivian," he called into the vacuum. He peeked in her room. He didn't expect an answer, but he also hadn't expected to see all of her stuff gone. The only thing left in the closet was one of the winter coats he'd bought her and the slight smell of jasmine. "Why did you leave the coat? What am I supposed to do with it?"

He looked by the front door, expecting to see her packed bags—perhaps she had taken a walk to clear her mind. But nothing was there.

Her aunt was on the other side of the country in a state where Vivian knew she couldn't find a job.

Where else would she go? He breathed concern—not panic, not yet—out of his chest. He'd said he would find her somewhere else to live. She was practical enough not to run off—she was pregnant! Resourceful, her father had called her.

She must be just on a walk.

Between the knitting and the cooking and the walks and the job applications, Karl had found her to be a doer, and she would be better served by *doing* her walk quickly and getting back to the apartment.

He walked into the living area and looked around. Then he looked behind the couch and chairs. No bags. There weren't bags near the dining table, in the kitchen, in his room or out on the balcony, either. The only evidence in his apartment that Vivian had ever been here was the coat in the closet, the bird on his counter and the smell of roasting meat in the kitchen.

She wouldn't leave the bird. Her father may have won that bird in some scheme or another, but she'd driven the bird across the country. It didn't matter that she'd had a destination in mind when carting the bird across five states and she might not have a destination now. Vivian held family dear, and the bird was family. She wouldn't leave the bird. Perhaps she was waiting in the lobby.

When he finally exited the elevator in the lobby, Karl looked around for his wife. It would be some kind of slap in the face if she'd been sitting in the same seat where she'd originally waited for him, her bags piled at her feet. But the only person sitting in a lobby chair was a man—definitely not Vivian.

"May I help you, sir?"

Karl turned to face one of the building's doormen. "Phillip, I'm looking for my wife."

"She left about three hours ago, in her car. I offered to help her with her bags, but she didn't seem to want my help."

"She had all her bags?"

"Yes, sir. I think so."

"Thank you for the information and for offering Vivian help with her bags." He turned to walk away, but thought better of it. "Phillip?"

"Yes, sir?"

"Ask management to see to those elevators. The ride from my floor to the lobby was inexcusably slow."

"Of course, sir."

The maddeningly slow elevator ride from the lobby to his apartment gave him plenty of time to consider his next option. A note. Vivian wouldn't have driven off without leaving a note. Despite cheating and casinos and her wastrel father, Karl believed her when she said the baby was his.

His words had been said in anger, not in truth.

He also believed that she thought his role in the baby's upbringing was important—and not just for financial reasons. She wouldn't have cut him out entirely. And there was the stupid bird to care for. If she didn't leave a forwarding address, she would've at least left instructions for the damn bird.

He kept calm and refused to hurry through the door and into the apartment to find the note—it would be there, next to Lucky or whatever that bird's name was.

Except it wasn't. It wasn't next to the birdcage, under the birdcage or even in the birdcage. Karl threw his tie over his shoulder and got down on his hands and knees to look on the floor. The note wasn't under the bar stools. He went around into the kitchen. It wasn't on the kitchen floor, either.

He was exhaling trepidation—still no need to panic yet—when his cell phone rang. "Vivian," he said, not bothering to check the number on the screen. "Why did you leave me the bird?"

"Karl Milek?"

Karl vaguely recognized the male voice on the other end of the line. "Who is this?"

"It's Jan. You know..."

"Officer Czaja, what can I do for you?" An image of a ten-year-old boy following his sister Tilly around the neighborhood flashed in Karl's mind. Until he'd run into Jan's mother at Healthy Food proudly showing off a picture of her son in his police uniform, Karl hadn't known the boy existed anywhere other than within spitting distance of his youngest sister.

"I wasn't sure if you knew, but Makowski heard it on the radio. Your mother's in the hospital."

TILLY, DAN, MILES and Renia got to the hospital at almost the same instant Karl did. They all stopped short in the hospital waiting room as none of them had expected to see Vivian sitting in a chair, her head in her hands.

"What are you doing here?" Karl asked.

She looked up at him, the normally warm undertone of skin a deathly white. "I came to the hospital after your mom left in the ambulance."

"That's not what…" Karl stumbled to a halt. He normally asked the exact question he wanted an answer to. "How did you know she was in an ambulance?" Only that wasn't the question he wanted to ask, either.

Nothing about this scene made sense. Karl wanted to go back to this morning when he and Vivian were riding a wave of happy family over rice porridge. "You disappeared."

"What Karl means to say—" his sister Renia shot Karl a dirty look before continuing "—is that we are wondering how Mom is doing."

"I don't know very much." Vivian's gaze traveled over the group before settling on Karl. "I called 911 because I thought she was having a heart attack. I don't know how long she'd been in the bathroom. The coffee on the floor was still warm."

Karl couldn't parse that statement in any way that made sense, his confusion overriding any feelings of fear for his mother. And being confused was easier than worrying about his mother.

"The doctors told me it was a heart attack, but they should be out soon with more details." *That* sentence made sense. Karl's heart clenched.

As if on cue, a doctor came into the waiting room and headed directly for Vivian. "Mrs. Milek?"

Hearing his wife called by his mother's title while she lay in an unknown state somewhere in this gargantuan hospital made the situation seem even worse. The doctor could be coming out to tell him he was an orphan. His child might never know his—her?—grandmother or get the chance to make a lamb cake at Easter.

Karl might be parentless. The University of Chicago Hospitals were supposed to be the best in the city for cardiac care, but even the best doctors made mistakes sometimes. His anger rang through his ears at that thought. If one of the doctors made a mistake with his mother, he'd make sure they paid for their error.

He was still too young to go to a parent's funeral, even if he'd already been to his father's.

Vivian's talking broke through the fog. "I'm just the daughter-in-law. Her kids are here now."

The doctor blinked a few times before shifting to include the rest of the family without excluding

Vivian. "Your mother had a heart attack. We've done an angioplasty and inserted a stent. She'll need to stay in the hospital tonight for observation, but she can go home tomorrow, Thursday at the latest. She'll also start receiving some lifestyle instruction about weight loss and exercise, and it's important that she follow those instructions after discharge."

My mother is alive. His heart didn't unclench, but at least he began breathing again.

Everyone started talking all at once, asking if she'd be able to go back to work, the risk of another heart attack, if she'd need a nurse at home and how she'd come to have a heart attack. Karl didn't know which questions were his and which were asked by his siblings and their partners. Each question was asked at least three times by different people.

Vivian's soft voice broke through the din. "When can we see her?"

Karl stopped midquestion to look at his runaway wife, who was avoiding his gaze.

"She's sleeping now," the doctor replied, "and will probably sleep through the night, but you can see her if you want. She'll be able to receive visitors in the morning."

The entire family turned as one unit to follow the doctor and assure themselves their mother was still alive.

Karl didn't speak to Vivian at all as they were led through sterile hospital hallways to view their sleeping mother, back through more hallways to fill out paperwork, back through a few more hallways to get to the hospital parking and finally through the cold, dark garage.

He walked Vivian to her car, calmed by the fact that she was still in Chicago. The sheer relief that his mother was alive overpowered his uncertain feelings about Vivian for the time being.

He'd stood at his mother's bedside with the din of the hospital thrumming around him and thought about the *almost* adult-size coffin that his brother, Leon, had been buried in. But every time the panic at the death of another family member started to overtake him, he'd get a whiff of Vivian's jasmine perfume. The exotic scent grounded him in the present. His mom was not dead, she was sleeping. She would wake up and the doctors said she would be back at work within a week or two. His grandmother's funeral would continue to be the last family funeral he'd been to.

As he watched Vivian unlock her car door, he wanted to reach out and grab her hand, to feel the warmth of her dexterous fingers and to know his future shared the lifeblood that pumped through her veins. His mother was in the hospital, but the present still had hope.

VIVIAN BEAT THEM all to his mother's and was unlocking the door to the kitchen when Karl pulled into the driveway. Without jasmine clouding his brain he'd had fear to muddle his emotions and he got out of the car angry.

"What in God's name were you doing at the hospital?" he yelled up the driveway as he walked to her. "I get home, expecting to find you waiting for me, and instead I find that stupid bird, no note and a call from some neighborhood cop saying my mom was in the hospital." His fears were exploding out of him, and years of practice at showing the world only the face he wanted it to see couldn't stop the outburst. If she cared she didn't show it, she just unlocked the side door with his mother's keys and let herself into the house. "Just as I'm thinking you've driven off to God only knows where, I find you sitting in a hospital waiting room, having been at my mother's house when she had a heart attack."

His wife's eyes were drooping and her face was drawn when she sank into one of the kitchen chairs. "By the time I realized I hadn't left you a note about Xìnyùn, I'd changed my mind about leaving."

Karl walked over to the sink, thought about what she'd said and pushed off the counter. *She was only going to leave a note about the bird?* When he got back to the table, he was too angry to sit. "Leaving to go where?" he asked, still hoping her answer would be the grocery store.

"Nevada. I was on my way to my aunt."

"You were on your way to Nevada and the only

note you were going to leave was about the bird?" His clenched jaw meant the words barely made it past his lips.

"Well, I…"

"You didn't think I'd want to know where you were going and, you know, about the baby?" How was he supposed to be able to find her if she only left a note about the bird, with no indication of where she was going? Did she even know if her aunt would take her in? He was going to find a place for her in Chicago, just not in his apartment, where he could smell her and she could drive him crazy.

"I think Aunt Kitty would have taken me in." She looked bewildered and Karl didn't know if it was because of his anger or the stupidity of her near cross-country drive. He didn't really care.

"You were going to drive across the country based on the uncertainty of the verb *think?*"

"And I was going to let you know when I got there. I wasn't going to keep information about Jelly Bean from you."

"Jelly Bean?" Tilly's voice asked. Karl looked up to see Tilly, Dan, Renia and Miles crowded in the kitchen doorway.

"How long have you been standing there?"

"Long enough to know there's a baby," Tilly said, her face radiating the innocence only youngest siblings could achieve.

"Does Mom know?" Renia asked.

"No," Karl growled. "Mom doesn't know. Vivian didn't want her to know."

"It's bad luck to tell people before the third month," Vivian said, defensively.

"I'm going to be an aunt," Tilly exclaimed, before glancing at Renia. "Again. I'm going to be an aunt again. How far along are you?"

"Seven weeks."

The room was silent as they did the math. Karl had avoided all questions about how he and Vivian met and got married, but everyone in the room knew he'd gone to Las Vegas alone for a conference and now everyone knew Vivian had gotten pregnant sometime during that week. A month later he'd been introducing her to people as his wife when nary a soul had met her before.

"Miles?" Renia asked her husband. "Why don't you look as surprised as the rest of us?"

"Sarah and I ran into the happy couple at the library. Karl was holding *What to Expect When You're Expecting* like it was a land mine he'd fished out of a Cambodian swamp and was afraid to put down."

"And you kept this from me?"

Miles shrugged. "Wasn't my secret to tell. If I'd known how good the secret was…"

"Neither Vivian's life nor mine is a soap opera to be dissected." His sisters stopped their chatter, but neither looked particularly apologetic. "Thank you, Miles, for trying to maintain my privacy."

"Hey, it was worth it to be here at the great reveal."

Now that his family was all here, he could think about something more concrete than his feelings for Vivian. "Let's focus on Mom's care. Even though the doctor said her recovery would be quick and she could go back to work soon, I think someone should stay with her. Maybe help out at the restaurant. Work is killing me right now, so I can't be here for her. Miles, Renia and Dan, you have the freest schedules. Can you guys care for Mom?"

WHY COULDN'T KARL see the obvious solution? "I can do it," Vivian said from her chair, her voice not quite rising to interrupt the arguing family members standing above her.

"I'm scheduled on a trip to visit some of our producers," Dan said. "But if I can get those postponed, or I can get someone else to cover them, I can definitely help Miles and Renia."

"I can do it," Vivian repeated. She really should stand up and assert herself, but she was too exhausted.

"I'll set up an online calendar," Miles offered. "Then we can coordinate schedules online and sync them with our phones…"

Vivian opened her mouth to repeat herself again

and was interrupted by Renia. "You men are so busy trying to manage the situation that you've not heard Vivian offer to stay home with Mom."

"Can you help at Healthy Food, Mom's restaurant, too?" Tilly asked. "Edward can manage the restaurant in Mom's absence, but they'll need someone to work the register."

"I can work the register." After two weeks of perfecting her cooking and walking down every street in the Loop, Vivian was grateful to have an opportunity to be useful and working again.

"She is *not* working at Healthy Food, nor is she staying home with Mom." Karl's voice didn't leave any room for argument, but Renia argued anyway.

"She's not fit," her husband said, finally.

As much as she wanted to let his words slide right off her back, they stung. She'd lived in his apartment for two weeks and not done anything but feed him and look for a job. What exactly did he think she would do to his mother?

"Is the pregnancy that risky?" Renia and Tilly's faces wore matching expressions of concern.

"It's not the pregnancy." Karl's mouth barely opened wide enough for the words to come out. If one of his relatives tapped him, he'd shatter.

"Just because I was fired from Middle Kingdom for cheating doesn't mean I can't work a register and remind your mom to take her meds." Four pairs of eyes blinked rapidly, but Vivian didn't care. Now that Karl knew her dirty little secret, she didn't see why the rest of the family couldn't know, too. Just throw the whole mess—one-night stand, drunken marriage, pregnancy, all of it—out into the light of day and see what happened.

She knew she didn't deserve the distrust emanating from Karl, especially as she was volunteering to help the family out by taking care of a woman who didn't even like her. "You wanted me out of the apartment. This would give me a place to live and something to do."

"But the register…" Karl protested.

"Whatever story your FBI agent cronies told you should at least convince you that I'm good at counting and have fast hands. I worked at that casino for sixteen years, and no one ever managed to pass a cheat by me. I can work a register."

"Let's not decide this now," Renia said. "We can all go home, sleep on it and come to a decision tomorrow. Maybe Mom wants a say in her future."

Vivian looked at Karl. While it felt like forever ago, it was only earlier this evening that she'd been driving out of Chicago to leave Karl and his suspicions behind. Now she was offering to stay in the city to take care of a mother-in-law who didn't like her on behalf of a husband who didn't trust her.

At least there was security in caring for Mrs. Milek, only…where would she sleep tonight?

"Vivian, perhaps you would like to stay at our place tonight?" Tilly offered. "We have a spare room."

Vivian flashed her blue-haired sister-in-law a grateful look. "I would really appreciate it."

"No, Tilly, you know you have to get to *your* restaurant early tomorrow. Vivian can stay with Miles and me in Sarah's room for the night, and we'll get her set up in Mom's house tomorrow."

The line of Karl's jaw tightened, as if he was thinking of arguing, but he didn't say a word in protest.

It was only when she got to Renia's house that Vivian thought to text Karl a short message with instructions for Xìnyùn's care.

CHAPTER THIRTEEN

KARL SLIPPED THROUGH the church doors and into the end of a back pew right before the priest proceeded down the aisle. Mass was the first time he'd come south of Cermak since his mother's heart attack.

He'd let his managing sisters get Vivian set up to work at Healthy Food and get their mother home from the hospital. He didn't want to see his mom shuffling around the house in a robe, maybe with an oxygen tank and definitely surrounded by pills. Nor did he want to be surrounded by the smell of jasmine and its ambrosial lie of a fake marriage and very real baby.

His feeble excuse was that he was swamped with work. After threats and some badgering, the law department had sent another disc—still heavily redacted. Plus, back at his condo there was that stupid bird to take care of. He didn't neglect his responsibilities, despite the bird being ahead in the H-O-R-S-E basketball challenge, fifty games to ten.

He recited the greetings in unison with the rest of the congregation, as he had most Sundays for as long as he could remember. People around him stood and kneeled and sat, and he used the familiar rhythm to let his mind wander into the thoughts he'd kept at bay all week. Despite his fears—which he knew were irrational—his mother was fine. She was going to survive the heart attack. She was going to learn to eat better food and maybe start walking to work instead of driving the couple of blocks. Another family member he loved hadn't died on him. He wouldn't be an orphan; he'd be a twice-divorced man with a child he hardly ever saw and a bird whose name he couldn't pronounce. Not exactly the future his father had imagined for him.

My boys! his dad would say. *Karl's going to do important things one day. My wife says he's going to be president, but I think he'll stay closer to home and his family.*

He was close to home and his family, and he was doing important things. What more could the ghost of his dad expect out of him? He had tried marriage, and it hadn't worked out. What he had with Vivian didn't count, as neither of them could define what they had with each other, and if they couldn't define it, they couldn't know what it was. She was pregnant with his child, and he was making sure he didn't neglect his responsibilities. Everything else was...fuzzy.

You're just going through the motions of marriage and family because it's expected of you, Jessica had accused him at the beginning of the end of their marriage. *The only thing you care about is your work, as if it will bring your family back to life. We could have a family of our own, but I don't think you can flex your mind even the slightest to see how that might be possible.*

Hearing the Nicene Creed said by the man next to him was a surprise and Karl wasn't able to catch up until the second line. He'd completely missed the readings and homily, moving in concert with the congregation but not hearing a word the priest said. When flashes of white moved about the altar, Karl closed his eyes, as he had every Sunday since his brother's funeral, to remember Leon in altar boy robes. Sundays, while the priest was preparing the Eucharist, was one of the few times he could remember his brother as alive, rather than dying in a hospital room. From the back of the church he could superimpose Leon's smiling face on whatever child was currently serving at the altar.

Karl never sat in the front pews.

Jessica's accusation had been unfair and proof she didn't understand him or what his dedication to his work represented about his feelings for his family. He'd left corporate law for the low pay and drudgery of the inspector general's office because the work was important, and despite what Jessica had believed and his mom had hoped, running for office was not a substitute for the work he did for the city. He wanted—needed—to do more to stop corruption than just pay lip service to ethics. He wanted to hunt down those who thought nothing of cheating the people.

Besides, he was the good son. He came to Sunday dinners at Mom's, often ate at Tilly's restaurant and had even worked a booth at the Taste of Poland for Renia. *The good son,* just as his father had expected, even if he wasn't around to see it.

He took a deep breath and opened his eyes. The present—Father Szymkiewicz holding the Eucharist up in offering and the warmth of the community around him—should be the focus of his attention, not anger at those who were in prison for their crimes. Anger had not brought his family back from the dead yet, and it never would. Justice and prevention were the key. And forgiveness. Surrounded by God's grace, he couldn't forget forgiveness.

"Peace be with you." Karl jumped at the voice and turned to see the man next to him with his hand out. He returned the greeting and shook hands with other parishioners, crossing the aisle to shake hands with Mr. and Mrs. Biadała, who asked after his mother. Karl informed them that his mother was going to be fine, which wasn't a lie. His sisters or Vivian would've called him if she'd gotten worse.

After taking communion, Karl knelt and rested his head on his hands, letting the edge of the wood on the kneeler bite into his knees and focus his mind. He looked forward to this moment of contemplation every week. No matter how many people interrupted him in a normal day—calls from his family or couriers with redacted and thus useless information—no one ever interrupted him during this moment of silence. And he could ignore the phone vibrating in his pants pocket while he talked to his father. Sometimes he used the moment to talk to his dad, and sometimes to his Father with a capital *F,* but he always took this moment to seek guidance.

The guidance he sought wasn't always available. Or, as today, he didn't like what he heard.

Forgiveness. Be willing to offer it, and don't expect it when you have done wrong unless you are also willing to apologize. He hadn't meant to expose Vivian's secret to his family. That Vivian's presence seemed to push him out of his comfortable stoicism was his responsibility, not hers. And he should apologize for any embarrassment he'd caused her—take responsibility for his actions.

Understand and have sympathy for your fellow man. He wanted Vivian to understand why he was so upset over her actions in Las Vegas—even if she hadn't actually cheated. She needed to see why the person responsible for the Sisyphean task of keeping cheating out of the city of Chicago couldn't be living with a woman who'd been one second away from cheating herself.

If you can't bring yourself to understand why she might have done what she did, you can't expect her to understand you. The truth of that statement was as uncomfortable in his mind as the kneeler was on his knees.

When Mass was over and he'd greeted the priest and several other parishioners he knew, Karl stepped out into the grey Chicago winter and checked the text message on his phone.

Working the lunch shift at Healthy Food. Your mom has been asking to see you. Be a good son.

What did Vivian know about being a good son? She was hiding from her father.

She's hiding from her father because he asked her to violate her morals and she's afraid she'll say yes if she sees him again. You should support that. And you are *hiding from your mother.*

Forgiveness and understanding should be easier with the realization that he shared something in common with Vivian. And that she was right about being the good son. He got into his car and turned out of the parking lot toward his mother's house.

Letting himself into his mother's house and finding her sitting in an easy chair with a blanket wrapped around her and a pot of tea on the side table, Karl disagreed with his conscience. He wasn't hiding from his mother—that would imply she could seek him out. He was avoiding seeing his mother's pale face and the pills on the coffee table.

"Don't look so scared. I just woke up from a nap." The rosy-cheeked, robust woman who nagged him about running for mayor was gone, replaced by a stranger with sagging skin at her neck. When had his mom gotten old? "If you'd come to see me after one of my short walks with Vivian, you'd see I'm hale and hearty."

He gave her a kiss on her dry cheek and sat on the couch. "You look fine, Mom. Better."

"You're lying, but you're doing it more to comfort yourself than me, so I'll forgive you." She smiled indulgently at him. "It took you three days to come see me."

"I've been busy." God, those words sounded hollow while worrying he would knock over her pill bottles. He counted three. Were there more? "Is Vivian taking good care of you?"

"She's a sweet girl."

"We were here for dinner, and you didn't like her at all."

"I didn't know you were having a baby." His mom patted his knee. The last time someone had patted his knee had been the doctor at Vivian's prenatal appointment—and before that it had been years. At least his mom's wasn't a pity pat. "She's caring and patient. Good at managing me without seeming like she is. She'll be a good mom to my grandbaby."

Vivian could have horns and spit fire, and his

mom would still love her because she was providing the grandchild. His sister Renia's daughter, Ashley, had been given up for adoption. And even though Ashley had gotten back in contact with Renia, an eighteen-year-old girl two states away wasn't the same as a newborn his mom could coo over. His mom was excited to have Ashley back in contact with the family, but Karl thought it only reminded her how much she wanted to be surrounded by grandkids. Not to mention she was still looking for someone to take over Healthy Food one day. Tilly wouldn't do it; a grandchild might, eventually.

"Which sister spilled?"

"Vivian told me. She said everyone else knew, so I might as well. I don't know why you were keeping it a secret."

Because Vivian wanted to, and I still wanted it to be a dream. Not wanting to change the past wasn't the same thing as looking forward to the future. "It's bad luck to tell people before the third month."

"Edward says she's doing really well at Healthy Food. The neighborhood is excited your wife is working there and she took to the register and hosting really naturally."

She took to the register really naturally... .

No, Karl stopped himself from thinking that. Vivian was doing the family a favor. He could be gracious and take her at her word that she hadn't actually cheated. She was carrying his child. They both shared the responsibility; he didn't have to be an ass, not even in his thoughts.

"Would you like me to get you some more hot water for your tea?"

"Are you staying?" He couldn't blame her for the doubt in her voice. He came for family dinners, but hadn't been in the habit of just dropping by to chat.

"Sure. I'll stay, at least until Vivian gets back from Healthy Food." The work he had to review wasn't going anywhere. His mom had just had a heart attack. He could spend the afternoon with her. "I'll even fix us lunch."

"Vivian put a list of good post–heart attack food on the fridge. None of it is kielbasa and pierogies, but what she's fixed so far hasn't been terrible."

CHAPTER FOURTEEN

WITH CAREFUL PLANNING, Vivian had managed to avoid Karl and the accusatory set of his jaw recently. Texting served as their primary means of communication, and he only visited his mom when the house was otherwise empty. As far as visits from her son were concerned, for Mrs. Milek ("Call me Susan, you're going to be the mother of my grandchild"), her heart attack had been a stroke—no pun intended—of good luck. Vivian had been under the impression that Karl was a dutiful son, only he seemed to have been *just* dutiful, nothing else. Now, instead of only visiting his mother for the expected Sunday dinner, Karl had taken to dropping in daily for tea and a chat.

Though she felt a little guilty thinking such a thing, Susan's heart attack had been lucky for Vivian, as well. Instead of being at loose ends, Vivian had a job and a place to live—all without being a burden to a judgmental prig. She was being useful, and it felt good.

For the first two days Susan had been nice to her strictly because of the baby. Then Vivian lost to her

at backgammon several times and taught her cribbage. Whatever problem Susan had had with her
before the heart attack disappeared completely with
the card games. They now played several games of
cribbage almost every night before bed.

In their first game of the night, Susan dealt first.
"Pawel, Karl's father, and I used to play card games
all the time, but of all my kids, only Leon enjoyed
them. I miss sitting around a table like this."

Vivian put down a four, a solid opening card. "I
know more games."

She had gotten a job dealing because she'd been
playing cards all her life. Her father had tried to
teach her how to count cards while they were playing Go Fish, but the concept had been beyond the
thought processes of a five-year-old.

"Karl said you were a dealer in Las Vegas."
Susan put down an ace. "That's where he met you."

"I was a dealer. And he met me at a bar." She
put a ten on the table. "Fifteen, for two." Vivian
counted her two spaces on the board. "Remember, don't make a five when we're counting. There
are too many tens in the deck and those are easy
points."

"Pawel always used to win at card games, too.
But I could beat him at backgammon." Susan had
beat Vivian at five straight games of backgammon.
"Though he would never play bridge with me."

"Bridge was one game I was never able to get

good at." Vivian counted two points for a pair and one point for the "go," then waited for Susan to put down another card. "My dad and I moved around too often to find a regular foursome, and it's not really a Vegas game."

Based on the cards she'd seen and what could be left in the deck, the only card Vivian had left would probably give Susan easy points.

"I have some girlfriends who I play with. You can take my place and I'll teach you the tricks. Then you can teach us to count cards at blackjack for the next time we go to the casinos." She laid down a card with a triumphant smile. "Fifteen-two and a run of three for a total of five."

"Susan!"

"What?" Susan looked up. "I counted the points correctly."

"Karl would be horrified if he knew I was teaching you to count cards."

"My son is a dedicated public servant who believes in the importance of his work. He should also be more mindful of the mother of his child. If he doesn't want you teaching me to count cards, he should pack you up and move you back into his apartment."

Vivian counted up all the points in her hand and moved her peg on the board. "I'm here to take care of you and help out at Healthy Food."

"That's bull and we both know it. I've noticed he never comes to visit when you're here."

"It's his schedule...." Vivian didn't entirely know why she was defending Karl, but Susan was his mother, and just because family had to love you, warts and all, didn't mean your warts needed to be gossiped about.

"Count this for me to make sure I got all of my points."

Vivian counted up the points in Susan's hand. "You got eight."

"That's what I counted." She pegged her points. "Now back to my son. His father and I raised him with enough decency to provide you with health insurance and some money for that baby, but he shouldn't have kicked you out of the apartment. Whatever you did."

Vivian wasn't sure whether the Milek family hadn't told Susan about her out of kindness or because they thought Susan knew already. "I was fired from my job at a casino under suspicion of cheating. I'm in the black book and can't get another job at a casino, ever again. Karl wants nothing to do with someone who cheated, even if only nearly."

"I only got a pair."

Vivian looked at the cards in Susan's crib. "You also got the matching jack, so three points."

Susan pegged her points before asking her question. "Did you cheat?"

"I thought about it." Vivian collected all the cards and began to shuffle, the still-new cards slick in her hands.

"I loved Pawel with every bit of my soul, but I also thought about smacking him upside the head with a frying pan more than once." Susan collected the cards Vivian dealt her and arranged them. Putting two cards in the crib, she said, "I don't care what the Church says about thought being the same as action. They are not the same, and Karl shouldn't punish you for something you didn't do."

Vivian added her two cards to the crib. There was a trick to building a cribbage crib. One option was to give yourself easy points, but leave little room for your opponent's cards to give points. The other option was to give yourself cards that provided opportunity for—but didn't guarantee—points. Despite all her father's lessons, she usually went with option one. Pregnant, barely employed and a thousand miles from the apartment she'd called home for sixteen years, Vivian took a risk and put a seven and a nine in the crib. Not just no points, but pulling for an inside straight. *I am living life in the fast lane,* she thought with a smile.

"It's fine, Susan. It really is. Ours is an accidental marriage and an accidental pregnancy. I know he won't forsake the best interests of Jelly Bean, and that's really all that's important." She turned over the top card when Susan cut the deck. The six wasn't so good for her hand, but could help the crib out a bit.

"I don't care how drunk he was, Karl never would've married a stranger unless he would've wanted to while sober." Susan put down her first card. The ace on the table marginally improved the odds of what was in the crib.

"Two," Vivian said, trying not to think about Karl wanting her, sober or not. If she didn't think about it, then she didn't miss him. Or miss him so much, she corrected herself. A girl could be spoiled by waking up to coffee on her nightstand every morning. "I hate to tell you this about your son, but he wasn't even sober when I met him, so I don't think that's a good starting point to judge."

"Run of three." Susan pegged her three points with a gleeful smile on her face. "If he didn't have feelings for you, he wouldn't be working so hard to avoid you."

Vivian looked down at the ace, two and three on the table, then back up at her mother-in-law. "You set me up for that." And she'd fallen for it, even though she knew she shouldn't have.

"I may only be learning about cribbage, but I'm right about my son."

The lure of a stable family was too enticing, especially when she knew it couldn't happen. Her past and Karl's stringency was too big a wall standing in the way of a happy-family future. "Did I tell you that the Biadałas came into Healthy Food on Monday?"

Susan raised an eyebrow, but allowed the change in subject. "What's Sharon's latest diet?"

Happy not to be thinking about Karl, and a baby and a future that wasn't going to turn out the way she wanted—as if futures ever did—Vivian shared the latest restaurant gossip with Susan until they'd finished their game and it was time to go to bed.

HEALTHY FOOD'S NEON Open sign blazed through the dark winter night as Karl walked up to the door and inside, expecting to shake hands with various people—as happened every time he entered his mother's restaurant. Not a soul greeted him, but there was a crowd of people surrounding Vivian and his mother at the cash register. Father Ramirez and Mrs. Czaja were welcoming his mom back to work, but the other customers hovered around Vivian. Mr. Czaja even appeared to be flirting with Karl's wife.

Not that he blamed the man. Amidst the crowd of Poles, Vivian was noticeable—and not just because she wasn't Polish. Her entire body buzzed with joy, and her face glowed. And then there was her outfit. He'd been trying to get his mother to change the Healthy Food uniforms for years and Vivian wearing one gave him more ammunition against the ridiculous things. On most of his mother's waitresses, the flowered, puffy, butt-skimming skirts, green T-shirts and black half aprons looked absurd. On Vivian, the teenybopper uniform made her look a plaid pattern away from a woman dressing up for her lover's Catholic schoolgirl fantasy.

No wonder Mr. Czaja was flirting with her, even with his wife standing four feet away. The true astonishment was that Karl didn't have to peel more men away from his wife to approach the register.

"Karl," Vivian said with a wide smile that brought a bit of pink to her apple cheeks. "It's your mom's first day back at work." She pushed a plate across the counter to him. "She made these tasty doughnuts for the occasion."

"Pączki." He bit into one of the Polish doughnuts traditionally eaten before Ash Wednesday, hoping it was filled with plum and not with rose hip jam. Bright sweetness and rich, eggy bread flooded his mouth. Strawberry filling. Not his favorite, but a pleasant surprise. "Enjoy the treat. Tomorrow Healthy Food will serve nothing but herring and potatoes."

"There are powidła pączki in the back for you to take home. And some for the office, as well," his mom said from behind him. "I was going to ask your wife to drive them up to you." Turning to Vivian, she said, "The powidła—plum ones—are his favorite."

"Welcome back to work, Mom." He wrapped his arms around his mother, who smiled up at him. He felt such relief at seeing her pink face. And the power behind the hug she gave him actually caused him physical pain, but the hurt was welcome. He was so happy to see her looking healthy that he was willing to overlook her machinations.

"It's good to be back. I missed all the hustle and bustle."

"You're not tiring yourself out, are you?" She looked so much better than when he'd first seen her after her heart attack, but the thought of being an orphan still caused heart-seizing panic.

"No. I'm only working half days for a week or so. Then I'll be back to my regular schedule."

"Are you sure it's not too much?" As he followed her to the kitchen doors, he noted the certainty of each step she took and kept his eye out for any hesitation in her walk or weakness when she pushed through the swinging doors. His mother looked nothing but robust. Was it hope or health he was seeing?

She shoved the sack of frozen doughnuts she'd grabbed from right inside the kitchen door into his hands. "Vivian has been a big help. After your grandmother died, I couldn't bear the thought of someone else sitting in her place at the register, so I didn't replace her. I should have. Managing the restaurant and the kitchen, working the register and hosting—it all got to be too much. It'll be better now."

Karl looked back at Vivian, who had added Father Ramirez and Mrs. Czaja to her circle. Whatever she was saying to them made Mrs. Czaja giggle and grab hold of her husband's arm. Vivian looked as though she'd been a part of the Archer Heights community for years, not just a couple of weeks.

"She's not a permanent solution, Mom."

"I thought I raised you better than to be one of those husbands who didn't want their wives to work after they had children. It should be a family decision."

"Maybe she doesn't want to live in Chicago." The thought of Vivian moving away gave him heartburn, even without wondering what would happen to their child. But she had no ties other than him in Chicago, and before their night of near lovemaking they'd bandied the word *divorce* between them like kids playing an easy game of catch. In truth, he knew that night of near lovemaking had changed the tone of their relationship to something softer. Something that might tie them together, not simply for the sake of the child, but for the sake of each other.

Then he'd found out why she had been fired and hurled the word *divorce* at her like he was a major league pitcher and she was still playing T-ball. When he'd said it, he'd made it ugly, rather than matter-of-fact. Not to mention the accusations he'd heaped upon her in front of his family. If she gave birth, arranged visitation rights with the baby and then headed off to Alaska, he wouldn't be surprised.

"Karl." His mother's voice lowered into a lecturing tone he hadn't heard since high school. Not even during his divorce from Jessica had she pulled that tone out for him. "It is your responsibility to make sure that child doesn't grow up without a father's guiding hand."

"I grew up without my father."

Her face tightened and she looked as if she was about to slap him. A slap he would richly deserve. He had lost his father when he was sixteen and felt the gaping hole in his life each and every day. To inflict that on a child because he refused to make an effort to be nicer to the mother was unjustifiable.

Karl allowed himself the satisfaction of closing his eyes. The problem wasn't his duty to the child. He *knew* what he owed his child. The problem was how to negotiate his responsibility for his child with his relationship with Vivian and her pink lips and near felony.

When he looked at his mom again, tears were welling in her eyes. Tears his thoughtless words had caused. *Perfect son, my ass.* Apparently when he failed, he failed spectacularly. "I'm sorry for what I said. Every time I think I've reconciled myself to having a pregnant wife, I learn something about her that kicks me right back on my ass."

"If Pawel were still alive, he would throw you over his knee and smack your behind for the sentiment." She sniffed.

"I am sorry, Mother. It was thoughtlessly said. You're right, of course. I have a responsibility to both my child and my father's memory not to be an absentee father."

He looked over at his wife, who was waving goodbye to the Czajas. She pulled at his soul. Not her pink lips, not the knobs of her spine and not her small breasts that his palms carried the memory of. Vivian *attracted* him. Her very essence— which was what made his attraction so frightening.

Lust could be rationalized away. *Of course* he lusted after Vivian. She was an attractive woman. But to be interested in her as a person, knowing why she had been fired and being appalled that she could have even gotten herself into that position in the first place—that was a different kettle of fish. An unacceptable, stinking, rotting kettle of fish. He had a responsibility to be against all forms of corruption and cheating, and his inner conflict only weakened him.

"It'll be okay." His mom patted him on the shoulder. The pity in her eyes should've been shocking, but instead felt inevitable. No matter how stoic he kept his face, she was his mother.

Karl walked over to his wife, taking care to note how the pull on his body eased with each deliberate step, until he was next to her and felt both relaxed and tense at the same time. The smile she greeted him with started out shy before widening into an open, honest grin.

"Hi there." God, he'd missed the spiciness of her voice and the way it washed over his entire body. "It's nice of you to come for dinner on your mom's first day back. She was hoping you'd come."

"My mom is hoping the entire neighborhood notices how devoted her children are to her."

Vivian blinked at him and he winced. "I'm sorry. That was a terrible thing to say." His second of the night. "Between Mom and work and…"

"And me."

"Yes, and you, I've not been sleeping well." Somehow, even just her presence in his apartment for those short weeks she'd been there had improved his sleep.

Imagine what sharing a bed with her would do to your energy levels.

She placed a hand on his arm, the caress seeping through the wool of his winter coat and under his skin. Sharing a bed with her wouldn't help him sleep better. He shouldn't even be thinking such things.

"It's okay." Vivian gave his mother an indulgent look. "I know that your mom would be pleased you came even if Healthy Food was empty and she was sworn to secrecy not to tell anyone. That doesn't mean she's not happy everyone will notice."

The affection in her voice gave him pause. He'd assumed his mother had changed her opinion of Vivian because of the grandchild and the help she'd been providing at Healthy Food, but he'd underestimated them both. Vivian squeezed his arm, and he wondered what else about her he was underestimating.

"Your wife has been quite the success at Healthy Food, eh, Karl!" The smack on the back jolted him forward. The guy paying Vivian for his dinner had been a couple of years behind him in high school and now worked at Midway Airport as a baggage handler. Karl couldn't remember his name. "I always expected your future wife to wrinkle up her nose at living in Archer Heights and now you've got one helping out your mom at Healthy Food."

Jessica *had* wrinkled her nose up at living in Archer Heights. And she never would have worked at Healthy Food. She'd liked the glamour of Chicago living and hadn't been interested in a house in a middle-class, ethnic neighborhood. At the time, he'd agreed with her. Now he had the sneaking suspicion that he'd underestimated his neighborhood and community. He was underestimating a whole hell of a lot of people recently.

"Here's your change. See you tomorrow," Vivian said with a wave.

"You seem to be fitting in well," Karl said when his wife turned back to face him. *Better than I thought you would.* How awful to have thought that.

She shrugged. "There have been a couple remarks about my obvious lack of Polish heritage...."

"Let me know who said things and I'll—"

"You'll what?"

Silence. Not knowing what he'd do from his office building downtown was an uncomfortable and unusual feeling.

"I've heard worse, and I've heard it from you."

He looked around, but Healthy Food had emptied. The only table occupied was in the back, where two cops were surrounded by empty plates and would probably be here until their radios went off or his mom kicked them out.

Her words bit into his skin. "I couldn't care less which country your ancestors immigrated from, or if you're Catholic."

"I can't do anything about being a Chinese-American, rather than a Polish-American. You questioned my character."

You nearly committed a felony. "Vivian, I..." He didn't know what to say. He couldn't apologize or wave off his words without sounding false. Because they would be false. Because he wasn't sure what he thought about her character anymore, only that he wanted to know more about her. Uncertainty was not a feeling he was comfortable with.

Worse, even if she confessed that she had actually cheated the casino for her father, he would still want to know more about her. Still want to touch her. The desperation with which he wished she wasn't pregnant, wasn't working at Healthy Food and wasn't taking care of his mother was physically painful. Her entrance into his life had been like a jolt to everything he believed in. If only he could expel her from his world....

But then he'd miss her jasmine perfume.

"That's what I thought." She looked more disappointed than angry. How to tell her all the emotions rolling inside him? How her presence both relaxed him and put him at odds with himself?

"When enough information about George Ryan and his corruption was made public for me to understand what cut my family in half, I made a commitment to myself and to them. I don't bend the rules for anyone, Vivian."

"Even if I didn't actually break a rule?" She spit the question out, angry.

"That you could even have considered it..."

"Vivian," his mother called from behind the two cops she was shooing up to the register. "After you take care of these two officers, close out the register."

"Of course." She smiled at the two cops as she

rang up their dinner, though it didn't quite reach her eyes. He had removed the smile from her eyes. That had been him, and his inability to overlook her past.

"Have a good night, officers." Vivian closed the register and turned the key. "Are you going to loom over me while I count the money?"

He took a step back. "It is not my intention to loom."

I just want to be close to you.

He was stupid to be in this situation. He didn't consider himself a Lothario or Casanova, but neither had he been alone and dateless since his divorce. He was also self-aware enough to realize that he was considered a catch. So, why *this* woman?

Not *why did he get this woman pregnant?* They'd had sex, and no birth control in existence was infallible. Not *why did he marry this woman?* He'd been drunk, maudlin and in Las Vegas.

But why had this woman burrowed under his skin and detached his self-control? Why was this the woman he wanted to be near? Why not an easier woman?

"I should go," he said, knowing he was running away and unable to stop himself. "I have to be at work early tomorrow morning."

The sound of Vivian ripping receipt paper against the teeth of the cash register tore at his ears. He wanted to be home, where he could blame missing her presence in his apartment on wishing he didn't have to take care of the stupid bird.

But she stopped him before he was out the door. "I'm far enough along in the pregnancy for a paternity test."

"It's not necessary." She was correct that he questioned her character, but he'd only questioned the pregnancy in anger.

"I think we both know it is. I don't want you to be able to throw your doubt at me again."

CHAPTER FIFTEEN

KARL WAS READING over his notes when the smell of cigarettes invaded his nose. Greta must have just been outside smoking because it was almost a full minute before his assistant entered his office, following the potent smell.

"How's your wife?"

Vivian had looked lovely each time he'd seen her at Healthy Food this week. "She's fine."

"Which means she's still living with your mother. Tell your mom thanks for the doughnuts, by the way."

Greta wasn't here for anything more than gossip, so Karl ignored the first statement, said, "Okay," to the second. Then he turned his attention back to the papers on his desk.

His assistant wasn't dissuaded so easily. "It's a real shame your pregnant wife is living with your mom."

How did Greta know Vivian was pregnant? He'd been a fool to think he could keep anything a secret in Chicago. It may be a big city, but between the neighborhoods, churches and close-knit immigrant communities, he might as well have gotten a plane to write a message in the sky. Or had Dan told Mike at the blog CarpeChicago. He knew as well as anyone that eventually all secrets found their way to the glaring light of day.

He flipped his legal pad to read what he'd written on the next page. "My mom just had a heart attack. Vivian is very graciously taking care of her and helping out at Healthy Food."

Hell, Vivian sounded like a saint when he described her like that. Karl reevaluated his words, then decided against correcting himself. His wife *was* taking care of his mother and helping out at Healthy Food, a job she had taken on before his mother had known she was carrying the beloved first grandchild. Vivian either had nerves worthy of Captain Cook or had desperately needed a place to stay that wasn't in Nevada—and wasn't his apartment. Karl didn't discount the possibility that both factors had played a role.

"You're newlyweds. You should be cooing over each other. Giggling and otherwise being cute enough to make your dearest friends barf."

Karl didn't look up from the page he wasn't reading. "Greta, we're at work, and my wife and I shouldn't be subjects of work-time discussions." He didn't expect the admonishment to have any effect, but it was worth a try.

"How do you expect to keep your marriage

healthy if you and your wife aren't living together?" She put her hands on her hips and peered down her nose at him. "And you're having a child together."

"Greta," he said, trying to put a warning into his voice.

But she didn't care. She'd mothered previous inspector generals and she'd mother future inspector generals. "I never met your ex-wife and why you got a divorce is none of my business."

Nothing about his personal life was any of Greta's business, but that'd never stopped her from interfering before.

"But that baby is more important than any little argument you may have had that sent your wife to your mother's. And, next time you fight, *you* should have to go live with your mother. Seems only fair."

"Thank you, Greta."

"Oh—" she produced papers from behind her back "—these came for you." Her piece said, his meddlesome assistant left.

Karl glanced at the papers she'd given him. If he'd known what she'd held, he wouldn't have listened to a word she'd just said about Vivian—probably why she'd kept them hidden behind her back.

HEALTHY FOOD'S FRONT door squeaked open, accompanied by a strong wind, and Vivian looked away from the customer she was helping to see Karl unwrapping the scarf from his neck. The knit cap she'd made him was pulled over his ears, the smudge of ashes from an Ash Wednesday service poking out from under the wool. Almost everyone she'd served today had a cross of ashes on their forehead and Mrs. Milek had offered each employee some extra time off to go to Mass if they wanted.

Vivian was worldly enough to know what the ashes meant, but the significance of Karl wearing the cap was beyond her experience. She'd find out soon enough, so she swallowed her anxiety and turned back to the customer, barely managing to say "thank you" and "have a nice night" as she returned the woman's credit card. Apparently she'd swallowed her anxiety away, but hope still choked her up.

"The cap looks nice on you." She could be polite. Even if he couldn't get over his issues with her past, she could be polite. He was the father of her child. She liked his family and was working for his mother. He was her link to stability and security.

Even if *she* knew her politeness was just a cover for wanting his respect and friendship, she didn't have to tell him.

"When it was given to me, I was too preoccupied with other things to thank its maker."

She searched his face for some indication that he wasn't as distant as his words indicated. Even though she hated herself for caring, she wanted them to be more than polite strangers sharing a child. She could pretend it was all for the baby, but lying to herself would be more damaging to her sense of self than keeping a secret from Karl had been.

She didn't acknowledge his roundabout thank-you, though. Graciousness only went so far. Instead, she lifted an eyebrow.

His eyes softened in his otherwise unyielding face. "Thank you. The hat is very nice."

"You're welcome."

"Is my mom around?"

"She's in the kitchen."

"Thanks." And then, as though they were cashier and customer instead of man and wife, mother and father, Karl walked off to find Susan.

Despite the banality of their exchange, Vivian felt as if the air between them had become clearer. Bright sun breaking through an otherwise cloudy day. Maybe even a possible rainbow.

VIVIAN'S FACE WAS lit up with amusement when she opened the door to let him into his mother's house on Saturday, though her eyes had a guilty cast to them. Not guilt as if she'd done something criminal. More naughty—like he'd caught her with her hand in the cookie jar and crumbs at the corners of her mouth. His mom had many cookie jars, of both the literal and figurative type.

You have to stop suspecting your wife of being

a petty criminal. And that was his problem. He knew—*knew*—she wasn't doing anything other than watching over his mom and working at Healthy Food. He had to stop thinking such things or he and Vivian would never progress to anything remotely like parents who could raise a child together. And that would all be his fault.

Of course, his suspicions were worse because he understood why Vivian had nearly cheated—and could even understand why she might have followed through with her father's plan. Watching her with his mother or working at Healthy Food, he saw how important family and community were to her. How loyal she was to the people in her life. Her father had trapped her with those loyalties, and if Karl had been in her position, he might have followed a similar thought process. He wouldn't have let it get as far as Vivian had, but that doesn't mean he wouldn't have explored all possible options.

Fate was scuffing up his line in the sand so that he could no longer see it.

Living together in his apartment may have seemed like a good way to get to know his new wife, but now he saw how trapped she had been, with no job and all her friends still in Las Vegas. He would never have been able to fully appreciate Vivian's personality and her principles had she not moved out. In his apartment, he would have continued to see the down-on-her-luck woman who'd appeared on his doorstep rather than the effervescent woman who flirted with old Polish men while asking after the health of their wives.

Then he heard giggles, and Vivian's lips pursed and the sparkle in her eyes changed from guilt to merriment. "You might as well come in," she said as she opened the door wide enough that the laughter sailed out into the front yard. "Though I don't think you'll like what you find."

Three of his mother's friends and his mom sat around the kitchen table in a semicircle, small piles of gambling chips in front of them. The fifth place, which must have been for Vivian, had piles of playing cards and more chips.

"Karl." His mom didn't even get up from her seat to greet him. "There's plenty of food on the counter if you want, and we have an extra seat. Vivian hasn't dealt the next hand yet."

"Christ, Mom. Is Vivian teaching you to gamble? It's Lent." He'd never known his mom to gamble and it was certainly against the spirit of the season to *pick up* a bad habit during Lent.

"If you've not given up taking the Lord's name in vain during Lent, Karl, perhaps you should worry about your own behavior first," his mom answered primly. "Get some food. Being hungry always makes you crabby."

Karl turned his indignation to Vivian. "Are you teaching them to gamble?"

"No." By the way the corners of her mouth danced, she was trying to keep a straight face, though not succeeding. "They already know how to gamble. I'm teaching them how to win."

"By cheating?" And he'd just convinced himself to stop thinking of Vivian as a petty criminal.

"By counting cards. Which isn't illegal, by the way. It's frowned upon, and casinos in Las Vegas will kick you out if they catch you, but it's not illegal."

"That's a straw man if I've ever heard one."

She shrugged. "They're having fun. What's the harm?"

"You're teaching my mother to cheat."

"I'm teaching your mother to play the odds of the cards she's dealt with the brains God gave her, not to stick cards up her sleeve. Do you stop thinking the moment you walk into a courtroom so the opposing attorney has an advantage over you?"

"That's not really what I do every day." Even as the words came out of his mouth, Karl knew he sounded like a lecturing prig. Had been sounding like a lecturing prig since he'd walked into the house. His mom and her friends were having fun. Vivian wasn't really teaching them anything illegal. Hell, casinos were designed to favor the house; what was the harm in a few old ladies learning how to count cards *in case* they ever went to a casino—which, as far as he knew, his mother had never done.

He sat at the last of the chairs. "Deal the cards and I'll play, too."

Vivian raised an eyebrow at him. One of his mom's friends tittered. Karl stood—well, *sat*— his ground.

His wife pushed some chips over to him. "Do you want to learn the counting system I've been teaching your mom?"

"No. If I'm going to make such a big deal about counting cards being akin to cheating, I might as well play in ignorance and get my ass kicked." His wry tone was rewarded by a small lift at the corner of Vivian's mouth before she shuffled the cards.

"Okay. We'll play some hands with everyone but Karl counting cards and no direction from me. Then we'll see how everyone fared and people can ask questions. Ready?" At nods from around the table, including Karl, Vivian dealt a hand.

After five hands, Karl hadn't lost much more than two of his mother's friends, though his mom's constant murmuring was getting on his nerves. He blamed any stupid bet he made on the distraction of constant droning in his ear, not on a lack of ability to count cards.

When her two decks were nearly dealt out, Vivian stopped play. "The first rule of counting cards is to not say your count out loud when I deal."

"It's just practice," his mom said defensively.

"Practice or not, if you get into the habit of advertising that you're cheating—"

"You said it wasn't cheating," Karl interrupted.

"Using your brain," Vivian corrected herself. "If you ever do go to a casino, you'll chatter there, too. Even though counting cards like this in blackjack is little different from counting cards in a bridge hand, casinos do frown on it." Vivian said the bit about bridge with a prim look at him, her eyebrows raised and her lovely pink lips pursed.

If they weren't at his mother's, surrounded by his mother's friends, and if she wasn't the near felonious wife he married while he was drunk, he would kiss her. Just a peck on those lips, enough to mess with her starchy defense of counting cards as though it was something old ladies did on Sundays while drinking tea and eating cookies.

Of course, his mom and her friends were drinking tea and eating cookies while learning to count cards, so—point of fact—it *was* something old ladies did. Which was further evidence that Vivian was turning his world upside down and inside out.

That he was sitting here eating cookies and drinking tea while gambling—even if there wasn't any real money on the table—was a sign that he liked the new Vivian-addled world. As hard as that may be for him to admit. And more than the lectures from his mom, more than Greta's mothering, his sitting at this table while Vivian discussed the hands that had been dealt and played was a sign that he had to give this relationship a try.

The child she carried was important, but still abstract. However, the joy he felt while in Vivian's presence was real and palpable. He'd be a fool to let those feelings slip out of his life because of some misbegotten sense of justice for a crime she'd never committed in a state he didn't live in.

He wasn't committing himself to anything. Exploration of a relationship wasn't the same thing as a marriage proposal—or a divorce retraction, since they were already married. This was just him getting to know the real Vivian, with faults to match the kissable knobs of her long neck. He could learn to see her as a person. Not just as the person he'd married, or the mother of his child, or the near criminal or the woman he thought about before he fell asleep every night, but a *person*—complete and flawed and perfect.

Karl loved his father—missed his father—even though his father hadn't been a paragon of humanity. Occasionally his father had imbibed too much vodka, had fallen asleep during Mass and had clearly looked at his daughters and wished they were boys whenever they talked about dolls and princesses or asked for a pony. If Karl could reflect honestly on his father's memory and still love the man, then Vivian deserved the same openness while she was alive and carrying his child.

Though, he still didn't let Vivian explain to him how to count cards as they played the next several hands. He could be open-minded about his wife without actually cheating. Because no matter what she called it, he still felt as if it was cheating.

Since he didn't lose too much—and his mother and her friends didn't win too much—his self-righteousness was justified. The women at the table were indignant at their lack of obvious advantageous winnings. Vivian explained that counting cards at blackjack often meant finding a "hot" table and the better odds of winning depended largely on how many hands were being dealt an hour—which meant how many players were at a table, the skill of the dealer, the skill of the other players, etc.

"Really," he interrupted their complaints, "if you're going to complain about how little cheating pays, you should probably find another game." He said the words with a smile, so everyone at the table would know he wasn't serious. "I understand there are some very profitable tax fraud schemes out there."

His mom gave him a friendly shove. "If you're going to go back to being judgmental, you can leave the table."

"I have to leave, anyway." He kissed his mom on the cheek. "There's some work I need to get done by

Monday, and I'd rather not have my Sunday taken up with work instead of family dinner and Mass."

As he stood, an idea came to him. "Vivian, would you walk me to the front door?"

She nodded and followed him. They must have made some progress in their relationship over the course of the day, because she looked curious, rather than suspicious. And his mother and her friends giggled like a pack of teenagers.

"Are they drinking?" He hadn't bothered to notice if the liquid they'd poured in their tea was actually white or if they were just calling it milk.

Vivian's eye roll was more indulgent than judgmental. "When you got up to use the bathroom, one of them put brandy in the creamer and they've been adding it to their tea when you weren't looking."

"Why?"

She shifted uncomfortably, but he just raised an eyebrow at her and waited. "You were so disapproving when you saw what they were doing in their card game that your mom made a joke about you being a strict father and them being teenagers. It devolved from there."

He sighed. The realization that his mother, who should understand where his sense of right and wrong came from more than anyone else, made jokes about his principles was disheartening.

Vivian's long fingers were strong when they squeezed his shoulder. "Their games—both about you and the cards—are all in good fun. Your mom is really proud of you. I hope you realize that."

"I know." And he did. He was the perfect son who had never done anything to disappoint his parents. The one who could find the right path in a dark forest at night. What was it Jessica had crudely said once, during a fight?

You're a parent's wet dream, but I want more than a dutiful husband.

What the hell was wrong with having a sense of duty and justice?

Then Vivian squeezed his shoulder again and suddenly he didn't care that his mom made fun of the integrity his father's death had forced upon him or that Jessica had never understood it. He wanted to feel those fingers on him again—and he didn't want them squeezing his *shoulder.* There were better places on his body for her fingers.

He wanted sex with Vivian. Call it sleeping together or making love, he didn't care. He wanted the physical connection of his naked body against hers, of his breath and sweat mixing with hers, of him inside her.

Saying he wanted a relationship for the sake of their child, that he wanted to know her as a person, and thinking about the joy he felt when around her was a justification for the elemental truth. If Vivian gripped his shoulders again, he wanted it to be because he was on top of her, pushing into her and she was leaving scratches down his back while screaming his name.

The truth wasn't elemental so much as it was primal.

"Are you going to fuss at her for drinking, too?"

"What?" It took Karl a few seconds to remember Vivian wasn't privy to the lustful thoughts ranging through his brain. "Oh, no. I don't care about that." Dreams of Vivian's hands and those pink lips had taken his mind off any irritation at his mother. "Would you like to go to the opera with me on Friday?"

The seconds in which Vivian blinked and said nothing ticked away on his mother's grandfather clock. Finally, when Karl thought he'd finally met someone who could wait out his silence, Vivian responded. "I've never been to an opera. I don't think I have anything to wear."

This was a problem Karl could solve. "I'll buy you a dress."

She wrinkled her nose, but her protestations had a new aim. "I don't know. I think I'm working at the restaurant Friday."

"I know your boss and I think I can talk her into giving you the night off."

"I'm not sure you asking your mom to give me the night off is the proper channel. It might constitute special treatment, which I thought you were against."

"If you don't want to come to the opera with me, just say so." He wasn't used to feeling unsteady when asking a woman on a date. Being irritated was more familiar and comfortable than feeling inept.

Vivian cocked her head, and her answering smile radiated light through the room. "I'd love to go, and I'm sure your mom won't mind if I take the night off for an evening at the opera. I'll think about you buying me a dress, but maybe I can borrow something."

"An evening at the opera with me." Karl didn't know why he felt the need to specify the details Vivian already knew, but he wanted there to be no misunderstanding.

"The part where *you're* involved is the part of the evening your mother will be most supportive of."

"Have you been getting the 'be friends with the mother,' er, 'father of your child' lecture, too?"

Her eyes and smile softened, but were no less beautiful. Even if they broke his heart. "I've wanted us to be friends from the beginning."

VIVIAN SHUT THE door behind Karl. The living room was silent except for the beat of her heart and the giggling of the women in the kitchen. That the pounding of her heart reverberating through the room was nearly loud enough to drown out the giggles didn't bode well for her sanity. She had wanted to be friends with Karl from the beginning…but she'd seen the heat in Karl's eyes when he'd insisted on repeating, "An evening at the opera with me."

He wanted them to be more than friends. *She* wanted them to be more than friends.

She rested her hands on her belly. It had just stopped being flat. Growing inside her was a baby. Under other circumstances, they could explore this relationship without concern of consequences for anything other than their hearts. Jelly Bean changed things. If they plunged into a sexual relationship—again—and it failed, where did it leave their shared parenthood? Could they retreat from a romantic relationship back to friendship? Possibly, but it would be difficult.

The knot of her ponytail pressed into her head when Vivian leaned back against the door. Was she talking herself out of letting a date progress because she was scared? She had wanted to be friends, had allowed herself the security of hoping they might be more than friends, and he'd hurt her. Only a fool would open herself up to Karl's prim self-righteousness again.

Apparently she was a fool. But why?

Because Karl's eyes twinkled with mischief when he was caught off guard, and his smiles were more precious for being so rare. Because his judgmental mind had a kind heart and a wish for the world to be right and fair for everyone in it—a sentiment that was hard to be too critical of, even if his judgmental mind had fallen upon her.

Mostly Vivian knew she would be a fool because his arms offered the security of a man who knew how the world should be and fought for that reality. And because her fingers wanted to trail down his lean body and pierce his expressionless countenance; the rest of her wanted his strong embrace.

The sound of something falling, then gales of laughter, blasted the reflections out of her mind. Once in the kitchen, she saw that Susan had knocked over a mug of tea and the entire room smelled of brandy.

"Okay," she said with a clap of her hands. "I think all of you have finally had too much to drink. Even if we played more hands, I'm not sure any of you has enough head on you to count past one, much less make a bet on your count. Let's clean up, then I'll give you all a ride home."

"I call shotgun," Susan yelled, pumping her fist in the air. When Vivian gave her a curious look, Susan smiled innocently. "If you're going to treat us like children, we're going to act like children." The words had no irritation to them, so Vivian just reminded all the women not to forget their coats and hustled them into Susan's car.

As soon as the last of Susan's friends had gotten out of the car and was wobbling through her front door, Susan turned to Vivian and said, "Has my son come to his senses yet?"

Vivian gave her mother-in-law a sideways glance. "I'm glad most of the drunkenness was an act. I don't think alcohol mixes well with the medications you're on."

"You didn't answer my question."

"Can I have Friday off? Karl asked me to the opera." She didn't know if that meant he'd come to his senses—and she wasn't sure what his senses were. She wasn't sure what *her* senses were.

"Good." Susan's cooing of the word made Vivian uneasy.

"Why good?"

"Opera is very special to him."

"Oh."

"Don't you want Karl to come to his senses about you?"

"I don't know." She needed to know what Karl's senses *were* to be able to recognize them and decide if she wanted them in her life. Vivian looked at the houses around them. She'd not seen so many swan planters in one neighborhood before. "I think I got us lost."

"What? I should've been directing you. We've gone too far south and east, so make a left at the next light."

Unfortunately, the process of getting back on track didn't distract Susan from her questions.

"Don't tell me you're not interested in Karl as more than the accidental father of your child. I've seen the way you look at him. Not to mention how he looks at you."

"We've had this conversation before, Susan. Karl thinks I'm a suspicious character. No matter how hot he is for me—" she rolled her eyes when Susan tittered "—he's unlikely to look past what he thinks of me just because he wants me naked. And I can't believe I'm having this conversation with you about *your* son."

"I like to be reminded that Karl's human. Sometimes he doesn't act like it." Her mother-in-law reached over and squeezed Vivian's knee. "It would be easier to mother you both if you both wanted the same thing, but I'll be supportive no matter what. You've been a great help to me. And Karl's my son. Like me, he'll get past his snap judgment about you and see you for the person you are."

Susan's words brought tears to Vivian's eyes. "Thank you. And thank you for being a mother to me when I need one most."

CHAPTER SIXTEEN

"YOU DIDN'T HAVE to buy me a dress," Vivian said as she smoothed the silk over her hips.

Between the short time they'd lived together and his daily stops at Healthy Food, she could now read Karl's stoic face. Not a muscle moved, but the hazel of his eyes got warmer as they traveled from her curled hair down to her toes and back up again before stopping at her face. She felt a bit like a furtive teenager when her body responded with tingles while standing in Susan's living room. "You said you didn't have anything to wear to the opera."

"What I said was that I didn't know if I had anything to wear because I'd never been before. I don't understand why you bought it—"

"How about because I wanted to?" His intense eyes never left hers but she felt like he saw through the bronze latticework at her waist to her bare skin. "Because we're married and having a child together, and I am learning how to share my life with you. And because I like the way you look in the dress."

"Thank you. I like the way you look in the

tux." The way the wool clung to his shoulders and smoothed over his chest. The way his cheekbones made his face so stern, but she knew she could make him melt if she wanted. The way she was already melting.

But acknowledging what you wanted out of a night wasn't the same thing as being willing to risk getting it.

He held out her coat, and the lining slipped over her bare skin as she put her arms through the sleeves. She buttoned up the coat he'd bought her over the dress he'd bought her, and all the reasons she'd put the brakes on a physical relationship came screaming back. Was tonight different? She was still dependent on Karl for health insurance, but at least she had a job and a place to live—even if both those things were provided by his mother. She'd like to believe Susan's assurances that *that* little bit of security wasn't dependent on Karl.

"Will you be warm enough?" His hand was cool when he handed over the fancy clutch he'd bought her to match her dress. She wanted him to run that hand over her belly and down until his arctic tranquility melted under her heat.

She hoped her smile covered up the nonsense in her brain. "Of course."

Susan called out, "Have fun, kids," as they walked out the front door.

THEIR PROGRESS THROUGH the Civic Opera House lobby was slowed as Karl greeted people he knew. While he shook hands, Vivian took the opportunity to gawk at her surroundings. After living in Las Vegas, she wasn't a country bumpkin any longer and could recognize the difference between a historic building restored to grandeur and a modern building designed to look old. The towering white columns and red carpet looked like Hollywood glamour meets a downtown bank as reimagined for the opera. Or what she supposed opera was—over-the-top, loud and in a language she wouldn't understand. The only thing she knew about the opera they were watching tonight was that it was one of Karl's favorites.

She'd passed this building many times on her daily walks through the city while she'd still been living with Karl. The front of the structure looked like a towering office building, and she'd had to cross the river to see why it was called Insull's Throne.

In the midst of the women in elegant dresses and silver-haired men in tuxes milling around in the white stone lobby, she was glad Karl had bought her a dress. The black pants, white shirt and Asian-print brocade vest she'd worn dealing would have looked out of place and it was the nicest thing she owned—she'd sold her dresses before moving.

When they'd settled into their seats, Vivian opened her program to learn about the spectacle she was about to watch and blinked when she read the description. Then she read the description again. "You brought me to an opera about a woman whose baby is murdered?"

She flipped the program over to look at the cover, *Jenůfa*. She flipped back to the synopsis.

Karl looked at the program open in her hands. "The peasant girl is the title character, but the story is more about the decisions of the Kostelnička, the stepmother who murders the baby."

"I still can't believe you brought a pregnant woman to an opera about infanticide."

"Makes how my mom greeted you at that first family dinner seem insignificant in comparison."

She jerked up from the program to look at him. His eyes were twinkling and the corners of his mouth kicked up in a smile. She laughed. "It's even worse that you would joke about it."

The tightness in his jawline as he had walked through the lobby was gone and his smile was real—and blinding. "Don't tell anyone. It will ruin my reputation."

The lights dimmed and the curtain rose on a bare set. Even after having read the description, she was expecting castles and giant sailing ships— props to wow her, not a bare stage with a table and a couple boulders. The orchestra started and she peeked at Karl.

If she hadn't spent so much time watching him, she wouldn't have noticed the small evidence of his immersion in the music. His face wasn't void of emotion; his feelings were simmering just below the surface. The corners of his eyes dipped and his brows lowered as his shoulders relaxed. His body leaned forward as an extension of his attention reaching all the way to the stage. Seeing those small movements were her reward for paying attention to him.

When he blinked rapidly, she turned her eyes back to the stage in time to see Jenůfa grasping her face. One of the characters, Laca, had just slashed her cheek to make her less attractive to Števa, the father of Jenůfa's child and Laca's half brother. The music swept through Vivian and she didn't turn to look at her husband again until the curtain dropped and the lights came back on.

Karl sniffed and his eyes were red, but the look on his face was pure joy. They walked through the lobby, his arm around her as he occasionally stopped to press a kiss into her hair.

"I don't believe Jenůfa would forgive the Kostelnička so easily after the woman murdered her child. Or that she would forgive Laca for slashing her cheek. Sins out of love, indeed," Vivian said after they'd settled into a cab.

Karl slipped his gloves off and reached for one of her hands, taking his time to peel *her* glove off, staring down and intent on his task. Once her hand was bare and wrapped up in his, he looked at her. "Like I said, the story is only nominally about Jenůfa. It's more about the Kostelnička, who has a duty to care for Jenůfa—her stepdaughter, not her own child—and who understands the social pressures and prejudices acting against a young girl, even a pretty one, who allows herself to get pregnant by a drunk and whom no one will marry. Jenůfa is too overwhelmed with love of her baby to see her future. The Kostelnička is responsible for Jenůfa's future and fixes it the only way she knows how."

"By murdering a baby and marrying Jenůfa to the man who knifed her?"

He shrugged and said matter-of-factly, "Better than the drunk who got her pregnant, then tried to marry the mayor's pretty daughter."

Karl's eyes twinkled in the passing streetlights and Vivian was surprised enough to laugh. "I thought you didn't have a sense of humor, but now I realize you have a macabre one."

His head fell back against the headrest. He lifted her hand up to his lips, kissed her palm gently then closed his eyes. "The world is full of pain. If you can't find humor in it, you'll drown." He raised his head and turned to look at her. "You can imagine people wouldn't find my sense of humor appropriate in my current job."

"So you think the Kostelnička was right to do what she did?"

"Not right—crimes are never *right*. She will be tried for drowning the infant and deserves death. That is justice. But there is also social justice for Števa, who got a girl pregnant when she was pretty and abandoned her when she was disfigured."

"Laca seems to come out all right. He gets the girl."

"Neither social justice nor legal justice work perfectly. Maybe Laca will come to realize he is complicit in the death of an infant because he refused to marry Jenůfa, the woman he says he loves, while she still had his brother's child." He was resting against the headrest and his eyes were closed again. "Or maybe he will never take the time to evaluate the consequences of his actions and die confident in his infallibility."

"His sins are sins of love."

His voice was sleepy as he replied, "That's the stupidest line in the whole opera. I think it's supposed to be romantic, but love doesn't excuse sin."

Which, Vivian supposed, was why she was living with her mother-in-law instead of with the man she loved.

CHAPTER SEVENTEEN

INVITING A PREGNANT woman up to his apartment for a nightcap had been an obvious pretext, but Karl had done it and Vivian had said yes. He hadn't even bothered to smooth out his ploy with "before I drive you back to my mom's." They both knew a "nightcap" meant she was sleeping over.

His fingers brushed the skin of Vivian's bare arms as he helped her out of her coat, and the smoothness burned through his body. He walked over to the closet to hang up their coats before she could turn around and notice his increased heart rate.

He'd spent years practicing how to cover up his emotions so that when people looked at him they saw who and what they needed to see—and who and what he *wanted* them to see. But Vivian read *him*. Not the perfect son, not the Golden Pole overcoming tragedy for a greater purpose, not the man in a suit on a woman's arm. She saw him. He had felt her perceptive gaze the first time she'd sat next to him in Las Vegas, and in his drunkenness it had been invigorating. When she'd sat on the couch in his Chicago condo and begged for health insurance, it had been scary. Now he wasn't sure he could live without it.

He also wasn't sure how to reconcile his need for her with his opinions of her past. Tonight would surely jumble any hope he had of being rational about her, but he found he didn't care.

"Thank you." She swept her hair over her shoulder, revealing the length of her neck. The neck he still wanted to kiss his way down. "For the dress, for the night out, for the music, for everything."

"You look beautiful." Bronze silk the color of her eyes glistened next to her pale golden skin. The dress skimmed over her slight figure, peaking over her nipples. She glowed like a goddess risen from the molten depths of the earth.

The copper in her eyes blazed when her mouth curved in a knowing smile and she took a step forward, slipping her hand into his. He had called her Helen of Troy. A siren. Some temptress risen from the deep to test him on his journey through life. But then he'd seen her at Healthy Food, smiling and teasing the regulars, and with his mom, taking care of her. And now he knew she was more Penelope than Lorelei. Underestimated for her cleverness and resourcefulness, like Penelope, using tricks to keep her unwanted suitors at bay. Her femininity and softness made her a tougher character, not a weaker one as a less confident man might think.

Her dress rustled when he tugged her close to him. He lifted one hand to her face and ran it down the length of her neck to smooth the stiff neckline of her dress away from her collarbone. She wasn't wearing a bra. He could sweep the dress completely off her shoulders and worship at her breasts until his body burst into lava. He could melt with her.

He bent to kiss the juncture of her neck and shoulder, just once, feeling her heart beat against his lips, and someone moaned. "I could barely pay attention to the opera, wondering what your skin tasted like."

"Liar." She tilted her head to the side in offering, and he didn't hesitate. When he licked the line of her clavicle she gasped and lifted herself up onto her toes. "I was sitting right next to you. You were entranced."

"I'm a good actor." He slid one hand down to grasp her butt. Silk slipped under his fingers as he lifted her leg up, pulling her so that his erection was settled against her belly and she had to rely on him to stand. He was beyond want; he needed her. He needed her to need him.

She righted her head and turned her eyes on him, her lips opening in invitation. He would be engulfed in flames if he didn't kiss her lips. Still...

"You don't have to do this." He'd said similar words once before, and that night had ended with him taking a cold shower, but the words needed to be said again. "The dress, the opera—none of that has a price."

"I want to." She hadn't finished her sentence before he finally felt the lush softness of her lips melt under his.

KARL SLIPPED HIS tongue into Vivian's mouth and all her reason disappeared, replaced with a blessed insanity and the knowledge that his cool lips burned. She thrust her hips forward, but he was too tall for her. She didn't want the feel of dress and wool against her skin. She wanted him—his cool skin, his fine brown hairs, his hard length and lean muscles. She moaned and shifted, meeting his tongue with hers. When she ran her tongue over his bottom teeth he grunted and lifted her leg higher, pushing himself against her but still not meeting her where she pulsed with desire.

She broke the kiss. "This will never work."

His chest rose and fell in exertion as he closed his eyes and nodded. "I understand." His hand slipped from her butt.

She reached around to keep it there. "No." She smiled, and the uncertainty she hadn't even been convinced was in his eyes disappeared. "Standing. This will never work standing. Either I grow several inches or you shrink."

He pulled back enough to sweep her into his

arms. "It'll be more expedient if I carry my wife across the threshold—any threshold."

She tilted her head back and allowed herself to be a princess, swept off her feet into the arms of a waiting prince. A fairy tale of a girl plucked from daily toils and lifted into a castle tower. There was no question of whether she deserved this—all women deserved to be swept away at least once in their lives.

A down comforter embraced her when he set her gently on his bed. She'd not been in his bedroom before. Two weeks of living in his apartment and she'd never been willing to broach the doorway and invade his privacy. Now she was too overcome by his hand running down the length of her body and hiking up the skirts of her dress to do more than notice that his pillows smelled like his shaving cream. Desire coursed through her body, and she lifted her arms over her head to give the craving an escape. All she succeeded in doing was speeding up her heart rate.

Two thunks sounded as her shoes hit the floor, followed by two more, his shoes. Then his hand skimmed up her body, dancing over her hip and stalling under her arms. "Ah, zipper." Butterfly kisses followed the rasp of the zipper down her side. She wiggled as he pushed the dress over her head, cool air streaming in to zing newly revealed parts of her body. When she shifted to sit up and help him undress, he pushed her back on the bed and took her mouth in a consuming kiss.

"I want you undressed," she said against his mouth. She clicked open the buttons of his tuxedo shirt and smoothed her hand over his hard chest, coarse hairs catching in her fingers. He bucked and groaned when she ran a thumb over his nipple.

He hopped off the bed, shucking his bow tie and clothes. Under his pants, where she had expected him to wear staid tighty-whities or gray boxer briefs, were lime-green boxers with pink flamingos on them. Buried deep down along with his macabre humor, her husband also had a sense of whimsy. She smiled, both at the silliness of his underwear and at the sight of the erection nudging open his fly.

He answered her smile with a wry one of his own, his hands stalled on the waistband of his boxers. "Now you know all my secrets," he said before shedding the last bit of fabric.

The mattress bounced when Karl hopped to all fours on it and climbed such that he was above her, an unexpectedly playful smile on his face. She waited while he tilted his head to the left and the right, her body tense with desire, afraid movement would wreck the moment. "Finally, those wonderful breasts are bare and waiting for me." He shifted back and sat on his heels, his erection *so close* to being inside her that her body clenched in anticipation.

She ran her hands up his legs. When she reached the thickening hair at the juncture of his thighs and pelvic bone, his playful smile grew wider. She kept one hand tickling his thigh while the other ran over the slight bulge of her belly to her breasts. When his eyes darkened in response, she pinched her nipple. "Are you going to do anything with them?"

"I have been waiting a long time to get you naked and under me." His hand followed the same trail over her belly to her breasts that her hand had just made, stopping just shy of her breast. She shifted her hand to touch his, stopping when he shook his head. "I've had lustful thoughts about you while at my mother's restaurant talking to my priest."

Finally, his fingers grazed the underside of her breast and her body trembled. Her breasts had been extra sensitive and had just stopped being tender, but the edge of pain and pleasure that his hand walked stilled her breath with anticipation. "If I want to take all night to fully appreciate the value of what I am about to have in my hand, I will." When he slid his hand under hers and pinched her nipple, her hips bucked. "I'll make the anticipation worth your while."

"*I'll* make the anticipation worth my while," she said, not so far gone with desire that she didn't miss the twinkle in his eye as he bent his head and took the other nipple into his mouth. When he bit down, she amended her statement. "But you can help," she said and felt his smile.

His thighs tightened around hers when her hand traveled from the indent of his hip to grip his erection. His answering moan sent trembles through her body, though he didn't stop his veneration of her breasts. Desire burned within her, such that she could feel the electricity between them. Even where their bodies didn't touch, the heat off his body sizzled.

When she could no longer stand the hunger, she shifted her knees in an attempt to get him between her legs and inside her.

"I know what you're doing," he murmured as he licked his way up her neck to nibble her ear. Sometime during his attentions, her free hand had found his shoulder and was now gripping it. He ran his tongue along the outside of her ear, and she closed both hands, digging her nails into his shoulder with one hand and clenching his cock with the other. "That was interesting," he said before shifting to catch her mouth with his. He teased her lips apart with his tongue, slipping into her mouth as she wished he'd slip into her.

The movements her hand made on his cock echoed the pulling and tormenting of her lips on his tongue, but no matter how she aroused him, she couldn't get him to reposition himself so that she could put him inside her. He wasn't so much denying her as taunting her with what she wanted. *Tantalus,* she remembered from her Greek literature class, satisfaction within sight but never within reach.

Her head lifted to follow him when he pulled away from her mouth. Her moan was intermingled with frustration and hunger for completion.

"I wonder if it will work with the other ear." He kissed a path along her jaw. Involuntarily, when he licked the edge of her other ear, she gripped his shoulder and cock again, and he chuckled with satisfaction.

This time, she got her revenge by tickling his balls with her fingernails. Satisfaction flooded her when he stilled in his ministrations and groaned. Loudly. But as with all revenges, this one left her unfulfilled. Karl was still not inside her. She pushed at his shoulder in frustration. In response, he rolled onto his back, pulling her with him so that their positions were reversed.

Before she could accustom herself to their new arrangement, he was using one hand to guide her hips to where his other hand held his cock, keeping her hovering just above him. When she shifted to— *finally*—have him inside her, he raised his eyebrow at her and shook his head. Then he moved his hand from her hip to her wet folds of skin. One finger slid in and then two.

Her arms shook with pleasure before she stead-
ied herself.

"I like to be in charge," he said with satisfaction.

"And I'm not going to let you."

She said the words, but didn't have the inclina-
tion to do more than reposition herself so that his
fingers hit a spot to make her moan. His fingers lingered there as her body tensed around him. When
he pulled his fingers out from her, her hips curled
to follow them, bringing her close enough to graze
against his erection.

"That's what makes it so fun," he said before lifting his hips and filling her.

She whimpered with pleasure as her body
wrapped around him. Neither of them moved for
several heartbeats as they enjoyed the feeling of
connection. Then Karl began to lift his hips and
Vivian lowered hers until they found a rhythm. His
hands found her breasts again, fondling and kissing
as they moved together. She clutched his shoulders,
bracing herself above him and leveraging herself
down so that she felt the entire length of him as
he slid in and out of her. The tip of his cock would
nearly withdraw and then push back into her. She
clenched around him. Their cries and grunts min-
gled together, echoing off the walls. Their smells
blended, filling the room.

She leaned over to lick his neck and then, irrevocably joined together, she found his mouth. They kissed and came in unison.

CHAPTER EIGHTEEN

WITH VIVIAN TUCKED against him, her butt cradled by his curled legs and his fingers absently stroking her breasts, Karl realized what he had forgotten to do. With some regret, he dragged his hand away from her breasts and lifted her hair off her neck.

"There you are." He drew his chest away from its comfortable resting spot against Vivian's back and allowed his fingers to bump along the nubs of her neck bones. Spent and satiated, he still felt the anticipation of her presence in his life.

He rolled her onto her stomach and she responded with a drowsy, "Hmm?"

"The bones along the line of your spine." He leaned in to kiss one. "Since I woke you that morning to inform you of our marriage—" he was willing to broach the subject again because she couldn't go back in time and undo the night they had just spent together "—I've dreamed of putting my lips to each bone of your spine and kissing my way to the small of your back."

"Better enjoy it while you can." She sounded both smiling and sleepy. "In a couple of months

I won't be able to sleep on my stomach and then you'll have to wait until after the baby is born."

He hoped she was too tired to feel his lips still against the last and largest of her cervical vertebrae. The baby was still unbelievable to him. The woman lying against him was carrying his child— their child. She would give birth and he would have a little stranger to nurture into a responsible adult. Knowing this—having his mother and Greta lecture him on his responsibilities regarding the child—was not the same thing as lying in his bed with his wife in his arms, able to reach around and feel the slightly thickening waist that covered their child.

Not the same thing at all.

He still didn't know what to do with himself or with the woman in his arms. Providing money for a child's care was one thing. Being a husband and a father was another. Could they build a *family* out of a one-night stand? Not a family in the sense of being related to each other—there was no escaping the connections his mother would draw on the family tree in his great-grandmother's Bible. Could they be a family together in its most elemental sense? When Vivian was pissing him off beyond all sense of imagination, could he still look at her and be thankful she was in his life? Could a random night in Vegas lead to a relationship he could rely on to be supportive, no matter what else was happening in the world?

Karl didn't take his responsibilities lightly, but could Vivian be more than just a responsibility? Could their relationship be a joy?

And could he find this joy with a woman who'd nearly and with forethought committed a felony? He understood her reasons, he just wasn't sure he accepted them yet or that they fit into his understanding of how the world should be.

"Listening to you think is exhausting."

Lying in bed, his body heavy with sexual satisfaction and a woman in his arms, was not the time to be having these thoughts. He probably should have resolved them before bringing Vivian back to his apartment with sex in mind.

But she was here, and he had missed her presence so he shifted in the bed until he was embracing her again. His lips grazed the sensitive skin at the back of her ear. "You can't hear me think."

She clasped his hands in hers against her chest and said, "Go to sleep so we can do this again in the morning."

That was the most sensible thing he'd heard all day.

WHEN HE WOKE up for the second time that morning, the winter sun was streaming into his windows and Vivian was missing from his bed. He pulled on the boxers that she had found so silly, ran his hands through his hair and stumbled into the kitchen. Vivian was in her panties and his T-shirt, sitting at the bar drinking coffee and playing basketball with Xìnyùn.

"I made plenty of coffee, and I can make breakfast, too," she said simply. He wasn't able to judge the expression on her face.

"I'd rather take you back to bed and eat breakfast later."

"I have to be at work soon. Plus I have to go—" she paused "—back to your mom's to shower and change." Her lips curled up in a smile and the strange look on her face disappeared. "I don't think I can work the register in my opera dress."

"No, I don't suppose you can," he said in the strangest morning-after conversation he'd ever had. She was his wife, pregnant with his child, and he was going to drive her to his *mother's* house where she lived.

He noticed she hadn't called his mom's house home. Even with a place to live, Vivian was still adrift. Her moorings at his mother's were tenuous, at best. He opened his mouth to suggest she return to his apartment, but said instead, "I'll find you a pair of sweats."

Such a hollow offer, but were he to ask her to move back in, where would she sleep? Either of them crossing the expanse of his living room seeking sex was ridiculous. Yet the thought of her moving into his apartment and into his bedroom was uncomfortable in a different way. If he were to stand outside himself and watch their relationship unfold it would be like watching a movie run backward—child, marriage, moving in, first fight, sex. He wasn't sure the courtship had reached its beginning and was ready to move forward instead of in reverse.

Which hadn't stopped him from undressing her last night instead of driving her back to Archer Heights. He was a fool for her, and that knowledge was scarier than the child she was carrying.

The bird chirped, "Hit me," and hopped back and forth on his perch.

She nodded. Vivian couldn't know what he was thinking, but he felt as if her nod was for more than just the offer of clothes to wear home.

"You're still reading the Melville stories," she said.

The book was on the bar, the bookmark not much farther in than when Vivian had left.

When he'd kicked her out. He should be more honest with himself.

"Between exercising your bird—"

"It's my dad's bird."

"*Your* bird, work and visiting Healthy Food for dinner every night, I've not had much time to read." He picked up the book and flipped through it. "I wanted to reread 'Billy Budd, Sailor,' which I read when I was in law school. I should've skipped the other stories."

"You're not a man to skip to the good parts."

"No." He gave her a wry smile. "About the good parts…I'm not going to ask you to move back in. It's…"

Karl honestly didn't know how he wanted to finish that sentence. He'd never worried before about a woman's expectations after one night of sex, but he'd never had a night of sex with his pregnant wife before, either. The rules—as he understood them—for sex with your wife didn't apply in this case.

Vivian was wreaking havoc with his life and, instead of doing his duty to the child and being done with a sexual relationship with the mother, he wanted to share breakfast with her. He still hadn't worked his way to sharing his life with her; breakfast was scary enough right now.

"I never expected happily ever after. Not when you bought me that first drink, not when I waited for you in this building's lobby and certainly not now."

That Vivian was understanding about it only made him feel worse. She would be perfect, except for the danger that waited in the wings of their relationship. Friendship was already more than he'd planned.

Sex just complicated things further. It certainly complicated this morning after.

Blessedly, Vivian changed the subject. "You have quite the collection of bookends." When he only nodded, she continued. "And they're all hidden away in your bedroom rather than for people to see."

That was the point. "They're private."

"What made you start collecting bookends?"

"My brother, Leon, gave me some for my birthday right before he died."

If Vivian had continued to ask questions, he might have dodged her curiosity with one-word answers. Since she just sipped her coffee, he continued. "Leon gave me the hockey players." Their mom had given him an *Encyclopedia Britannica* and Leon had so proudly bought bookends to match it. At the time, the fake-gold-plated hockey players had seemed garish and beneath Karl's teenaged dignity. Now, they were a reminder that families could be wiped out in an instant. "I took those with me to college and was the only person in my dorm with real bookends, as opposed to those bland metal ones. So people gave me more bookends."

"And now you have more ends than books."

"Yes." Because she was Vivian, he offered her more information. "I have several boxes of bookends in storage. These are just my favorites."

"When Jelly Bean is born, I'm sure someone will make her baby booties into bookends."

"Baby booties, storks, naked babies sleeping with

their butts in the air. If they make a baby-themed bookend, I'm sure someone will give it to me."

"I'd like to make sure I get you something unique." She cocked her head and looked out the window, innocence blanking out all other emotions on her face. "Like bookends made with her umbilical cord or something."

Karl nearly spit out his coffee. "That was wicked."

Vivian's sly smile broke into a full-out, self-satisfied grin. "Yeah, but you thought it was funny." Then she stood up in her seat, leaned over the bar and kissed him on the mouth.

And suddenly the morning wasn't so awkward after all.

CHAPTER NINETEEN

THEY SAT IN companionable silence as Karl drove Vivian back to his mother's house. Which was good, because Vivian had a lot on her mind.

She'd meant what she said to Karl about not expecting happily ever after. It didn't mean she didn't *want* it, just that expecting it seemed a surefire way to get her heart broken. Plus, there hadn't been any courtship in Las Vegas or when she invited herself to live in his apartment. Even if a traditional happy family was in her future, she didn't want to miss out on the getting-to-know-you part of the relationship. Pregnant or not, she wanted to get a couple of dates out of the deal.

If she went back in time and told her eighteen-year-old self—the one desperate to escape the unstable world her father lived in and thrived on—that she wouldn't be pushing for absolute security at this point in her life, that younger self would smack her upside the head and call her crazy.

And crazy she might be. But seeing Karl's silliness last night made her wistful for a marriage based on more than a certificate and a baby. She wanted the trust that he'd shown her last night to underpin their entire relationship. No more doubts and no more suspicions. She wanted them to raise the baby in a home with two parents who loved and supported each other.

It was the best and most unrealistic thing she could hope for.

Up until that night in Vegas, Vivian hadn't purposely avoided marriage, but she had been afraid to tie herself to another person whose potential impulsiveness could ruin both their lives. Karl's impulsiveness—though she shared the blame for their situation—had changed her life completely. However, knowing him meant knowing that he took care of his responsibilities without question. If she was going to ask for the moon, she might as well ask for the stars, as well.

For the first time in her life, she wasn't going to take the safe road. Or be nervous that she didn't even know what the safe road was. She wasn't going to settle for something subpar because she was afraid of falling off a cliff. She was on the hunt for perfect, whatever that might be.

VIVIAN SPENT THE next week learning about Polish Easter traditions. When they weren't working, she and Susan cooked food for Sunday. There were the foods Vivian had expected—hard-boiled eggs, bread and ham—and the foods that surprised her, including making a cake in a lamb mold. Susan told Vivian to frost the cake, "so that you can learn and help my grandbaby when he's old enough."

At Vivian's apologies for the alien-looking monstrosity of a dessert, Susan showed her pictures of the last cake Karl had decorated. Vivian protested that Karl had frosted that cake as a teenager and she was thirty-four, but Susan waved her off. "He might have been younger than you when he frosted that cake, but he'd been frosting them for years. This is your first one." Then her mother-in-law took a picture of Vivian's creation, to add to her collection.

Everything they did to prepare for Easter seemed to involve lambs. Vivian helped Susan shape softened butter into a lamb mold. The greeting cards Susan had mailed out on Monday had lambs on them and many of the linens were embroidered with lambs. Susan even brought home sugar formed into lamb shapes.

Saturday morning and after a couple times practicing the word in front of a mirror, Vivian helped Susan pack a *Swęiconka* basket. Into the basket went bits and pieces of each of the foods they would eat tomorrow, including enough hard-boiled eggs for each family member to have a good-size wedge of egg. Susan was going to take the entire basket to church so the food could be blessed.

As they packed the basket, Susan explained the symbolism of each item. "This is for joy and abundance," she said, as Vivian handed her the small ham Susan had purchased especially for the blessing. Susan tucked the ham next to the ball of cheese (though it wasn't a cheese ball as Vivian recognized the term)—abundance (the ham) and moderation (the cheese) bundled together.

Before Vivian handed over the bacon—the last of the three pork products that went into the basket, all related to generosity and abundance of some kind, which Vivian found amusing though pigs probably found it less so—she asked her mother-in-law the question that had been on her mind since seeing Susan get into her car on Palm Sunday. "Does it bother you that I'm not Catholic?"

Vivian hadn't gone to any church services in the month she'd lived here. Since most of that month had been Lent, and Easter clearly meant more to the Mileks than an Easter egg hunt in the city park, Vivian felt as though her lack of religiosity was a bit of a scarlet letter on her chest. But, despite all the time they'd spent in the kitchen preparing food and now sitting around the table preparing a basket to take to church, Susan hadn't mentioned Vivian's lack of church attendance once.

Honestly, Vivian had felt more pressure to go to a church service on a Sunday during a very brief stay in Provo, Utah, before her father had decided that he wasn't cut out for fleecing people by preying on their religious beliefs. "It's easy money, but a man's got to have some standards," he'd muttered to himself as they packed one night—quickly, so they could leave before dawn.

Susan gestured, and Vivian handed over the bacon. Her mother-in-law packed it in silence, her brows furrowed. Vivian had given up expecting a response and was passing the little container of salt when Susan sat back in her chair. As soon as she started talking, Vivian put down the salt and listened.

"Karl's ex-wife, Jessica, was everything I wanted in a daughter-in-law. And she was everything I thought Karl wanted in a wife. She was Polish—from Milwaukee—and Catholic and as smart as he is."

Vivian ignored the unconscious insult; she wanted to hear what Susan had to say.

"But they couldn't make each other happy. They just expected too much out of each other. Karl doesn't expect anything from you." Vivian didn't have to say anything about that insult because Susan realized what she'd just said and looked up in horror. "I didn't mean that the way it sounded. I meant Karl doesn't know what to expect out of you, so he's taking the time to get to know *you*, rather than his ideal of you. And it's the flesh and blood person that's going to make him happy, not the woman he thinks his wife should be like."

Not sure what this had to do with going to Mass,

Vivian kept her mouth shut and waited for Susan to finish her thought. "So I guess my answer to your question is that I'd rather Karl be happy than his wife be Catholic. And I expect that between the two of you, you'll raise my grandbaby to be a responsible citizen."

Vivian wasn't sure if parental values were a perfect indicator of a child's values. If they were, she would've cheated when her father asked her to, the cheating wouldn't have bothered her, she wouldn't have gone to the bar to drink herself forgetful, she wouldn't have met Karl and she wouldn't be in Susan's kitchen right now, stuffing a basket full with symbolic food.

But the present didn't seem like the time to mention any of this to Susan.

"I'd like my grandbabies to be raised Catholic. I hope there will be many of them and that I live long enough to see their First Communions. However, one grandchild has already been raised Lutheran and I survived that." Susan must be referring to the child Renia gave up for adoption in her teens. "And Maria is still my favorite sister, Buddhism and all."

So the answer was that her daughter-in-law not being Catholic bothered Susan, but not enough for her to say anything, and she was respectful enough of their relationship not to pressure Vivian. They packed the basket with a few other foods, and Susan continued to tell Vivian the meaning of each item they added. Only when Susan was covering the basket with linen did Vivian realize their previous conversation wasn't yet over.

"What I really want," Susan said, "is for family traditions to continue. I think it's important for children to know that their great-grandparents also made eggs on Easter for the priest to bless and that they have a connection to those long-dead family members."

"Back in the old country."

Though Vivian said the words with a smile, so Susan would know she meant them kindly, she needn't have worried. Susan just laughed and said, "Yes, back in the old country. Learning Pawel and I shared some of the same traditions that first Easter we were married—even though my family has been in the U.S. since before the Revolutionary War and his parents were new immigrants—made me feel like it was meant to be. You see, I'd made a rash decision and was looking for signs I'd made the right one."

That search for signs was familiar. Vivian had felt the same way the first night in Karl's apartment when she'd woken up to a cup of coffee. Her coffee had been cold, but the gesture was unmistakable. "Karl speaks about you and his father as if you were a perfect love story."

"I saw Pawel at Healthy Food and knew he was going to be my husband. Even still, the two of us spent many years, with young children in tow, figuring out what being husband and wife meant. Karl probably isn't too young to remember those days, but he wouldn't focus on them. He idealizes Pawel."

Susan patted the basket. "Traditions adapt, as they should, for each generation. I hope you and Karl will keep them up after I am dead, even if you have to change them a little to fit whatever future I could never imagine."

Vivian stopped herself before responding with, "You're too young to be talking like that." Susan was only a month away from a heart attack. Her mortality probably still weighed heavily on her mind, even if the doctors said she was doing everything she needed to do in order to see another twenty years and more grandchildren.

Instead, she promised her mother-in-law they would continue the traditions so their children would know their history. The promise was easy to make. Vivian had grown up with few traditions, though her father talked about some he had been raised with. As it had just been the two of them, they had always gone to the fanciest hotel in whatever town they were in for Thanksgiving, and they'd exchanged presents at Christmas, though, as she got older, Vivian had begun to suspect some of the presents were ill-gotten. When she was a teenager, her father had put money into her college fund for Christmas and her birthday.

What was harder for Vivian to promise was that she *and* Karl would teach their child these traditions. The *and* part of that promise was still up in the air.

"We can add in traditions you grew up with."

Like the Easter egg hunts that Vivan would attend, if whatever town she and her dad were in at the time offered one.

"If you want," Susan said softly when Vivian didn't respond.

"My dad wasn't really into traditions, but my aunt may know a few that she and my mom grew up with." Vivian made a note to call her aunt and ask about them. And her grandparents? She didn't even know if they were still alive. When her aunt Kitty had left, so had Vivian's connection to her maternal grandparents. And her father had never talked about his parents, except for regularly reminding Vivian how much freer her childhood had been compared to his.

"So, yes, I want." She had friends in Las Vegas and had shared some of their traditions on holidays—if they weren't working—but never allowed herself to think about her family. Thinking about what her dad had denied her growing up just made her mad, and she didn't want to spend her time mad at her father. No matter his faults, he was her father and she wasn't going to get another one. However, if she concentrated too much on the good memories, she was easy prey when he called and asked her to send him money. Her relationship with her father was the two-faced Janus and she just tried not to look.

Could being a part of a family give her the courage to face both sides of her father without losing herself?

"Good, dear." Susan patted her hand with affection. "And, even though I've not asked, you're always welcome to come to Mass with me."

"I know. I appreciate both the welcome and the not asking."

Vivian had spent sixteen years in Las Vegas and developed a community around herself. She'd had friends and known the folks who worked at her favorite coffee shop, but it was different than the community that Susan was inviting her to join. Las Vegas had been transitory, especially toward the end when the economy was crashing and so many of her friends were leaving for greener pastures.

Chicago—and Archer Heights—felt permanent.

CHAPTER TWENTY

FOR THE FIRST time since they had all been living in Chicago as adults, his mom had convinced all her children to go to Mass. Easter Mass was especially long, and by the end Karl was pretty sure most of his siblings and their significant others were regretting their decision, though only Miles's daughter was saying anything. Dan was elbowing Tilly and rubbing his behind, making his sister laugh. Once, Dan had made his sister cry until she was almost empty of tears, and now he could make her laugh as easily as he could blink his eyes.

And that's what Karl had always enjoyed about the Easter service, long as it was. Easter and spring represented rebirth and second chances. During the worst years of his first marriage, second chances had always seemed like a burden. A burden to Jessica to grant and a burden to Karl to have to keep asking for. With Vivian, asking for a second chance seemed glorious—as though the sanctuary had been dark and all the lights were now being turned on in celebration.

Disgorged from their cars, the Mileks and their

significant others spilled into his mom's kitchen. Vivian was sitting at the table reading. She looked both at home and as though she didn't belong there.

"Where's breakfast? I'm starving." Sarah looked put-upon, as only well-cared-for teenagers and dogs can.

"First things first." His mother bustled through the crowd to sit at the table. She buzzed with energy, her face alight with the pleasure of being surrounded by family. "Before the boys get to work on breakfast, we all have eggs to eat."

"Easter is a day of rest for Polish women. Dan, Miles and I will finish whatever is required for breakfast while the rest of you sit in the living room," Karl explained at the puzzled look on his wife's face, coming around to stand behind her and placing his hand on her shoulder. She leaned over to drop a peck of a kiss onto his hand. A small, insignificant gesture that she probably didn't even notice she made but that started Karl's heart racing.

"It seems like cheating, since your mom made most of the food already, and all you have to do is put it on the table."

Tilly laughed. "It's even more of a lie because our job is to keep Mom from busting into the kitchen and 'resting' by telling everyone what to do."

"Trust me, there's nothing restful about that task," Renia said.

"I'll be good this year," Karl's mother said, as she got up to walk over to the *Święconka* basket.

Miles stopped her. "You can start by letting me get out the eggs while you sit back down. Dan will get you coffee."

"As the only male foodie in the group," Dan said with his good-natured grin, "I think I should be responsible for the food. You're married to the woman who searches the internet for intravenous coffee drip patents once a month. You can do the coffee."

"And it begins," Karl whispered into Vivian's ear. He stood up straight and addressed the crowd. "I'm the oldest and only Pole with a Y chromosome in this crowd. I'll decide what everyone does. Dan, you peel and slice the eggs. Miles, you make coffee. If you don't have a Y chromosome, go sit in the living room."

"I don't think it's very restful to be bossed about by my son," his mother murmured, but she said it good-naturedly *and* while walking out of the kitchen on Tilly's arm. The clamor in the room was cut in half, which Karl was grateful for, but Vivian was no longer in touching distance, which he wasn't so grateful for.

Dan dug the hard-boiled eggs out of the basket and took them over to the sink. "What do you think the chances are they'll stay in the living room?"

Karl felt rather than saw Vivian return to the kitchen. "Not good," she said. "I came in to get a glass of water, but if you really want to keep us out, you can give me a bell to ring whenever we need something."

"I'll bring you a glass of water. Go back and sit with Mom before she gets any ideas." He leaned over and kissed Vivian's cheek, grateful she had come into the kitchen so he could see her again and smell her jasmine perfume.

When he turned back around, Miles and Dan were both looking up at the ceiling a little too obviously. Miles was whistling.

Sometimes life was easier without family.

Karl thought about his family members, dead on the side of the road or dying in the hospital, and reevaluated his thoughts. If Leon could be here in this kitchen, Karl wouldn't mind any teasing his brother would subject him to.

The coffeepot and the other things he needed were in the same place they had been since the first Easter he could remember. The platter for the eggs was new—*Babunia* had dropped the original sometime when her hands had started to shake—but the silver coffee set had been a wedding gift from some family friend his mom didn't even keep in touch with anymore.

Miles filled the coffeepot and gathered cream and sugar. Karl made several trips to the living room with coffee cups for everyone. Dan, foodie that he was, wasn't satisfied with slicing the eggs and sticking them on a plate; he arranged a smorgasbord of *Swęiconka* foods decoratively around the eggs. Miles waited until Dan's back was turned, then rearranged the food on the platter so that the sugar lambs looked like an army led by the butter lamb, ready to conquer the pile of sliced ham. Dan just sighed and rolled his eyes when he saw the platter again.

In the living room, Vivian was using her ultrasound images to successfully distract his mother from her normal "resting" state of offering helpful suggestions to the kitchen. Even though she'd seen the images many times before, his mother still cooed.

Karl could understand some of the amazement. At eleven weeks, the ultrasound images of the baby had so much more detail than they had just a few weeks ago. He couldn't believe that the mouse he'd seen at Vivian's first doctor's appointment now looked something like a baby with a head, arms and legs.

He finally understood what people meant when they said pregnant women glowed. Sitting in his mother's living room, surrounded by family, Vivian lit up his life. And he knew why he'd thought she didn't look as though she'd belonged at his mother's kitchen table. Karl didn't want Vivian living with his mother. He wanted her back at his apartment, living with him. He wanted her to look as if she was *visiting* when she sat at his mother's kitchen table, not as if she was *home* there.

Vivian was family. She was his wife. She was carrying his child. She should be in his apartment, with him.

THE HOUSE HAD fallen increasingly silent as each of the Mileks had left for their own homes. Now, only Susan, Vivian and Karl were left and Karl was about to leave. Only he wasn't leaving. He was standing in the doorway wearing his coat, scarf and hat saying, "Vivian, I think you should come home."

Did he think she was going to grab her coat and walk out the door with him?

Vivian couldn't help recalling a similar scene in his apartment, while he stood, bundled in his winter clothes, telling her where to live....

Wherever she was, she was never in the right place, as far as Karl Milek was concerned.

She wouldn't cry, not when he was looking like somber business-Karl even though they were talking about where she should live. It wasn't business, but she could pretend it was just as well as he could. The emotion he'd shown over Easter breakfast, little touches and that familiar kiss, made treating this conversation like business harder, but not impossible.

Now he looked detached from the emotional

world and she was back to wondering where—as
his pregnant wife—she fit into his life. She turned
her back to him and walked to the couch, leaving him to shut the door and follow. "When I first
showed up at your apartment, you insisted my home
was Nevada. I can't go back there, so where do you
mean for me to go?"

She sat on the couch, trying to lounge, as if this
conversation was no big deal. As if he couldn't
break her heart again. When she lifted her head to
consider him with what she hoped was the ease of
a woman regarding a painting of fruit on the wall,
his face had tightened and the little tic at the base
of his jaw had started. Reading all of his emotions
from that barely visible twitch was getting tire-
some. "Home with me, Vivian. I think you should
come home with me."

Maybe if he had shown more emotion—maybe
if he had asked her while making an inappropriate and macabre joke or while she could see what
the silly pattern on his boxers was tonight—she
would've said yes. But everyone said "yes, sir" to
Karl when his jaw tensed, and so she lifted her
elbow to rest on the arm of the couch and said,
"Why?"

"The doctors have told us repeatedly that it's fine
for Mom to live by herself again."

"That's only a reason for why I don't need to
live with *her* anymore. Why should I move back

into your apartment?" She wanted him to say the words. To say he wanted her and that he not only understood why she'd nearly cheated, but also that he didn't care.

"You're my wife." He stepped farther into the living room and reached out for her thickened stomach, but didn't come close enough to touch. "You're carrying my child."

Vivian could no longer distinguish between heartburn and anger, but Karl was causing one of them. "Until we get a divorce..."

His hand recoiled back to the side of his body. The tic in his jaw sped up and his face darkened. At least his emotions were strong, even if he would never reveal them.

She repeated herself. "Until we get a divorce, I am your wife no matter where I live. This baby—" she put her hands over her belly as if she could protect the growing child from a father who would never laugh with it "—will always be your child."

Karl didn't say a word. He just stood in silence and she didn't have the patience to wait him out. "Besides, I like your mom. I like living with your mom. I like working at Healthy Food. Why should I leave a place where I'm content to go where I'm not completely welcome?"

"For God's sake, Vivian!" The vehemence in his voice pushed her back into the cushions. "I just asked you to come home with me. How much more welcome can you be?"

He was right. If she continued to live with Susan and work at Healthy Food, she and Jelly Bean would be fine. If they got a divorce, the Mileks wouldn't stop being a family to her just because she wasn't married to Karl. He would provide child support, she could slowly build up her savings again, and she would have a measure of security and family.

If she moved back with Karl—if she stayed his wife because she was his wife—she would never want. Jelly Bean wouldn't want. Tilly and Renia would stay her sisters-in-law in actuality, not just because they liked her. Susan would stay her mother-in-law, not just the grandmother of her child. She wouldn't be working at Healthy Food to build up her savings; she would be working there because she enjoyed it. Family and security—permanence—beckoned from Karl's apartment.

She pulled herself out of the cushions and sat rigid on the couch. "It's not enough."

"What's not enough?" He stepped closer to her, but still not close enough that he would be able to touch her. Was he afraid to touch her? "My apartment's not enough? My money's not enough? The opportunity I'm offering you to have a *home* isn't enough? Tell me, Vivian, what about my offer isn't enough?"

"I want more." Living a half-life because it was a secure life wasn't enough anymore. "I want to live with my husband because he loves me, not because I'm his wife."

"You *are* my wife." Another step closer. "You're carrying my child. You belong in my house."

"Belong?" She arched an eyebrow at him.

Karl's bottom jaw jutted forward until Vivian was afraid his entire face would crack. "You risked driving from Las Vegas to Chicago because you knew I wouldn't abandon my obligations, so don't look at me like you suddenly think I'm a caveman."

"I don't want to be your wife because I'm pregnant and you are a man who meets his obligations. I want to be a wife because life is better with a partner. A month ago, what you're offering me now would have been enough for me. It's not, anymore. I want it all."

He took a step back. "I don't have any more to offer."

"Then I'll stay with Susan and work at Healthy Food for as long as she'll let me."

"And after that?"

These were the scariest words Vivian had ever had to say, but she said them anyway. "If Susan fires me and kicks me out of her house, then I'll figure out what to do. I'll be fine. But I'm not willing to give up happily-ever-after for a guaranteed roof over my head. That's not good enough for me."

Then she stood and fled to the kitchen, before she could change her mind.

CHAPTER TWENTY-ONE

KARL WAS IN the conference room at one of the laptops, comparing the notes the staff attorney had made with an email, when he heard Malcolm's heavy footfalls come down the hall and into the room.

"Don't you have someone else to do that for you?" Malcolm asked.

"I'm looking for something specific." Reviewing documents occupied his hands and keeping his hands occupied kept his mind busy. Not engaged, but at least he wasn't thinking about Vivian. Otherwise, his thoughts had a tendency to wander to her shiny black hair, pink lips and how her skin tasted when he kissed it. Then he would remember how much he had come to enjoy sharing his apartment with her in the short time they'd lived together. Then his mind would slip further and turn to imagining her sleeping next to him every night.

He wouldn't think about the circumstances that had led to her being in Chicago and living with his mother. He wouldn't think about the failure of his previous marriage or how he couldn't get Vivian to move back in with him unless he said words that weren't his to say. He would simply think about her. Then he would think about *them* together. And he would think about a family—their family.

Idle hands were the devil's workshop.

"I don't mean to pry," Malcolm said with false primness, "but why isn't your wife living with you yet?"

"Between you and Greta, no one in this office ever means to pry."

Karl looked back down at the laptop screen. Without seeing Malcolm's face, Karl could feel the feral grin spreading across the face of the director of investigations, and the man's smug sense of satisfaction pushed all the air out of the room. Malcolm was great at his job, which meant his inquiries weren't easily fobbed off by a short remark and a metaphorically turned back.

Even though it was a battle he was going to lose, Karl continued to ignore Malcolm in hopes he would give up and leave the room. In response, Malcolm sat down and started spinning in one of the chairs. The heavy chair creaked as it turned and rocked under Malcolm's weight. Karl didn't have to occupy his hands to keep his thoughts away from Vivian; the screeching chair meant he couldn't think at all.

"Would you stop that?"

"Stop what?" Malcolm rocked back and forth,

the chair squeaking in time with his movements. As Malcolm was looking for a reaction, rather than an answer, Karl didn't give him either.

For several minutes the only sounds in the room were Karl clicking the mouse and Malcolm squeaking the chair. Then the squeaking finally came to a halt. "I'll stop if you tell me why you're not living with your wife yet."

Finally. Karl's determination to wait out his friend was successful. Only Malcolm hadn't given in by leaving, but by further pursuing his question.

"You're the one who told me why she got fired from her job." Karl spoke to the laptop, even though he was no longer seeing the words on the screen well enough to process them.

Malcolm's shoes clumped on the wood floor. "Since she's living with your mother and working at Healthy Food, I assume she's actually innocent of any crime."

Innocence wasn't the question. Whether or not he cared about her *near* crime was. And, if he didn't care about her near crime, what other near crimes wouldn't he be able to care about? And would he be able to rationalize away the small crimes, the ones that *seem* insignificant, but were just part of a larger problem? Karl's back started to ache and he leaned back in his chair, rubbing the crick like an old man.

"And—" Malcolm wasn't done "—you've been

even more silent than usual around the office, so I know something's on your mind. Being the experienced investigator that I am, I can only conclude that you're thinking of how your pretty and pregnant wife is living with your mother instead of with you."

"She's helping my mother out at Healthy Food."

She was still in Chicago, but she didn't need him any longer. Not that Karl wanted her to be dependent on him. No. He preferred the Vivian with a sense of independence over the Vivian who had been trapped in his apartment. But he didn't have anything to offer her, and she expected something before she would move back in.

Her refusal was more frustrating because her "no" wasn't an "absolutely not." Instead, it was a "not until you give me what I want." He didn't think he could give her what she wanted. And she wouldn't take what he could give.

"And she can't help at the restaurant while living in your apartment?"

Karl finally looked over to see Malcolm had rested his arms on his legs and was bent over in his seat, his eyebrows raised in concern. Or maybe curiosity. Either way, the man didn't need to know Karl's business. "It's more complicated than that."

"Explain it to me."

"We're at work."

"You're the boss and it's nearly quitting time for

normal people. Let's go to a bar and you can explain it to me over a beer."

Sharing his problems with a coworker, even a coworker he respected and nearly considered a friend, was almost as scary as Vivian and his soon-to-be child.

Something in his face must have given his thoughts away because Malcolm's expression turned sympathetic. The man's expression was near enough to pity that Karl bent over the laptop again and waited for Malcolm to go away.

"Do you have friends?"

"Of course I have friends."

"I don't mean the people you shake hands with when you see them at the opera, I mean someone you relax and share your problems with. Or maybe someone you just get a beer and watch basketball with."

Vivian. He relaxed and shared his problems with her. She'd probably watch basketball if he were interested. "I'm a hockey fan."

"So the answer is no. You smile and shake hands with everyone in Chicago, from the guy selling *Streetwise* on the corner, to visiting senators, and then you go home to your silent apartment and—what? Watch hockey?"

"I'm rarely at my apartment." And with Xìnyùn there, his apartment was no longer silent.

"Maybe the reason Vivian isn't living in your

apartment is that no woman would want to be subjected to that tomb."

Karl's head snapped up so quickly he got a headache and the oppressive wood paneling in the conference room blurred.

"Ah, you've never considered that Vivian's 'no' might be permanent. And, from the horror on your face, you're afraid to confess your feelings because she might turn you down. And that might suck."

Karl folded his arms on the table, finally giving up any pretense of reviewing the staff attorney's notes. "You're right that she didn't commit the felony she was fired for. Middle Kingdom could never prove she cheated because she didn't. And I believe her. But that's not the issue."

"What is the issue?"

He sighed. Malcolm was right that he didn't have anyone to talk with about this, but he didn't *want* to talk with anyone about this. But Malcolm was also probably right that he needed to talk with someone before he exploded.

"Her father came to her for money because he lost more than he could repay while playing poker. Vivian agreed to the scheme and then changed her mind at the last minute."

"People have committed felonies for less compelling reasons. Does she regularly help her father out with such schemes?"

"No." Karl thought about the conversations he'd

overheard her have with her father. "I gather she sends him money when he asks, but also tries to avoid hearing him ask. She keeps him at arm's length as much as possible."

"So, she has a scheming father, but is otherwise all sweetness and light."

Karl stood up so he could shut the door. Talking this over with Malcolm was one thing. The entire office hearing it was another. "The lesson she seems to have learned from her father is that schemes don't pay and an honest living is better." Her father's schemes had cost her dearly twice that Karl knew of—first her college fund and then her livelihood. Of course, it was the rare child who watched their parents' mistakes and didn't repeat them even as they tried to do something differently.

"So, what's your problem?" Malcolm looked confused.

"I understand why she considered cheating. And I appreciate that she didn't cheat—I respect her for that. But I think I would even understand if she *had* cheated." He thought back to what he remembered about the waste of Melville's "Billy Budd," when those who had been responsible for dispensing justice had chosen to *not understand* and what a tragedy that had been. Was that why he had decided to pick up the book again?

"But if I forgive my wife for being willing to let her moral standards slip because her father was in hot water, how do I hold a man accountable when he took a bribe because his salary won't pay his wife's hospital bills?" The words sounded so simplistic, but his arteries clamped around his heart as he said them. "I'm not talking about the alderman who's trading favors for the extra slice of power or a few more pennies in her campaign fund, but the guy just trying to live his life."

His entire worldview had been snapped in two. And there was no clamp that would fix that rend. The confession exhausted Karl so completely that he had to take a seat in one of the damned squeaky chairs before he fell over and further humiliated himself.

"Ah," Malcolm said with understanding. "You've worked with corporate lawyers and inspector generals, but you've not had enough interaction with law enforcement to know your problem isn't unique."

"Of course it's not unique," Karl snapped.

Malcolm kept talking as if Karl hadn't just splintered into pieces. "But in your favor is the fact that the gray world you've happened upon will make you better at what you do. Maybe the guy taking bribes because he's trying to keep his wife alive is guilty, but he's not guilty in the same way as the alderman. You can be understanding of the first guy's motivations while still believing he's guilty. Life in the gray is harder, but it's more rewarding. And more fair. Compassion can only help you."

"Justice can't always be fair. And it's rarely compassionate." *Or just*, if Karl were being honest with himself. Watching *Jenůfa* should have reminded him of that fact.

"Justice is a theoretical concept constructed by society and understood differently by different cultures. It's only as good as the people responsible for enforcing it. But people do have feelings. They can be compassionate. And, by seeing the gray you can be a part of making justice more than a noble goal. You won't always succeed, but it's better to at least try."

Karl pondered Malcolm's argument for several seconds. "I never imagined you as a touchy-feely guy."

"I have depths you will never uncover." Malcolm's laugh was full and hearty. "My wife will tell you that I can be as tenderhearted as the next guy."

"Love really does give people rose-colored glasses." The words came out false as Karl tried to follow Malcolm's lighter tone and failed. If Malcolm noticed, he ignored it.

"So what does all of this have to do with Vivian living at your mother's?"

Instead of answering, Karl stood and walked over to the laptop he'd been working on. Slowly, deliberately, he saved his work and closed the screen. Then he put the notes back in order. The sharp slice of pain through his finger meant he now had a paper cut along with the embarrassment of confessing his soul to his coworker.

Malcolm was silent until Karl stood back up. "What does all this have to do with Vivian living at your mother's?" he asked again.

"She says she won't move back while I still judge her for being fired."

"But you no longer judge her for being fired. I don't even think you're certain of your position to judge her at all."

"I don't. I'm not." Karl shoved a chair under the table. "I don't *care* anymore."

"Have you told her that?"

"No." The next chair wasn't sticking out from the table, but Karl gave it a shove anyway. The hard plastic of the arms clinked off something under the table. He shoved it again before moving on to the next chair.

"Have you at least told her that you love her?"

Shove. "No." Shove. "She hasn't told me she loves me, either."

"Didn't you learn anything about women in your first marriage?"

"Apparently I never learned anything about Jessica, much less something I could extrapolate to the greater world of women." The next chair caught on something when he shoved it, and Karl caught the back of it in his gut. He had to take a deep breath before he could get the next words out. "This is the twenty-first century. I shouldn't have to say 'I love you' first."

"No, but what's stopping you?"

She could be one less person he'd have to worry about driving down the road, at the mercy of drunk drivers, people texting and the old man who should've given up his license years ago. If a fireman did pull her broken body from a collapsed car, Karl wouldn't have said "I love you," and so the loss would hurt less. If she had to have a closed-casket funeral because the damage had been so severe, the face covered by wood wouldn't be the face he had woken up to every morning.

"I just don't think I can do it," was the answer Karl gave Malcolm.

Marriage to Jessica hadn't been this hard. But Jessica hadn't been the wife he'd wanted; she'd been the wife he'd thought he was supposed to have. If Vivian really became his and he really became hers, how would he survive if something happened to her?

Malcolm stared at him for several *long* seconds before responding. "I didn't take you for a coward."

"Self-preservation hardly makes me a coward." Didn't it make him a survivor instead?

"Even if you don't believe it makes you a coward, trying to preserve some sort of self that is much less than who you *could* be certainly makes you stupid." Malcolm waited, one eyebrow raised, but

Karl didn't respond. Finally, Malcolm huffed in disgust and left the room.

If Karl could have done the same, and left the stupid part of himself behind, he would have.

CHAPTER TWENTY-TWO

AS FAR AS Karl was concerned, the only pleasant part of this shopping experience was spending time with Vivian and watching her fingers trail over the pale wood of the crib. But because the world had a mean sense of humor, watching Vivian's long fingers touch every item in the store was also the worst part of shopping for baby furniture.

His wife bent a little at the waist to read the tag on the crib. "It says this crib converts into a bed, which would be nice. I like the color, too." She straightened. Her lips were puckered and shifting from side to side.

"But?"

"But it's a bit too big for your mom's house."

This entire shopping experience was proof that Karl could lie to himself. Watching Vivian's fingers *was not* the worst part of buying baby furniture. Listening to her assess each piece of furniture in terms of his mother's house was.

"It will fit fine in the second bedroom in my apartment." They were a broken record. She would say it wouldn't fit in his mother's house and he would remind her of the cavernous space in his apartment.

She assessed the crib again, then shook her head, her long black hair swinging against her shoulders. "I think the crib and the guest bed would be a tight fit."

At the first crib they'd looked at, Karl had managed to say, "We can get rid of the guest bed," before Vivian walked away. Now, in a series of cowardly moves at odds with her character, she scurried away each time he tried to bring up the idea of them living together, baby in one room, parents in the other.

And each time he'd opened his mouth to call her on her cowardice, he remembered his conversation with Malcolm and his lips slammed shut. She wouldn't move back in with him until he released his judgment of her near felony. He couldn't release his judgment because, well, because there wasn't much left of him if he wasn't judging people.

Is that all I am? God, what a horrible thought. He hurried to catch up to her before he lost any more of the precious time they were spending together. He at least wasn't so cowardly that he couldn't continue after his wife in the baby store. Malcolm was sure to be impressed, Karl thought wryly.

"Maybe we can buy a bassinet now and a crib later, when we figure out how much space we really have." She was fingering the fabric canopy of the bassinet and not looking at him at all. Two people, having a baby together, picking out baby furniture, and they couldn't be further apart if she were still in Las Vegas. "Of course, there's still the changing table and the rocker that we need to get. I guess we don't *need* a rocker. Your mom has something I can use, and anyway I can't imagine my dad had much more for me than a dresser drawer when I was a baby."

Karl seized on the possible change of subject. Anything to stop the scratch of the needle on whatever album of broken relationships they were playing. "What was your childhood like?"

"Besides moving in the middle of the night because my dad was caught up in another failed scheme?" She gave the bassinet a little push, but it didn't rock.

"You never imagine your parents excitedly looking at baby stuff?" Not that Karl could imagine his father ever stepping into a giant, baby-stuff-filled store like this one, but his father had enjoyed his children. He'd been strict with the boys and a little afraid to break the girls, but Karl had never doubted that his father had *wanted* them. Catholic prohibitions on birth control hadn't been the reason his parents had had four children.

Vivian bent to look at the tag on the bassinet. It was on the tip of Karl's tongue to tell her to stop looking at the price—that he could afford whatever she wanted for their baby—but he stopped himself. He wanted to know the circumstances that had made her who she was, and being frustrated with her for being frugal—clearly a result of her childhood—wouldn't help.

"Maybe buying a bassinet first and a crib later is a waste of money," she murmured. "But we have some time to think about it."

When he caught up to her, she was ready to respond. "My parents got married because my mom was pregnant." She smiled wryly. "I mean, at least we got married on the same night I got pregnant. The marriage even came first, really."

This bassinet rocked when she pushed it. They watched it in silence until it came to a stop. Karl took Vivian's hand and gave it a squeeze.

"My mom lost everything because of her pregnancy. No one actually said those words to me, but my aunt Kitty used to remind my dad of that when they fought, and I often overheard." This time, she was the one to give *his* hand a squeeze. He squeezed back, to support them both. "My mom's parents *hated* my dad, and they eventually disowned her. She dropped out of college. She died in childbirth. When I got older, I wondered if my aunt Kitty tried so hard to get custody of me because she felt guilty for her family abandoning my mom. I don't know and I'm afraid to ask."

Karl stepped closer to her so that he could wrap

his arm around her, a full understanding of her childhood finally beginning to form in his mind.

"Even though I was an accident who forced him into marriage and then killed the woman he loved, my father never let me believe I wasn't loved." She tucked her head against him and he pressed a kiss against her hair. "I'm not pretending he was a great father. He's a liar and a cheat who could never figure out how to make sure there was food in the house for his kid. But he always had time to listen to my stories from school. He would take me to the library and the park. And when he told me I could be anything I wanted to be, I believed him. My dad's greed is just the negative side to his vision for a better future. He always believed in me."

Vivian shifted a bit, as if to pull away from him, but Karl kept his arm tight around her. He wanted her against him as he processed what she said. Their respective fathers had each fought for their belief in their children, only they each seemed to be fighting for a different team. His dad also believed in his children and in a better future. Only Pawel had taught him to believe in justice and fairness. That there is a *right* answer, even if it is the hard answer, and that usually right and easy are on opposite sides.

Karl opened his mouth to say the words Vivian wanted to hear. Not just "I love you," but also that he didn't judge her past decisions. That he understood them and, more importantly, he didn't care anymore. That he wanted her more than his sense of self-righteousness.

But his memory of his father grounding him for an illegal hit during a hockey game was as fresh in his mind as if it had happened yesterday. The ref hadn't seen the hit, but his father had. Not only had Karl been grounded for a month, he'd had to call the opposing player and offer an apology. "Just because the ref didn't see you, doesn't mean you can get away with cheating," his father had said before Karl had taken a deep breath, dialed the number and prepared to ask forgiveness, all the while knowing any absolution would have to wait until the next time he went to confession.

So the words never came out. He put down the shopping basket he was carrying and turned so that he faced Vivian, putting his cold hands against her warm face. The fire of her lips melted his as soon as he touched his mouth to hers. Her lips were soft and, when she opened her mouth to welcome him, moist. He could feel the puffs of her exhaled breath on his cheek.

If only he could say the words, then he could have a kiss like this every night of his life. And every morning. And before he left for work and when he came home from work. And just because his wife was amazing. Her tongue slipped into his mouth before he could pull back and say anything.

If he was going to pull back and say anything. His track record so far wasn't very good.

Vivian slid her hands down his back and grabbed the waistband of his pants. Karl stopped thinking and just let himself feel.

Vivian was the one who finally broke the kiss. Her lips were shining from a mixture of their kiss and her lipstick, and her eyes were bright.

"I'm sorry," Karl said. Not for the kiss—he could never be sorry for the kiss—but for his inability to say the words she wanted to hear.

Vivian closed her eyes for several seconds. When she opened them, their brightness had been replaced by pity. She nodded, patted his cheek with her hand and walked off. Karl was left standing in the middle of a field of baby furniture alone.

He caught up to her in the forest of baby toys.

When people accused Karl of having a stick up his ass, he was never shocked. He just preferred the term *straitlaced.* Like he also preferred *righteous anger* instead of *judgmental fucker.* An administrator for the Illinois Department of Human Resources had called him that last name once. Karl hadn't particularly cared for the sexual affair that the administrator had been having with a key figure in the state's Department of Human Resources office, but the high-pay, low-work jobs that her family got without ever seeming to have to interview *had* been a concern. The administrator had been arrested the day after giving Karl his epitaph.

The problem was not that Karl didn't know who he was; it was that he didn't think he could be flexible without breaking. Even for Vivian, who was shaking a rattle with a wide, bright smile on her face.

But he was willing to try. "What are you doing on the twenty-ninth?" he asked her.

"Probably working. Why?" Before she could shake the rattle again, Karl took it from her and put it in the shopping basket he was carrying. "Why'd you do that?" she asked.

"Even if our baby has no interest in the rattle, you seem to like it."

Vivian raised one eyebrow at him. Maybe the people who called him overbearing were right. He pulled the rattle out of his basket and handed it back to her. She gave it one loud shake, which reverberated through the store, then handed it back to him. "Why do you ask about the twenty-ninth?"

"It's Phil Biadała's wedding. I'd like a date."

Vivian put down the set of colored rings she was holding and assessed him. He didn't squirm—he never squirmed—but he did relax his stance. Just a little.

"Okay. Let me clear it with your mom first, but okay." She picked up another rattle, giving it several shakes.

He smiled. "My mom will say yes."

"She's still under the impression we will kiss and make up." She put down the second rattle and picked up another. If she was trying to make each rattle more annoying than the first, she was succeeding.

"Is a perfect nuclear family no longer the goal?"

Karl had a feeling she was now shaking the rattle because she didn't know what else to do. He'd made her nervous, which hadn't been his objective. But he was pushing himself, and there was no reason she couldn't be pushed along with him.

Finally, she set the rattle down and lifted her face to his. Her expression was perfectly smooth, with no wrinkles to reveal how she was feeling. Only her eyes betrayed her nervousness. "It's still the goal. But I've not changed my mind about what I deserve."

As much as it hurt to admit it, Malcolm was right. "You do deserve it." He picked the rattle off the shelf and handed it to her. Then he picked another off the shelf and handed that one to her, as well. "And I'm trying."

As HE HAD been for the past several nights, Karl was the last customer to leave Healthy Food. It didn't seem quite right to call him a customer, but he never stayed to help clean up, so he wasn't an employee. He offered to help, but Susan always shooed him out the door with a reminder about his real job and its importance to the city. Despite his protests, he always looked relieved when he walked out the door as the mops came out. Relieved and tired.

Vivian didn't blame him for either. Cleaning up a buffet restaurant was a nightmare—people managed to get food in the strangest places when it was their responsibility to carry it to their tables. Plus, Karl had a job. One that was important to him. More important to him than she was.

Not that she could blame him for that, either. She could be angry with him—often was angry with him—but she'd been around the Mileks long enough to know that Karl had idolized his father. She'd also learned that Papa Milek had been more willing to say "I love you" than "good job," and all the Milek children were expected to hold to his high standards of being a good citizen. Susan spoke with such praise about how Karl had stepped into the role of man of the house after the car accident. Up until he'd married his ex-wife, Karl had tried to play father to his sisters, even when his pep talks and advice had fallen on deaf ears.

His struggle with his expectations of himself and the imagined expectations of his father had looked physically painful, especially when surrounded by baby furniture that was all supposed to be about joy. She could feel sorry for him, and even have to restrain herself from smacking him, but she couldn't *blame* him.

She moistened her finger on the little sponge next to the register and began to count the money in the till—something else to do so she didn't think about Karl and his inner-little-boy struggles with his grown-up self. The register made satisfying crunching noises as the Z-tape printed out. Her brain must make similar noises when she thought about her situation and how easy it would be to pack her bags and move into Karl's apartment to play family. He cared for her; Vivian didn't doubt that. He would be faithful and honest. Frustrations or not, they were friends. It would be so easy to believe that was enough.

When he kissed her, she believed it was enough.

She looked down at the money in her hand and sighed. She'd lost count. It would have to be recounted—this time with actual attention paid to it. The longer she spent counting the money, the further away her bed got. She restacked the bills and started over. Then began the long process of checking credit card receipts against the record in the till. And checks from the few old Poles whom Susan still allowed to pay with a check.

Healthy Food was full of traditions—things that were "just the way they were when Pawel's mother was still alive," to quote the old-timers. Grandfathering in people who could pay with a check—a

privilege that was *not* passed down to children—
was cute and homey. An ancient cash register that
had to be repaired every two weeks and an old dial-
up credit card machine were not. Vivian would love
one of those fancy systems with the credit card slot
attached to the monitor. Then there would be only
one receipt for the customer to take and one receipt
for her to count.

Vivian had suggested the idea to Susan once. Her
mother-in-law's response had been a halfhearted
"I'll think about it" followed by "people love to
chat while we ring them up. Would a faster system make them think they had to hurry along?"
And that was the rub of having a restaurant passed
down from Milek to Milek. Modernizing anything
was too easily seen as an affront to tradition. Some
people *still* complained about the new, clear sneeze
guards over the food, even though it was incom-
prehensible to Vivian that people could prefer the
green light the old sneeze guards had cast on their
mashed potatoes.

Being in Susan's position when the waitress uniforms finally disintegrated into rags would be terrifying. But also an awesome challenge.

The first week or so Vivian had worked the register at Healthy Food, someone had counted the
register a second time. Not out of suspicion, but
to make sure she'd done it right. It hadn't taken
long for Edward and Susan to realize that Vivian

was never wrong in her count. She hadn't counted money in her years of dealing, but she'd counted almost everything else. Now Vivian prepared the deposit with no one looking over her shoulder, a new feeling of trust after years under the 360-degree cameras. Fate had an ironic sense of humor.

Her chores for the night done, Vivian set the register so it would be ready for the morning, packed the deposit away in the safe and helped out until Susan was ready to go home.

CHAPTER TWENTY-THREE

KARL SAT AT one of the big round tables with the one old man too feeble and the two teenagers too cool to dance at the wedding reception. He was neither, but—he looked out over the conga line snaking around the dance floor—the abandonment everyone else seemed comfortable with just wasn't his thing. He could walk around the room, talk with people and otherwise be social—but no dancing. The thought of a conga line made him shudder in horror.

Vivian's exuberance made it difficult for her to hang on to the person in front of her, but she laughed every time her hands slipped off Chuck Biadała's shirt and he turned back to admonish her for not keeping up. She'd not known a single person from the neighborhood the first time she'd sat at Healthy Food's register and started ringing up customers. She'd been a stranger—an outsider—and not just because she wasn't Polish. She wasn't from Chicago, she hadn't gone to Mass or Catholic school with these people and she was suspicious of sweet cheese pierogies, but her smiles and kindness had integrated her with the neighborhood. Now, when he walked around Archer Heights with his wife, she seemed to know more people than he did.

She exaggerated the kick of her legs out to the sides, whooping as she did so. Her face glistened with sweat, making her skin glow and her eyes shine. Sometimes it was hard to believe this exuberant person was the same woman who'd quietly played solitaire in his apartment and knit him a cap. He knew better than anyone the difference between public and private faces. But what amazed him about his wife was how her public face invited people in.

Karl knew how to smile and shake hands. He could ask questions and get people to talk with him, but he also knew that—even at his most friendly— he intimidated people. He was a serious person and people took him seriously. Until now, he'd been content to raise his eyebrow and have people tell him their problems out of fear. Fear, intimidation or friendliness—he didn't really care why they told him about city problems, just so long as they told him. He had a responsibility to the city and he couldn't fulfill his duty without the help of the citizenry.

However, watching Vivian, he wished people would tell him out of love. Because people loved her. His neighborhood adored her. His family treasured her. Everyone she met warmed to her immediately. When she'd been cooped up in his apartment, terrified he'd learn about her past and kick her out into the street, he'd been completely unaware of how welcoming a person she was. Wasn't that how the saying went? He couldn't see the forest for the trees? Karl had been so close to Vivian that he'd only been able to see her fear. Now, with a little distance, he could see her courage, too.

She tripped over her feet, stumbled into Mr. Biadała and laughed. When Mr. Biadała turned back with concern on his face, she waved him off.

What a terrible shame it would have been if he'd won the argument over her working at Healthy Food or living with his mom. If his suspicions of her had triumphed, he would never have gotten to know this lively, laughing woman. Knowing this vivacious side of her made the quiet, contemplative side more special. That was the side she saved for him, just as he saved his macabre sense of humor for her.

The song ended. Vivian had one hand on the slight bulge of her stomach and was resting the other on Mr. Biadała's shoulder. She looked happy and was smiling but the skin around her eyes was tight and... *My mother died in childbirth.* His heart stopped at the memory of those words. The doctors said everything was fine, there were no complications, but what if they were missing something?

When he stood up the chair scraped against the

floor and would've toppled if he'd not grabbed on to it. He didn't bother to tuck it under the table. Worries over Vivian trumped manners.

By the time he'd stumbled past other wedding guests and up to Vivian, her hand was off her stomach and resting at her side again.

"Are you okay?" he asked. She was more than just the mother of his child—she was a part of his life, and he didn't want anything to happen to her.

"Hmm?" Her voice was dreamy as she smiled up at him, her skin electric with joy. He cushioned her face in his hand and rubbed his thumb over her cheek, which was puffy and still lovely. "Hmm…" she murmured, as she rested the weight of her head in his palm. He relaxed with her, able to support and help her for the first time in what felt like months. Since she'd moved in with his mother and started working, he felt as if she didn't need him anymore. Being needed by his wife, if only as a headrest, felt nice.

"Are you okay?" he repeated. "You were holding your stomach and I'm…" He was scared to lose her and scared to say that fact out loud.

"I'm fine." Her cheek curved as she smiled against the palm of his hand, and she turned to kiss the fleshy part of his thumb. "I'm a little out of breath, but I'm afraid if I lean over, I'll get lightheaded." His worry must have shown on his face because she kissed his palm, the tip of her tongue brushing against the hollow of his hand, and said, "It's normal for me to get breathless and light-headed at this point in my pregnancy. It's fine. I'm fine."

She might be fine, but he wasn't. The kiss she'd pressed into his hand had woken up all the atoms in his body, and all he wanted to do was take his wife back to his apartment—what should be *their* home—and make love to her. And he wanted her to still be there when he woke up the next morning.

Warmth and sweat from dancing made her jasmine scent more potent. If he could figure out how to swing her over his shoulder and carry her, caveman style, to a closet, he would. He would then have to figure out how to make love to a short, pregnant woman in a janitor's closet, the physics of which he wasn't certain of, but was willing to try.

"Come on." He slid his hand around her waist and pulled her in close, letting everything about her wash over him.

"Where are we going?"

Somewhere I can act like the crazed, lusty man you've turned me into. But he didn't say that. She'd rocked his equilibrium, and he'd gotten her pregnant. "We're going to sit down so you can catch your breath and I can get you a fancy virgin something to drink."

"Oh, I love virgins," she cooed. "Mr. Biadała was right when he said you were a keeper."

"A keeper?" The thought of his American history teacher and the father of his best friend from high school telling his wife to keep him made him smile. Being with Vivian made him smile, period.

The deep carpet stopped the sharp clicking noise her short heels had made on the dance floor as she walked with him to their seats. "He also said he didn't know why I was still living with your mom, but one of us would come to our senses soon and, even if you were being a 'stubborn fool,' that I should forgive you."

He'd like to believe he was the one who should have to forgive Vivian, not the other way around. But Mr. Biadała had always known the right answer when Karl was in high school, and he probably knew the right answer now.

"Here." He sat Vivian down in his chair and she sighed as soon as her butt hit the seat. "Catch your breath and I'll be back with a Shirley Temple."

"Double cherry," she called after him.

Karl was glad he'd brought himself a glass of water because she finished her drink in three gulps, then reached for his water. "Do you need more?" he asked when she put down his glass, now empty.

"No, but I wish I had some antacid in my purse." She put her hand to her heart. "I'm not sure drinking all that liquid so quickly on top of all that dancing was a good idea."

He placed his hands on hers, grateful to be close

to her when not also surrounded by his family. "There's a drugstore not far. I can go get you some."

"Ah, that's sweet." She picked up his hands and kissed his knuckles. More tender, affectionate kisses. Not the crazed sex in the closet he was fantasizing about.

He didn't want to be sweet. He wanted her to come home with him. He wanted to strip off her clothes and make love to her until she didn't think about her heartburn anymore.

"But I think I hear the Electric Slide starting and I want to dance some more. Come on." She slipped out of the chair, yanking on his hands. A lock of her hair was plastered across her sweaty cheek and he wasn't able to get out of her grip long enough to brush it aside and escape for the hills.

Topping the list of things he *didn't* want to do was the Electric Slide. He set his feet. "You just said all that dancing gave you heartburn. I have Tums at my house."

His words halted her pulling. She cocked her head up at him, one brow raised, that lock of hair giving her two wicked smiles across her face. "I have Tums at your mom's house and I like the Electric Slide."

"But I'm not at my mom's house." *Come home with me, Vivian. I want you.* Was she going to make him say the words?

God, even the sight of her biting her lip made

him crazy, which just proved how badly he needed her and how far off his center she made him.

Then she smiled, and the corners of her eyes crinkled, and he knew he'd both won and lost.

"After you do the Electric Slide with me."

He'd won more than he'd lost, though she'd nearly made it a draw. But just because he didn't resist as she tugged him to the dance floor didn't mean he couldn't protest. "I don't know how to do the Electric Slide."

"Everyone knows how to do the Electric Slide."

"I can't dance." She had a smaller stride than he did and he could have easily caught up with her. But she was enjoying cajoling him and he was enjoying being cajoled.

"I can't, either. We'll be the cutest couple on the dance floor."

The din of wedding guests and music got louder as they got closer to the dance floor. Karl dragged his feet a little more. He would do the Electric Slide with Vivian, but he'd prefer not to. Then his shoes hit the wooden floor and he thought about how he'd look, tripping over his own feet and knocking his pregnant wife to the floor.

At the sight of thirty people crossing their legs front and back, front and back, Karl stopped. He could joke about it at the table, but he really didn't dance. He stood on the sidelines and watched others dance while remaining aloof and impassive. Straitlaced, never in anything more casual than khakis was his M.O.

He took a deep breath and let it out in a great puff. He hadn't danced since he was thirteen, and that memory alone was awkward enough for him to consider abandoning Vivian. His one middle school dance…his fingers skimming the girl's back, sliding down to the crest of her butt and then chickening out at the last minute for fear she would raise a fuss and his dad would find out. His erection and the step back he took every time she took a step forward. His certain knowledge that his deodorant—another new experience—had failed and she would be assaulted by his BO just before banging against his jutting erection.

By the time he'd figured out how to touch a girl's butt, control his erection and trust in his deodorant, no one expected him to dance. And he no longer had to worry about a lecture from his father on respecting women if his hand slipped from a girl's waist to the curves of her butt. None of which helped him with his current predicament. Boy or girl, his child was getting dancing lessons.

"Are you okay?" Vivian turned to look at him.

"Fine." He still didn't take a step forward.

Her lips twitched from side to side as she examined him. Finally, she wiped that stuck lock of hair from her cheek and said, "You don't have to dance." She looked over her shoulder at the dance floor. "We can just go back to your apartment."

Her eyes lost a bit of their luster as she said those words. Living with his mom and working at Healthy Food, Vivian had become part of the community he had grown up in, and he wanted to take her away from it—even if just for a night—because *everyone knew Karl Milek didn't dance.*

The newspapers liked to say he was a leader in Chicago's Polish community and leadership gurus liked to say leaders become leaders by not being afraid of making asses of themselves. He closed his eyes to gather his sense of dignity, then looked his wife straight in her copper-colored eyes and smiled. "Let's show this room how poorly the Electric Slide can be done."

His reward wasn't going to be taking Vivian home with him tonight; his reward was the way her smile brightened his life. Swallowing the last of his resignation, he followed his wife onto the dance floor, faced the wall and prepared to boogie-woogie-woogie.

And he immediately went to the left and bumped into Vivian, who laughed with unrestrained delight. He stood in one place to watch her feet and listen to her "step, cross, step, clap" instructions and the person to his right ran into him—Mrs. Biadała, who made mother-hen clucking noises and told him how cute he looked.

He hadn't danced since he was thirteen and he hadn't been cute since he was six. Past six, he'd been "an old soul" and "precocious." Tonight was a night of firsts.

"Back, back, back, clap." Vivian's amused instructions jarred some distant memory in his brain and he didn't even have to be told to lean forward, tap his back foot and make a stupid circle with his forearm. Or hop to turn and face the other direction. Apparently, bounding about like an ass in a line with other people was as much about muscle memory as riding your bike or ice skating.

He missed crossing his legs, but he moved to the right with the rest of the dancers and was only a millisecond or so behind them clapping. After the next hop and turn, he moved to the right *and* crossed his legs behind one another like he was supposed to, though he still clapped too late.

"See," Vivian said over her clap, "I knew you were a regular Gene Kelly."

What the hell. He was already dancing. He could say stupidly romantic things to his wife. "I'd prefer to be Fred Astaire and call you Ginger."

A bead of sweat on his neck dripped from his collar to his hairline when he leaned forward to rotate his arm. When he reversed course to stand up and hop to his left, the sweat dribbled back down between his shoulder blades. He should have taken his suit jacket off—or at least loosened his tie—before attempting this hoedown.

"I can do anything you can do—backward and in high heels," she said with a laugh.

His cockiness caught up with him. Mrs. Biadała didn't look nearly so amused this time as he tripped over his own feet and stumbled into her. "Better me than your wife," she said. He supposed she was right, given Vivian's pregnancy, but Vivian would've laughed, and he might even have laughed with her.

He got back on track when they had to step back and his clap was perfectly timed with the rest of the dancers. By the time the music stopped, Karl had figured the dance out and was no longer making a fool of himself. A wasted lesson, because he never planned on dancing the Electric Slide ever again.

"That was the worst four minutes of my life," he said as he tucked Vivian under his arm and steered her toward the door before she heard another song she wanted to dance to. He snatched her purse from her chair when they walked past their table, not willing to slow down. Whatever song the deejay had put on next was obviously another line dance, as the instigators of such tomfoolery and their victims were lined up in rows again.

Vivian turned her face up to him, impish, sweaty and beautiful. "I hate to break it to you, but you only danced for three minutes. Was it really so bad?"

Her warm, soft body fit perfectly against his and he leaned down to innocently kiss the top of her head while thinking of how slowly he would peel off her clothes once they got back to his apartment. And how she'd smile at him, but it would be a slow, private smile with melting heat in her eyes. "No. I'd do it again." He stooped a bit so he could kiss the top of her ear and whisper, "But if you tell anyone that—especially my sisters—I'll deny it until I have no breath left in my body."

CHAPTER TWENTY-FOUR

THEY HAD DRIVEN to the wedding separately, so Karl had to wait—aroused and cold as the sweat from dancing evaporated off his body—in the parking garage for Vivian to drive into her spot. He didn't want to risk her changing her mind between the wedding and the apartment; if he could have towed her car behind his, he would have.

God, she looked hot getting out of her car, her face glowing with perspiration and an annoyed scowl on her face as she pulled strands of her hair out of her pink lipstick. "I swear, every light was red by the time I got to it. Do you have some secret machine in your car to change lights to green when you pass by, like they say cops do?"

Then she smiled at him and held out her hand, and he didn't care how long he'd been waiting in the parking garage, so long as she was near him. "Does it increase my chances of getting lucky tonight if I say yes?"

If a yes means you'll move back in with me, I'll invent such a device and have it installed on any car you might possibly drive.

"You're already getting lucky tonight." She pressed a soft kiss onto his lips, her perfume overwhelming the stale air and exhaust, and her presence drowning out the cares of the world. Then she walked away from him toward the elevator, their fingers still entwined, tugging him behind her.

Determined to make good use of a slow elevator ride up to his apartment, Karl swept Vivian's hair off her neck and kissed the knobs of her spine until the lace of her dress impeded his progress. Undeterred, he kissed his way around her neckline to lick salt off her neck. She tasted better than any meal, and the soft murmurs she made sounded better than any opera.

Her dexterous fingers danced down his chest, unbuttoning his coat and slipping under his suit jacket to his belt buckle. She slipped her hand under his waistband and it was all of his janitor's-closet fantasies come true, complete with the physics problem of Vivian not being nearly tall enough. Even with her in heels, he couldn't quite position himself so that he could keep kissing her and she could keep her magical fingers tickling his balls. Karl settled for nibbling on the top of her ear while she panted into his neck.

His mind registered the slowing of the elevator, but he didn't do anything other than mumble a protest when Vivian pulled her hand out of his pants and smoothed the front of his suit. He wasn't aware of anything other than the brush of her hair against his nose until the elevator beeped and opened onto the lobby of his building. Vivian gave a sly smile before turning them both so that she stood in front of him, facing the group of women getting on the elevator.

Karl stood with his pants undone, his erection pressing against Vivian, unwilling to take his hands off her belly long enough to zip up his pants. Instead, he twirled the tie of her dress around his fingers and willed the giggling women to get off the elevator before his floor. One of the women looked at him, raised her brow and pressed the number for the floor directly under his.

Hours seemed to pass between the beeps of the elevator at each and every floor. Each echoed through his head, made worse by the smell of jasmine he now associated with Vivian in his bed and the pressure of her body against his.

Beep. And those women kept giggling.

Beep. The fingers that had only recently been down his pants tangled with his, the silk ribbon of her dress rough as it trickled first through her fingers and then through his.

Beep. Vivian shifted their interlocking hands like she was innocently scratching her neck, only her movement meant the back of his hand skimmed up against her breasts and, as the vixen delicately scratched her neck, his hand cupped her breast before falling back to her stomach. He leaned his head against the cool mirrored back of the elevator, fighting a groan, his only consolation that her games aroused her, too, if the slight tuck of her ass against him was any indication.

After an interminable ride the elevator finally began to slow and they all halted—Karl, Vivian and those interfering women—until the elevator doors opened. Instead of gushing out of the elevators the same way they had poured in, the women sauntered through the doors, one by one. The last one to leave, the same woman who had pressed the button for this floor, had to bang the elevator doors to keep them from shutting on her. Instead of taking the shutting doors as a sign that she should *hurry,* she turned back and looked Karl and Vivian up and down. Then she winked. "I actually live two floors up, but it seemed cruel to make you walk past us in that state."

The doors shut on the sound of uproarious female laughter, and he was so desperate to be in his apartment that he didn't care.

Vivian's ass shook when she giggled, and Karl tightened his hold on her. "Don't," he ground out, "move."

The ride between the two floors left him with just enough time to bunch up the stiff skirts of her dress and slip his hand across the softness of her skin and the silkiness of her underwear. By the time the elevator beeped for the last time, they were both panting heavily enough to fog the glass walls they were leaning against. As soon as the doors opened, he gave Vivian a gentle push and hurried after her. The cool, dry air breezing through his open fly only heightened his desire to bury himself in Vivian's damp heat.

When they got to his apartment door, Vivian leaned against the wood and slipped her hand back under his waistband as he tried to unlock the door. He concentrated on the lock so he didn't come in his pants. The third time he readjusted his aim and the metal of the key clicked against the metal of the doorknob. She tightened her grip on his cock and said, "I hope you've got better aim inside, cowboy."

Karl couldn't decide if he should bang his head against the door in frustration or groan with pleasure, so he settled for laughing. "Three months ago I was just sober enough to remember you saying almost the exact same thing."

"At the time, I assumed tequila caused your lack of aim, but now I know you were just horny."

The key finally slipped into the hole and the lock clicked open. Before he turned the knob to open the door, he leaned down to whisper in her ear, "We both know my aim improves the fewer clothes you're wearing."

"Apparently your aim was spot-on," she said with a raised brow and a gesture to her stomach. But before the mood could become too overwhelmed with the magnitude of how Vivian's pregnancy had changed both their lives, Karl turned the knob and they tumbled through the doorway.

Once inside the sanctuary of his apartment, Vivian didn't hesitate. Her coat came off first, spilling onto the floor. Then she turned to face him and slowly, tortuously untied that ribbon around her waist. The ribbon rasped as the silk slipped against itself and the knot was undone. Blood pounded in his ears as he focused on that one ribbon, knowing her dress wouldn't magically fall off her when it was untied, but he could still hope.

She smiled slyly at him, reached behind her back and the sound of a zipper being loosed resonated through the apartment. Her dress inched down her body, revealing her delicate collarbones with the thin strap of black against her skin, then the lacy cups of the bra covering her enlarged breasts, and finally, with a rustle, the dress was off completely.

Vivian stood in front of him in her matching underwear and heels, the dress pooled at her feet. "Let's see if you can hit the bull's-eye," she said, before turning and walking away from him.

Karl tripped over her clothes as he tried to follow her, taking off his shoes, coat and tie at the same time, not worried about the pile of clothes on the floor and only caring enough about his dignity not to fall on his ass as he stumbled. Her skin was warm when he caught up to her at the edge of his bed and wrapped his hands around her waist. She twisted in his arms, fumbling to unbutton his shirt as they fell together onto the bed, limbs intertwined.

Vivian opened her mouth, but before she could say anything Karl pressed his lips against hers and opened her mouth a little wider, her tongue meeting his as he cocked his head for better access. Her lips were soft. Her mouth was warm. Her teeth were sharp enough to keep him aware of every last cell in his body as he ran his tongue along the inside of her mouth.

God, she felt good under him. All the windows in his apartment could bust open, letting the cool April night air in, and he'd still be on fire with her hands pulling at his shirt and her nails skimming along the sides of his body.

He groped for her panties, shoving down and pulling them off over her hips, desperate to end the torture that had started on the elevator ride. When she kicked out with one leg and her panties came free, he was too intent on his newfound access to care that she'd nearly kneed him in the crotch.

"I'm sorry," she mumbled before taking his nipple between her teeth and biting down gently.

He tiptoed his fingers through her curly hair until he got to her moist folds, then slid a finger inside her. "Let's both be glad *my* aim improves when your clothes come off."

He lifted up on his elbow, watching his now-damp finger trail over her belly. Vivian lifted a leg over his hip, pulling him toward her in invitation and, unable to wait any longer, his pants and shirt still hanging off his limbs, Karl grabbed hold of his cock and pushed into her. She pulsed around him, and he tried to think of cardboard boxes, damp wool and his constitutional law professor from law school—anything to take his mind off the mind-blowing feeling of the woman wrapping her legs around him before he ejaculated with the finesse of a sixteen-year-old in the shower.

Luckily, he wasn't the only one struggling to last longer than two minutes; the elevator ride had nearly done them both in. Karl had only pulled out of her once when her breath started to catch and her nails dug into his shoulders. She bucked against him, tightening her thighs around his legs. She stilled, her eyes pressed tightly shut. For a moment he was worried she had stopped breathing, but she called out his name as her body shuddered.

When she opened her eyes, gave him a wicked smile and said, "Bull's-eye," Karl's balls tightened painfully and he released into her with a groan.

KARL BECAME CONSCIOUS when the bed shifted. He opened his eyes to find Vivian sliding out of the bed, the moonlight gleaming off her bare shoulder. As she leaned over to pick something—her underwear—off the floor, he could make out the cascading ridge of her spine. He loved seeing her naked, adored her breasts, but this was his favorite view of her. It was like sneaking into one of Renoir's paintings of bathers, intimate, vulnerable and inviting, the muscles of a woman's back soft and smooth. Then her underwear skimmed over her butt, and she reached down for something else.

"Where are you going?" She wasn't headed to the bathroom.

"I have to be at Healthy Food early tomorrow. It will be easier if I drive home tonight."

Her words grated against his skin. "Your home should be here."

Slight and short, with only her pregnancy breasts and her barely there belly to give any heft to her figure, she still managed to look formidable in just her underwear, her arms behind her back as she hooked her bra together. "Remember how after the last time I was naked in your bed, you said, 'this can't change anything'?"

Fuck. "Yes." And, at the time, nothing had changed. Now, three weeks later, having seen Vivian every night at Healthy Food, at family dinner and after having plenty of conversation but no sex, everything had changed. This wasn't about a one-night stand gone wrong. This was about his life. Their lives. Their life together.

She raised an eyebrow at him, but he didn't say anything else. He was going to make her say the words.

Her black-silk-covered breasts rose and fell with her sigh. "This doesn't change anything."

"So we're married and you're pregnant with my child, but you're still going to be living with my mom and we'll just be what—fuck buddies?"

He could tell he'd hurt her when she blinked rapidly several times, but she was hurting him by leaving.

"Would you prefer I found another fuck buddy?" And she walked away, the coward.

Karl scrambled out of bed, tripping over his pants as he shoved his boxers on and followed his wife. For the second time that night she was walking away and he was going to fall on his ass. Except time was working in reverse. When he stumbled into the living room, Vivian was at the entry, zipping up her dress. Her coat would follow and...

"You can't just leave."

"A month and a half ago you couldn't get me out of this apartment fast enough." She was tying that goddamned ribbon that had started this nonsense in the elevator. Irrational though it may be, he couldn't escape the feeling that once that ribbon was tied, she was lost to him.

"But a lot has changed since then." He winced at the whine in his voice. Years of practice at being unemotional and suddenly all his pent-up feelings were coming out over this one woman and the stupid, sexy knobs of her spine that smelled like jasmine. "We have different responsibilities to each other."

"Like what?"

"Like...like...like..." He couldn't bring himself to say the words she wanted to hear. The words that would convince her to climb back into his bed and stay there until morning.

The still-untied ribbon swayed with her movements as she put her hands on her hips. "Do you still judge me for nearly cheating Middle Kingdom and getting fired?"

"I understand better what drove you to it." The lessons he'd learned at his father's knees lingered at the back of his mind. How did those ghosts get enough strength to prevent him from telling the woman he loved what she wanted to hear?

He couldn't see the reaction on her face as he said the words because she was looking down, tugging on the ends of the ribbon to tighten the knot. When the bow looked as pristine as it had before the wedding ceremony had even started, she raised her gaze to his. Any emotion she felt had been worked into that knot. "But you still judge me for it, and so I am a fool for having come over here tonight."

"When you were sitting on that couch, all you wanted was a place to live and health insurance. I'm offering you that—and more. What else do you want from me?" He asked the question knowing what the answer was, hoping it had changed and knowing it shouldn't.

The apartment was silent as Vivian slipped her arms into her coat and buttoned up against the early spring night. Finally, when she was entirely bound up and so far from him that she might as well have been at his mother's house already, Vivian answered, "When I was sitting on your couch I was one step away from being homeless and pregnant. My situation has changed and I now know that I'm worth more—that I deserve more than just a place to live and health insurance. That's not good enough for me."

Then she walked out his door before he had a chance to tell her that she was worth *everything* to him.

CHAPTER TWENTY-FIVE

VIVIAN CAME HOME from work on Monday, exhausted from a busy day, and checked her email. Among the "buy now" spam from stores, a couple of "hey, you" emails from friends and a note from her aunt Kitty, was a message from her father.

After their last conversation, he'd gone to ground and she'd assumed she wasn't going to hear from him until he needed money—and he knew she had some to provide. He was either desperate for whatever spare pennies she might have, or...

Or Vivian wasn't sure what else. As a child, she'd idolized her father and looked forward to all of their games. Then she'd realized what he was and had never really been able to go back to that wide-eyed adoration. But, sadly, neither had she been able to pull herself away from him entirely.

She contemplated the complete break she could make from him now, while hidden away in Chicago. Then, as all the other times she had contemplated ending their relationship, she thought about how much fun they'd had decorating their house for Christmas one year with playing cards on string.

The mouse hovered over the delete button, then moved to the subject line and she clicked.

Her father had written the usual nonsense about how this job would be different, how he would be able to retire/pay her back/buy an island, blah, blah, blah. Not until the last paragraph of the novel did Vivian's heart nearly leap out of her throat. "And I have some new business partners in Chicago. Since you're not really working, maybe you'll want in on this next venture."

Her father had been studying up while AWOL from her life. Business partners. Venture. She'd almost believed he was legitimate, except that she knew he scraped a living by making people believe his lies.

And he was coming to Chicago.

It had always been a guarantee her father would find her. She wasn't really trying to hide from him, only she didn't want to have to listen to his pleas for money before she'd built up her energy stores again to tell him no. Over and over and over. She wanted to feel on firmer ground before he started knocking her about emotionally.

Nearly two months in Chicago and she was still skirting the same quicksand that had made her flee Las Vegas. Sure, she now had a job and Susan wouldn't kick her out of the house while there was a grandchild in the mix, but the stable base she'd come to Chicago for was still having its foundation dug.

Some of this was her fault. Despite saying no to her dad's pleas for money and ignoring his phone calls *most* of the time, she had given in enough that he believed she would give in completely, eventually. Because she always had. But now she was responsible for more than just her own well-being. She couldn't let her father bleed her dry because then he'd bleed Jelly Bean dry, too.

Karl could protect her from her father. She could call Karl up, apologize for walking out on him, appeal to his sense of responsibility toward their child and move back into his apartment. She wouldn't have to give up her job at Healthy Food if she moved back in with Karl. But she'd be right where she had been a month ago, relying on her husband for security rather than for love and companionship. She'd been trapped in that apartment then, and keeping a part-time job at her mother-in-law's restaurant wouldn't make her free this time.

"Hell," she said to no one but herself as she logged out of her email. "Being free now is all in my mind."

She was living in her mother-in-law's house and working in her mother-in-law's restaurant. The only difference between her current situation and the one she insisted she was too good for was that she couldn't sleep in Karl's warm bed with his expansive view of the city whenever she wanted to.

She could always look for a job that wasn't dependent on the Mileks, but she *liked* working at Healthy Food. She liked seeing the same old Poles come in for their buffet dinner every night at five-thirty, and she liked the rotation of cops that came in throughout the day for a meal when they had a free moment. Stability and vibrancy danced together, amongst new immigrant and third-generation Americans alike.

She wanted to be a part of Archer Heights—that odd woman with Asian features and a Polish last name defying everyone's sense of what should be—and have a marriage with Karl based on love and trust rather than dependency and suspicion. She wanted to have her *kolaczki* and eat them, too.

Turning the monitor of the computer off, Vivian giggled at her own joke. Maybe she could embrace what made her different from the neighborhood and use it to pull off what she had in mind. Maybe the idea wasn't that crazy, after all.

TILLY CAME OUT from Babka's kitchen, sweaty and energized. The sweaty Karl understood. After he noticed the twinkle in her eyes and she opened her mouth, he understood the energized bit, as well. "I heard you did the Electric Slide at Phil's wedding."

He'd known someone would tell his sisters, but he'd hoped they were mature enough to ignore the gossip.

"And that you bumped into Mrs. Biadała twice because you didn't know the steps."

He'd been wrong. Baby sisters grow taller. They find life partners and they become successful owners of popular restaurants. They even get a dish on the cover of *Bon Appétit*. But they stay baby sisters, confident that their role in life is to keep their older brother humble even though he'd outgrown being able to give *them* a noogie.

"Maybe Dan and I will get married just so I can see you do the Electric Slide in person, instead of having to hear about it."

"I didn't dance at Renia's wedding. What makes you think I would dance at yours?"

Even the bartender was barely able to contain her amusement as she reached around Tilly to hand him his glass of wine. He'd come to Babka for dinner because he didn't want to be alone in his apartment anymore, didn't want to go to Healthy Food and see Vivian and had mistakenly thought family would help his mood. Instead, Tilly's entire restaurant seemed to be determined to make him regret doing the Electric Slide.

Then the image of Vivian's smile and her swirling hair as she pranced about and clapped flashed in his head, and he knew he would never regret doing anything that made Vivian smile so brightly.

"Ah, but Renia didn't *know* you would dance. I know, and knowledge is power." She tapped her skull and he rolled his eyes. "The best part about that story was hearing how you nearly caveman-dragged Vivian off the dance floor and into the parking lot. I do so love it when your feathers get ruffled."

"Get out of the way of my wine and get back to work. I can't believe how intrusive the service is here."

His sister laughed. "That's what you get for walking in the door just before closing." Then she waggled her eyebrows at him and said, "Have you told Vivian that you love her yet?"

Karl might have needed many things to go differently during his last exchange with Vivian, but he didn't need to relive their conversation with Tilly. *That's not good enough for me.*

He wasn't good enough for her? His apartment wasn't good enough for her? She'd prefaced the pronoun with a reference to a roof over her head, but that didn't make sense. He wasn't just offering her a place to live. He was offering her himself.

That's not good enough for me.

"It's really none of your business." No matter how much Vivian's words thrashed about in his head, he wasn't going to share the conversation with his baby sister.

She smiled, not worried about his sour mood. "You've never let your family near your business before. One taste and we can't get enough."

His fights with Jessica had sent him to his office, not to a family member for company. *You think it's enough that we're married and you come home every night. Everyone look at Karl Pawel Milek, such a dedicated husband. But I want to be more than a duty.* And he'd tried. For their marriage's sake, he'd tried. He had bought her flowers, chocolates and jewelry. He had asked what her favorite flowers were because apparently it wasn't roses. *Good husbands bring home flowers, so you're bringing home flowers. It's like you're a robot husband.*

Tilly—his whole family—would've been fascinated by those fights.

"If Vivian wasn't living with Mom right now," he informed his sister, "I wouldn't let you near this business, either."

His sister raised her dark eyebrows nearly up to her ridiculous turquoise hair. "When is she moving back in with you?"

Karl sipped his wine, but the alcohol didn't make the track of this conversation any easier to bear.

"You think you can out-silence me, and you're

probably right. But I've got something to say and you need to hear it."

"Advice from my baby sister?"

"Your baby sister has figured out how to be in a happy relationship—something you never seemed to manage."

Karl put down his glass of wine and looked at his sister. He might as well listen to what Tilly had to say. Vivian wasn't coming to live with him; a lecture from his baby sister couldn't hurt his pride any worse.

"The interesting thing about watching you trying to woo Vivian—"

"She's my wife. I don't have to woo her."

Tilly ignored him. "Is learning that your pontifications about justice and stopping corruption and all that is a bunch of B.S."

"What do you know?" Anger built in his body until he had no choice but to stand before fury ejected him clean out of his bar stool. "You were eight when Dad died."

"Sit down, Karl," she said in a no-nonsense voice he hadn't even known she possessed.

He obeyed, shocked that his sunny, joking baby sister was talking to him this way.

"And don't look so surprised. Anyway, I'm not belittling your devotion to your job, just questioning the reasons you always give for it. All of us assumed your life was motivated by justice, when it's actually motivated by duty." She shook her head. "I don't know how we were all fooled for so long. It's never been justice that made you come to Mom's for family dinners or go to Mass every Sunday. You think it's your *duty* to come to family dinners because Leon can't and to go to Mass because Dad can't. You come to Babka for dinner out of a sense of responsibility for me. And worst of all, you didn't marry Jessica because you loved her, but because you thought you had a duty to marry a Polish Catholic girl."

Karl sipped his wine, though it could have been vinegar for as much as he tasted it. "Everything you've said *may* be true, but you didn't say anything about why I go to work every day. I do that because I believe bribery, waste and corruption hurts everyone in Chicago. If Bauer had done his job, the Willis children might still be alive."

"You've made a compelling argument for your duty to the memory of the Willis children." He blinked and she smiled in response. "I'll even prove I'm right."

"I'll admit you've articulated your point neatly, but I don't know how you intend to prove it."

She smiled brightly. "I bribed two health inspectors so that I could keep Babka open."

He blinked again. "You shouldn't lie just to prove your point. I'll think about what you said."

"Oh, I'm not lying." That gaping smile was still

on her face. "Exaggerating maybe, but not lying. You can ask Dan. Steve hid a rat in my kitchen and called the health inspectors on me. Dan took the rat to his house and I bargained with the health inspectors to keep Babka open."

Paulie the rat. Karl sipped his expensive, tasteless wine and processed what Tilly was telling him. He'd always assumed that pet was some joke of Dan's, but if what Tilly was saying was true, a city worker had let a health code violation slide for his sister. A small infraction—it wasn't as though Tilly ran a dirty restaurant—and she'd had an employee trying to get her restaurant closed, but he had stated on record that no infraction should slide. But, small or not, what she'd done was unethical, if not illegal.

"Why are you telling me this?" He'd have preferred not to know any of this. If he ever investigated the health inspectors' office, this information was too juicy not to come out in some exaggerated form and then he'd have to think about Tilly's restaurant and the legacy she'd given their grandmother and how intertwined it was with his public stance on corruption, no matter how small.

"If you're motivated by a hatred of corruption in all its forms, you're thinking about whether or not your office should investigate the health inspectors' office. If you're motivated by duty, you're trying to figure out if duty ties you to your family or to your office."

He harrumphed because she was right. "What do my motivations have to do with you sticking your nose in my business?"

"With my nosiness?" She shrugged and then leaned against the bar, her face close to his and sisterly love in her eyes. "Only that I feel like I have new insight into my big brother. But I'm telling you this because *you* might find insight into why Vivian's not packing her bags to move in with you."

He was sick of being lectured, but he was also sick of living alone with Xìnyùn for his only company. "Okay, *siostra*. How will this help me?"

She pulled back to look at him, her arms folded and her eyes glowing with pleasure. And, if he were being honest with himself, amusement. "I can imagine you asking Vivian to move back in with you because it's your duty as a husband to live with your pregnant wife." She tsked at him. "Those are sexy words."

"This conversation was bearable so long as you weren't being sarcastic." He hated to insult the mother of his child but... "Anyway, shall we go back to the beginning? Remember, Vivian was fired from her job at the casino because she couldn't prove she didn't commit a felony."

"The casino couldn't prove that she did. Innocent until proven guilty."

"She shouldn't have even considered cheating."

He pushed his empty wineglass down the bar toward the bartender.

"Why haven't you asked me the names of the health inspectors who let my code violation pass?"

Did she have to bring this up again? "You're my sister."

"Why did Vivian nearly cheat?"

When had his world turned upside down? If he hadn't let his emotions get the better of him, he wouldn't be losing an argument to his sister right now.

He sighed when all he wanted to do was kick the wood of the bar in front of him. "Because her father needed help."

"And?"

"And I know what you're trying to do." She raised her eyebrow at him. He sighed again—heavier this time, so she couldn't doubt how annoying it was to be badgered by his sister as though he was a first-year law student. "Vivian felt a duty to her father strong enough to question right and wrong. I feel a duty to my family—to you—strong enough to pretend I didn't hear about your experience with the health inspectors and to not wonder what else they might be letting slide and why. Thus, I should be more sympathetic to Vivian's choices. And I should apologize to her before asking her to come back home."

"Sometimes for a smart person, you can be pretty

dumb." Her laughter removed some of the sting of her words. *Some.* "Don't apologize to her because it's your duty to apologize to her. Beg her to move back in with you because you can't imagine your life without her."

"I don't have to imagine life without her. I'm living it."

"She's still within driving distance and if you're not at work, you're at Mom's house or Healthy Food. Life without her will mean she won't even be around for you to pretend you don't love her. Go home and think about what Dad would say about *that,* smart guy."

CHAPTER TWENTY-SIX

As soon as they got home from the night's work at Healthy Food, Susan collapsed into one of the chairs at the kitchen table. "The problem," she said, her voice muffled by the folded arms her head was lying on, "is that I want to close my eyes, and my legs want to tap dance."

Vivian filled two mugs with milk and stuck them in the microwave. While the milk was heating, she got chocolate syrup out of the fridge and some spoons. Hot chocolate was acceptable when both punchy and tired. What Vivian really wanted was a whiskey, but between Jelly Bean and Susan's medicine, hot chocolate was as much of an indulgence as either of them was allowed right now. When the microwave beeped, Vivian put the steaming cups of milk on the counter and made their drinks—heavy on the chocolate. Susan perked up at the click of the mug on the table.

Wrapping her hands around her mug and sitting across the yellow laminate kitchen table from her mother-in-law, both of them too hyper to sleep, was as good a chance as Vivian was going to get to broach her idea with Susan. If Vivian didn't jump now, she'd probably chicken out from jumping later, and then how would she ever learn to fly?

"I was thinking of taking over Healthy Food when you retire."

Susan didn't do more than blink at Vivian's bald statement. Now she knew where Karl had gotten his poker face. Her mother-in-law slurped her hot chocolate, leaving Vivian with nothing more to do than shift in her seat.

"None of my children are interested in Healthy Food," Susan finally said. That wasn't a no. "Do you propose to wait until I die and hope I leave it to you in my will?"

It wasn't a yes, either.

"Well, I was hoping to buy you out." Vivian took a noisy sip of her hot chocolate, hoping to cover the nerves making her heart beat a million times per minute.

Susan's mug clunked on the table. "Vivian, I enjoy having you live here and think you are great at Healthy Food, but, well, you're living here because you have *no* money."

The flat tone her mother-in-law used when pointing out the flaw in her otherwise great plan made Vivian squirm. She tried to cover it up by sipping more hot chocolate, but Susan probably saw through the ruse. "I know. And, since I am working, I should probably be paying you rent or something. I'm not family."

Susan's face darkened; Vivian had insulted her, which was the last thing she had wanted to do. "So long as you are the mother of my grandchild, you're family. I don't want to hear anything said otherwise."

The warmth spreading through Vivian had nothing to do with the hot drink or overheated kitchen. "Thank you. That means a lot."

"When the baby's born, you should invite your aunt Kitty and your cousins to visit. And your father—it would be nice to meet him."

Vivian grimaced. "You'll be meeting my father sooner rather than later, if his email was any indication. Just promise not to give him any money."

Susan cocked her head, her concern on her face clear. "Is that what buying me out at Healthy Food is about? Not having any money to give to your father when he comes?"

"No." Her father's email had prompted her to think about why she was working at Healthy Food and if Healthy Food offered her more than just money. So, the germination of the idea *had* come out of fear—fear for when her father finally tracked her down. But, before presenting it to Susan, Vivian had given herself time to think it over without her father's email bounding about in her head. "I like Chicago. I like the people who come into Healthy

Food. I know I'm not Polish and I'm especially not a Polish cook, but I'd like to stay a part of it all."

"You don't have to be a part of Healthy Food to be a part of the community. You're Karl's wife and," Susan continued before Vivian could interrupt her, "the mother of his child, no matter the state of your marriage."

"I want something on my own terms." *I want a solid foundation without relying on Karl for it.*

Susan picked up her drink and eyed Vivian for a long while over the edge of her mug. "This is what you really want to do?" she asked before taking a big swallow.

"Yes. The idea is new, but once I had it…" Vivian trailed off, not sure how to put how she felt into words. "Once I had it, I knew it was right." She played her trump card. "Right for both me and Jelly Bean."

"Humph." Susan knew what Vivian had done there but didn't seem inclined to argue. "Raising a child is hard enough, especially if you're going to be a single parent. How will you manage to do both?"

Vivian bit her lip. The hopeful part of her had expected Susan to be wholeheartedly supportive, even though the rest of her had known that wasn't realistic. Family or not, they were discussing a business deal. Vivian straightened her shoulders and faced her mother-in-law like a business partner—lip no longer between her teeth.

"I'm sure it won't be easy. But women have figured out how to manage a child and build a career before I got pregnant. I'll figure out how to do it after I give birth. And I'm sure I can start figuring it out in between."

She wanted to ask if Susan would help with childcare, but she chose to keep that to herself for now, since her mother-in-law seemed to be looking for shortcomings to pounce on. "Whether or not Karl and I divorce, I'll want to work." She'd been working ever since she was at an age that someone would hire her. "I'm sure he'd help pay for childcare."

"And when you're working the night shift?" It was a good thing that the mug was mostly empty of hot chocolate the way Susan was shaking it at her. "Who's going to help that baby with homework? Read bedtime stories and tuck him in at night?"

"You worked and had four—" Vivian almost said three and barely corrected herself "—children. You weren't a single mother when they were young, but you were by the time Karl was sixteen."

"And my working nearly screwed up Renia, even though I had my mother-in-law to help me."

"Will I not have you?"

"Will you need me?" Susan countered.

Vivian wanted to walk around the table and shake Susan for being so cold and unenthusiastic about this idea, but instead she gritted her teeth.

"I suppose I won't *need* you, but I would like your help. Even if I hadn't decided learning a new business while pregnant was a good idea, I'd want your help with Jelly Bean regardless."

Finally, Susan put down her mug and her face warmed into a smile. "I just wanted to make sure you were serious—and that you knew what you were getting yourself and that baby into. You should be around to love my grandchild, but I also hope you'll set an example for him or her about making your own way in the world."

Vivian's shoulders relaxed and she bit her lip again. "So, you like the idea?"

"I'm not against it." Vivian supposed that was close enough. "How do you propose to raise the money?"

"I know I should probably be paying you rent, especially now that I've been working, but maybe the rent I would be paying you could go in a separate bank account. Set aside, for when you're ready to retire." Vivian squared her shoulders again. This idea felt a lot like jumping off a cliff blindfolded, but that didn't mean she had to go about it in a slouchy manner.

"It won't be enough, Vivian. I don't plan on retiring soon, but even still, it probably won't be enough." Susan was taking her seriously. Vivian wanted this plan to work, even if she knew everything about dealing cards and next to nothing about running a restaurant. For Susan to have faith in her meant there was more than a zero chance she could succeed.

Vivian closed her eyes on all the problems, groping about for a solution in the dark. "I know. I'm... I'm not sure what to do about the difference. I'm hoping to have a plan figured out when the time comes."

"From what I know about you—and your father—you could probably use your seed money and spend a couple of nights at a casino to make up the difference."

"My father likes to believe his future is in the roll of a dice or the turning over of a card. I'm not interested in that." Her father would never stop at having won enough to cover the cost of buying out Susan. He'd be so enthralled with the feeling of winning that he'd play and play and play until he owed money to someone sketchy. Vivian's childhood hadn't been built on quicksand because her father was a bad schemer, but because he didn't know when to get out.

Vivian was pretty sure she knew when to cut her losses, but that didn't mean she wanted to ever walk into a casino again, even if she weren't banned.

"Karl has the money. He could give you everything you need."

Vivian knew that. And she also knew that Karl would probably do it now, if she asked. He'd like the idea of her buying Healthy Food. But then her ownership of Healthy Food would be dependent on him, and she wouldn't be more independent than she was now. "If, when the time comes, we're a regular married couple and we make the decision to buy you out of Healthy Food together, then that may be an option. Right now, I'm not going to ask."

Making a decision *as a couple* to buy his mom out of her restaurant was a far cry from Karl giving the money to Vivian while she was broke, pregnant and living at his mom's house.

Susan nodded thoughtfully. "I don't entirely understand what is keeping you and Karl apart, but he's the father of that child and needs to own up to his responsibilities."

An image of Karl, standing in his whimsical clock-and-watch-print boxers, trying to convince her to move back in with him because of his responsibilities flashed through Vivian's head. "Don't worry. He is."

"I won't do this with you on the shake of a hand. We'll find a lawyer to draw up a contract with an out for you. You might decide Healthy Food and the old Poles who eat there aren't your future, after all."

"I might." Anything was possible, after all. "And you might decide——" especially after meeting her father "——that you don't want Healthy Food in my hands. Or maybe those old Poles don't want me running their neighborhood restaurant."

Bigger than Vivian's concern over money was her fear that the neighborhood would never accept anyone as Healthy Food's owner who wasn't blood-Polish, even if she was married to Karl. Most everyone had been nice to her, but paying the Chinese wife for your dinner was one thing, knowing she was in charge of the Polish food coming out of the kitchen was another.

Susan rolled the bottom of her mug on the table as she appeared to consider Vivian's concern. "Some of the customers will say you don't understand the Polish community and they may say you don't belong here every time you make a decision they disagree with. They do it to me, and I have a Polish maiden name. But my Polish ancestors came to this country before the Revolutionary War and so I don't understand what it's like to be *really* Polish. Staple of this community or not, I'm lucky if I'm an eighth Polish. It will be worse for you, and you'll have to learn those people aren't worth your time. Concentrate on the customers who aren't blind fools."

Vivian let that worry slide for right now. She had until Susan retired to win the community over. Susan was right that it wasn't worth her time agonizing over it. She could nail down the tangibles of taking over Healthy Food and worry about the intangibles—such as discrimination—later.

Her mother-in-law smiled and the wrinkles at

the corners of her eyes deepened. Softened. "If we are to do this, tell me what you know about running a restaurant."

Susan probably wasn't going to change her mind about the deal now, but Vivian was still nervous saying, "Nothing. I took a couple of hospitality classes at UNLV, but with nothing ahead of me except more dealing, I doubt I retained anything. I'm hoping to learn from you, before you retire."

"If anything's going to change your mind about this plan, learning what's involved probably will. There's nothing easy about owning and running a restaurant."

"I never imagined there was." But to be a part of this community, it would surely be worth it.

"And I won't have you going into this like I did, learning the right thing to do because you made a mistake and it cost you. As much as I hated sending Tilly off to New York to learn what I thought she could learn at home, here at Healthy Food, that school taught her business planning and other small business basics. You should take courses at one of the colleges in Chicago."

"I'll do that." Vivian's shoulders relaxed. She stood, grabbed both of their mugs and filled them up with more milk for a second cup of hot chocolate. This called for a celebration, and hot chocolate was about as strong a drink as she could imbibe while pregnant.

Her sock slid a bit on the old linoleum of Susan's floor, but the slips only added to Vivian's feeling that she was walking on air—risky and glorious at the same time.

She poured some milk into her mug. Honestly, though, this didn't feel that risky at all. This was what it felt like to have a parent looking out for you. Guiding you—not trying to stay one step ahead of the scammed masses with a child in tow.

She could still fall. Best not let that thought stray too far from her mind. She was well aware that buying Susan out when she retired was not security now, and, hell, it wasn't even security in the future. Vivian knew just enough about owning a restaurant to know it was essentially gambling with a stacked deck of your opponent's making—but it was a place in the world that she was creating for herself.

"Do you want more hot chocolate?" Vivian asked before filling up Susan's mug, as well.

"No. Anything more to drink and I'll just have to get up in the middle of the night to use the bathroom." She pushed away from the table a little, eyeing Vivian thoughtfully. "You should let Karl pay for any classes you take. He's got the money. He's not spent a penny of that money his grandmother left him."

"Maybe." Vivian stuck her milk in the microwave to heat up, deciding against more chocolate. With so much to think about, she would need all the soporific powers hot milk could give her with none of the caffeine.

"They say that the more education the mother has, the better it is for the child."

"Do I have to agree to Karl paying for classes tonight?" If so, she was going to need more than hot milk to drink.

"Are you going to get more or less stubborn about it after a night's sleep?"

The microwave dinged and Vivian removed her mug, wrapping her hands around the warm crockery. "Neither. How about we work out the details of this whole idea before we decide who's going to pay for my college classes." The milk both energized and relaxed her as she drank it in one long gulp then put the two mugs in the dishwasher.

Susan was standing when Vivian walked past her. Her mother-in-law put a hand on her shoulder, then seemed to change her mind and pulled Vivian into her embrace. Vivian rested her head on Susan's soft shoulder, which smelled slightly of kielbasa and cabbages. The smell of Healthy Food's kitchen. "You're a good daughter-in-law. I'm sorry I didn't see that right off."

Vivian squeezed the older woman, almost afraid she would disappear and Vivian would be transported back to Las Vegas without the warmth of a guiding hand at her back. "You're a good mother-in-law, and I didn't see that right off, either."

CHAPTER TWENTY-SEVEN

AFTER HIS CONVERSATION with Tilly at Babka, Karl headed home. He unlocked his door and stepped into his apartment. Once, before Vivian, he had come home to silence and emptiness every night. He had *valued* the quiet. Now it felt like a vacuum and he strained to hear Xìnyùn whistling, terrified he would come home and there would be nothing but stale air to greet him.

He hung up his coat—the coat he'd given Vivian was still hanging in the closet because she'd refused to take it—and let Xìnyùn out of his cage. The bird wasn't his pet. Vivian said it wasn't even her pet, but Karl still had the responsibility to make sure the bird got mental stimulation and exercise, and stayed healthy.

There was that word again. *Responsibility. Duty.* Tilly talked about obligations as though they were distasteful concepts, when he had let Vivian stay with him in the first place because of duty and he was playing basketball with a miniparrot because of a responsibility to the bird. If everyone did their duty, there wouldn't be abused children, or homeless veterans, and his dad might still be alive.

The bird lobbed the ball of wadded-up paper into the cup and whistled. "Jackpot."

Karl laughed. He would never have thought a bird would be such good company, but the two things he looked forward to most in his day were playing basketball with the bird and the hour or so he got to see Vivian at Healthy Food.

Between a developing case at work and making the drive south every day to make sure Vivian was still there, he wasn't getting as much sleep as he needed—being beaten by Tilly in an argument made that clear. But not seeing Vivian wasn't an option.

He tossed another ball to Xìnyùn, who missed the cup and chirped, "Hit me."

When he'd first started driving to Archer Heights every day, he had done it out of a sense of duty. The paternity test was clear—he was the father of Vivian's baby. He never should have expressed doubt in the first place. He'd promised her they would be friends and partners in the raising of their child, and he was going to own that promise.

But at some point his feelings about the drive had changed. Maybe it was when Mr. Biadała had asked Karl if Vivian was going to Phil's wedding, and Karl had stared blankly at the man, wondering how he could have asked such a simple question to which the answer was obvious. Maybe it was seeing the guilty amusement on Vivian's face when she'd opened the door to him, using her body to shield his mother and her friends playing blackjack in the kitchen. Maybe it hadn't been one of those moments, but a culmination of them all that made him realize Vivian was as much a part of him as Healthy Food, Archer Heights and his own family were. More special, even, because he'd been born a Milek in Archer Heights, but he had *chosen* Vivian, and she had chosen him.

Now the drive to his old neighborhood was a pleasure. He liked to see the small changes in Vivian's body during the day and wished they shared a bed at night so he could explore those changes in more detail. To see the curve of her pink lower lip over her sharp chin. To have her be completely unimpressed by the seriousness of his life and make him laugh as only someone who loves you can.

Karl finished his losing game of H-O-R-S-E with Xìnyùn and put the parrot back into his cage, draping the cover over the bird. He wiped down the counters and headed off to his bathroom to brush his teeth. When he climbed into bed the sheets were cold and smelled of whatever flowers his dryer sheets were scented with. Not of jasmine, as they did after Vivian was here. Instead of the heady fragrance only his wife had, it was the generic smell of millions of sheets in millions of homes across the United States. If he wasn't capable of giving Vivian what she needed, this was how his sheets would smell for the rest of his life.

His hand hesitated over the lamp switch, knowing he should turn it off and also knowing he wouldn't sleep tonight, light or no light. And so he lay in his bed, blinking to calm the bright light of the lamp in his eyes. On another not-so-distant night that felt like eons ago, he'd jokingly handed Vivian books to help her sleep. Karl rolled over onto his side and faced the spine of the Melville book, still unfinished. He picked it up, opened to his bookmark and began "Billy Budd" where he had left off.

It was a gift placed in the palm of an outreached hand upon which the fingers did not close.

Melville's language, even so cluttered and impenetrable to a modern reader, could not hide the great wrong the British Navy was about to commit upon the person of Billy Budd. Though he was innocent of murder in the barest sense of the word, Billy Budd was guilty as a point of fact, and so he was about to hang.

And since he felt that innocence was even a better thing than religion wherewith to go to Judgment, he reluctantly withdrew.

Karl had read "Billy Budd" in law school, when the chaplain's opinions of the condemned Budd hadn't felt so personal. At the time, he'd felt the story was cut-and-dried. Billy Budd had killed someone; there was no arguing that fact. The Articles of War said the punishment was death. Ergo, Billy Budd must hang. Age must have added some gray back into Karl's life because he finally saw the tragedy in Billy Budd's story.

He closed the book and bounced it off his chest as Vivian's words echoed through his head. *Do you still judge me for nearly cheating Middle Kingdom and getting fired?*

Shades of gray notwithstanding, the situations weren't the same. Billy Budd had been wrongly accused of mutiny and, when too overcome by his stuttering to defend himself, had pushed his accuser, who hit his head and died. Vivian had nearly cheated her employer out of money to help her wastrel father. Billy Budd had been sentenced to hang. Vivian had been fired.

Not the same at all.

And yet—both were innocent of the crimes they were being accused of. Billy Budd had not been guilty of mutinous assembly, and the death of his accuser was debatable as murder. Vivian hadn't actually cheated. She'd thought about it, but the law didn't judge a person's thoughts to determine guilt or innocence. Actions were key, and Vivian's biggest problem had been the inconclusive video evidence.

They had both been punished according to the

rules of their employers. In both cases the justice was "by the book." And in both cases the justice felt like a waste.

When Karl bounced the book this time, his hands slipped and the paperback bobbed off his chin. Clearly it was time for sleep and not confused thinking about a Victorian writer—or Karl's wife.

He put the book back on his nightstand and turned off his lamp before he could change his mind. Karl flipped over onto his other side so that he faced away from the book. The other half of the bed was empty, unfortunately, and when he stuck his legs out the sheets were cold. Despite the shock of it keeping him awake, he left his legs there.

He wanted to sleep. He needed to sleep. But he'd had an epiphany he still wasn't sure what to do with.

CHAPTER TWENTY-EIGHT

SUSAN HAD ENGINEERED this week's family dinner so that Karl would be an hour early. Plenty of time, she had said, for Vivian to discuss her plan to buy out Healthy Food. Vivian had gone to the library during her time off and researched restaurant business plans. She and Susan had estimated the present value of Healthy Food and estimated its value in ten years, when Susan planned to retire. Together they had worked out different buyout plans, along with some classes that would benefit Vivian and a list of things she would need to learn from Susan at Healthy Food. Fortunately, neither of those was how to cook; Susan hadn't cooked in the kitchen in years. Vivian was a good cook, but she didn't think she was up to the burden of cooking in a professional kitchen.

When Karl swept into the house through the kitchen door, Vivian was waiting for him with coffee and a variety of *kolaczki*. He stilled, looking uncharacteristically uncertain hovering in the doorway for a moment before greeting Vivian with an obligatory kiss on the cheek and sitting down at the table.

They'd shared intimate touches and little kisses as though they were really husband and wife, each touch feeling both natural and fake. More Karl fulfilling his duties to his wife, Vivian supposed, rather than because he wanted to. She *wanted* them to be fully real. She wanted their marriage to be fully real.

"Am I the first one here?"

"Your sisters won't be here for another hour." She pushed a folder over to him. "I have something to discuss with you."

God, this felt like a business meeting rather than a discussion between husband and wife about their future. How much of that was her fault? Karl wanted her back in his apartment, living as his wife. She just wasn't willing to agree to his terms. And what an ugly word that was—*terms.* As if their very relationship had to be negotiated. You say "I love you" and I'll give up on my request that you stop judging me for my past.

Only it seemed the cost of being husband and wife was too dear for each of them. Each had to give up some essence of who they were. Or, in Vivian's case, who she had learned she could be.

The folder made no sound as Karl slid it toward himself. "I thought we were waiting to discuss the divorce until you had a job that could support you. And health insurance."

He didn't open the folder. Just rested his hand on it, like he was holding down a dragon.

"This isn't about the divorce." Of course he would assume it was about the divorce. She'd be mad, but she'd told him straight-out that she wasn't interested in a real marriage until he could honestly say he wasn't judging her past and that he loved her. Since he hadn't stopped actively disapproving of her, divorce would be the next logical step in their relationship.

Vivian was through making logical decisions. She wanted a relationship with Karl built on something other than sex and the child she was carrying. "I want to buy Healthy Food," she said. He raised his brow at her, as well he should, given that she had no money to speak of. "In about ten years, when Susan retires," she clarified.

He didn't say anything, but bent over the folder, opened it and read every word on every page. Halfway through, he reached for his coffee cup and a *kolaczki*. Vivian tried not to fidget. She and Susan had worked out many scenarios for her takeover of Healthy Food. Some of them included help from Karl. Most of them didn't. Still, even if she didn't need his financial help, she wanted his support. Married or not, living together or not, Healthy Food was part of his heritage. She wanted to believe he would support her in this. That maybe he trusted her—just a little more than he said he did.

Finally, when he closed the folder, he said, "My mom has an insurance settlement she's never touched. You don't have to buy her out. She could give Healthy Food to you."

"There are tax implications involved in a gift of that size." Despite Vivian's protestations, Susan had investigated the possibility of gifting Healthy Food. Susan had been willing to jump through the hoops needed to make it happen. Vivian wasn't.

Karl sipped his coffee. Then he took another cookie. He had a preference for the strawberry ones.

"I don't want to be given this," Vivian insisted. "I want to earn it. I want to work for it."

"Some of these scenarios involve substantial amounts of help from me." He retreated deeper into the cold, businesslike Karl she remembered from the first night in his apartment. The one who approached every decision as though it was a problem to be solved. Once again, she was a problem.

She took a cookie. "I'm not foolish enough to believe I can do this on my own. Just that I want to work for it. And help is different than a gift." He'd said similar words after the first disastrous meeting with his family—that a helping hand was different than a rescue. She finally understood what he'd meant.

"I have an insurance settlement that could buy Healthy Food."

She bit into her cookie and chewed, hoping the action would sooth her irritations. She could love his stony face, but being offered money when she'd just said she wanted to earn something was worse than being a surprise problem in his apartment. This was more like waking up in a hotel room finding out she'd drunkenly married a stranger. She wasn't just a problem to be solved; she was a problem to throw money at.

"I don't want a gift from you or your mother."

"We're married, so it wouldn't be a gift. We would be buying my mother out together."

She loved this man. Of that fact, Vivian had no doubt. She loved his steadfastness, his devotion to his family and his sense of duty. What she didn't love was when he was all of those things without the warmth of emotion to soften them. She spent the time chewing her second bite of cookie remembering that she had benefited from his problem solving and so could have patience with the stony face.

"This isn't about our relationship. This is about me and a future for Healthy Food."

"How are those not things about our relationship?" His voice had the cold edge of anger, which she hadn't expected. "We're married. I want us to stay married, and not just for the sake of the baby.

I want you living in my apartment, sleeping in my bed. How is that not about you?"

"You know my terms on that." There was that ugly word again.

Karl picked the folder up and shook it at her. "Is our relationship as quantifiable as this?"

Vivian opened her mouth to argue, but she was the one who'd used the word *terms* to begin with. "I don't want to move in with you as part of a plan for Healthy Food. I don't want our relationship to be based on practicality."

"What part of 'want' is unclear?"

All the parts of it that didn't sound like "I love you."

"And a relationship based on practicality didn't stop you from appearing in my apartment lobby asking for health insurance and a place to live." She watched his eyes as he said the words, but even in his anger they lacked fire. "Both of which I gave you with hardly any questions."

And there, right there, was the biggest reason why it was foolish for her to want to sleep in his bed and wake up next to him every morning. So long as he still thought about how she had been fired and how desperate she'd been every time he saw her, she would be less of a person in his eyes. Any desire to sleep with her didn't change the fact that he couldn't truly love her so long as he thought so little of her.

"I was a different person then, and willing to settle." She nodded toward the folder. "But now I know that I want the husband, the child, the career, the family. Maybe it's not possible, but I'm not going to settle for less."

Karl tapped his fingers on the folder, and for the first time in their relationship he was speechless. Not silent—he was often silent—but completely lacking in speech. He opened his mouth to say something, then shut it. Completely stunned and gaping like a fish. What had she said that she hadn't said a million times before, in each of their previous arguments? If their conversations about her moving back in were a broken record, the player was broken now, too.

Vivian stood and gathered the coffee cups and cookies. "Your sisters will be here soon. Keep the folder. You can let me know what you think about the idea later. When you're no longer confusing it with how you feel about me."

CHAPTER TWENTY-NINE

A STRANGE CAR with New Jersey plates was parked in Karl's mother's driveway when he got to Archer Heights after leaving work early on Friday.

"Vivian," he called into the house as he walked to the kitchen. She didn't answer, but the sound of an argument in the living room was easy enough for him to follow.

"I don't have any money to give you, Dad." Vivian sounded plaintive, and Karl didn't know who she was trying to convince—herself or her father.

He stood in the doorway between the living room and kitchen, eavesdropping but not hiding his presence.

"Come on, girl. Just because I've been gone, doesn't mean I haven't been keeping tabs on you. You landed on your feet, just like I said you would." Karl waited for the man to acknowledge that he had been the one to pull the rug out from under his daughter, but he never did.

"I'm working as a cashier in a Polish buffet and living on the largesse of the owner. How is that landing on my feet? I used to have my own apartment, a savings account and a job I worked to get—rather than one given to me out of pity." Interesting how she was hiding the changed nature of her job and relationship with his mother. How hard was it to say no to this man?

"You're married to an influential man and that belly of yours is unavoidable. The baby's got to be worth some gas money." Yap's tone gave no indication he considered his words to be offensive. The man must have no shame.

Karl could tell Vivian was crying silently by the way her head was bowed, her hair cascading around her shoulders, but her voice only cracked twice when she responded, "You told me I was just like my mother when you said I would land on my feet, but you keep thinking I'm like you. My pregnancy isn't a scheme. It's a child."

Yap scoffed. "Come on, Vivy, next you're going to tell me you married for love."

Was it stupid of him to hope her answer was yes? Even when he knew it wasn't and that admitting to such a powerful emotion in front of Yap would give his scheming mind something to grasp on to. Once this man got his fingers into something, Karl didn't think he'd ever let go.

"I got married because we were both drunk and it was Las Vegas. I stayed married because you got me fired and I needed health insurance. For the baby."

"Has all the makings of a great scheme." Now Yap sounded excited. This was the man who'd raised Vivian? How had she come out of it with *any* scrap of honesty? As far as Karl understood, if she hadn't balked at cheating, she wouldn't have gotten caught, and neither would she have gotten fired.

"Do you think I wanted to be here?" Did she use the past tense on purpose, and did that now mean she did want to be here? God, love turned people into doubting fools as surely as it gave them rose-colored glasses. "Dependent on Karl or his family for everything? Your last scheme got me fired and I didn't even do anything. You stole my life savings—"

"I'll get them back!" Vivian's father said the words with such forcefulness that Karl was certain the man believed them. Karl didn't know if he was relieved Yap was fooling himself and thus thought he was being honest, or disgusted that the man was so misguided about his own intentions. "I'm not the kind of father who would take his baby's money forever. I've always looked out for you."

"You raised me the only way you knew." Vivian looked up at her father, the silent tears streaming down her face, too intent on her conversation to notice Karl standing in the doorway. Her father was going to keep pushing her, wringing her for every penny until he broke her in half. "But you're promising to return my money in one breath and asking me for more in another. I can't do it anymore, Dad."

"Remember that time in Winnemucca when..."

"Stop." She was holding her hands out in front of her, both a physical sign to stop and a plea. "Reminding me of good times worked the last time, when you were the only family tie I had. But I have a baby's future to think about and—no matter how much I love you—the love and responsibility I have for my child comes first. Even if I had money to give you, I would keep it for the baby."

"I'll go ask your husband for it." And Karl would tell the man to get lost without even blinking. Except...

"Please, Dad. If you love me at all, just drive away and don't come back. Ever."

Vivian's love for her father and the struggle it caused her was written in every tear on her face. Karl could see her physically wrestling with herself as she said those words. He knew enough people that he could make her father go away and never come back, but that would be the easy solution. And it probably wouldn't be the right solution.

"You're asking me to never see you again and never know my grandchild." As much as Vivian's father was here to ask for money, Karl could hear the sadness in his voice at these words. The man loved his daughter and had raised her the only way he had known how, as damning as those ways were.

"I'm not like you," she pleaded. "I don't think moving in the middle of the night is exciting. I could have a permanent home here. I'm asking you not to destroy that for me."

There was silence, and Karl could almost hear the thinking coming out of the salt-and-pepper-haired man sitting on the couch. Finally his father-in-law said, "How much..."

Karl coughed to make his presence known before the man could ruin his relationship with his daughter forever by putting a price on their relationship. "I'll give you fifty thousand dollars, cash, to never ask your daughter for money again."

Father and daughter turned to face him, looks of surprise on both their faces, though Yap's was touched with unabashed greed. Karl would have turned the man out of his house without blinking, but he had to blink twice at seeing how similar father and daughter looked, from their golden skin tones to their pointed chins and rounded cheeks. Was the father disappointed to have the apple seemingly fall so close to the tree yet be of a completely different nature?

"Conditions?" the man asked.

"Dad! You can't take his money." She whirled her head from her father to Karl. "Karl, you can't offer it to him. I told him no." Her voice was sure for the first time since he'd walked in on the conversation.

"As long as he knows you have access to my

money—or any money—he'll keep asking." Karl was surprised at how calm he was.

"I'll tell him no again. I've told him no before." She stood and crossed the room to face him.

Karl put his hands on her shoulders in reassurance. "And he's returned to ask again. And he'll keep returning until you're so sick of it that you put off seeing him and our child will never get to know his or her grandparent." Karl didn't like Yap, would prefer to keep Yap on the other side of the country, but the man was his wife's father, and Karl understood the value of family. And he was beginning to understand how Vivian could love a family member she didn't approve of and maybe didn't even like.

"Then you'll start ignoring his phone calls," he continued. "Maybe he'll show up at our door again, maybe he won't. But your dad's greedy schemes will kill your relationship and it matters because we have a child to think of. A child who deserves to know his or her family."

"I get the money and you won't try to stop me from seeing my daughter or my grandchild." The greed in Yap's eyes was no longer hidden, but the man was looking at his daughter with love. Karl wondered if the man was self-aware enough to ever struggle with his greed and his love for his daughter, or if whatever emotion was strongest at the time was the one that came out.

"I won't try to stop you," Karl said over Vivian's shoulder and her objections. "But if I hear you've asked Vivian for money—or any of our children when they're older—I will send the hounds of hell after you. Your schemes haven't caught up with you yet, but I will make sure they do if you don't agree to these terms. If you need money, you will ask me and *I* will decide if you can have it, not Vivian."

"Can I talk with you in the kitchen?" his wife snapped, looking pissed at what he thought was a very fair offer.

Karl looked from his mother's television and stereo system to his father-in-law, who shrugged. "I admit to being a cheat and a liar, but I'm not a thief. Well," he amended, "I *borrowed* money from Vivy. I'm going to return it, though." At least one person in the world believed Vivian would get her money back.

Still, Yap's bald honesty about his faults raised Karl's brows. Vivian had said her father was well aware of his shortcomings, just not how they affected other people, so he trusted all his mother's stuff would be in the same place they left it.

VIVIAN WAS WAITING for Karl in the kitchen, her arms folded under her chest and resting over the bump of her pregnant belly. "Why would you make an offer like that? Do you think I can't handle my own father?" She stopped herself from wagging a finger at him and becoming an actual barefoot, pregnant, nagging fishwife.

"You're misinterpreting my offer," he responded, with all the calm in the world. "I think you are capable of telling him no until the cows come home. And every time you tell him no, he'll remind you of some good time you had growing up until he's poisoned all those memories for you. Let me help you preserve those memories."

Her hands fell to her sides as she thought about what he was offering her. She had wanted everything the world could give her, not thinking the world would or could let her keep her father *and* Karl *and* her child in her life together. Karl was offering more than she had thought possible. "And you would trust him with our child?"

"No. I barely trust him not to steal the crucifix off my mom's wall, but I trust you with our child. You say your father won't hurt our children?"

Vivian didn't miss that it was the second time Karl had referred to children, plural. "No. Other than the lying and the cheating and the constant moving, he was a good dad." She realized it was a bit like saying that, other than the burning, hell was like a warm beach. "He was the best dad he knew how to be and he protected me from harm—always."

She had to believe that her father never would've gotten her mixed up with Frank and the cheating scheme if he'd thought she might get hurt. And he did believe he'd pay her back the money he'd taken. *She* didn't believe it, but he did. Plus, she would be there to provide a buffer for her children, a role no one had been able to fill for her.

"Then I'll let you judge how often he can see our children. If he won't harm them, they deserve to know both sides of their family."

"He won't harm them." She knew that as surely as she knew the sight of her own face in the mirror. "I love your mother, but my dad will be the most fun grandparent our child—children—could ever know."

Karl put his hands on her shoulders again. This time Vivian didn't think he was doing it to reassure her, but to reassure himself. "I'm going to make him sign a contract, and I wasn't kidding when I said I'd hold him to it."

Vivian grabbed his wrists. Karl closed his eyes for a moment, and she waited until he opened them again before responding, "He believes you." She squeezed his wrists, both in reassurance and emphasis. Her father had made it this far in life without landing in jail by recognizing the people who could put him there—and staying far, far away from them.

"Good. I'll give him the money as he leaves town. I don't want my father-in-law in Chicago with that kind of cash." Karl's face hardened, a sign he was struggling with conflicting emotions. She'd been around him long enough to recognize the signs. "I have a reputation to uphold."

"Why did you make the offer?"

"I want you to come home with me."

"And that is worth fifty thousand dollars?"

"I was willing to give you more so you could buy Healthy Food." His hazel eyes warmed, even if his face was still a solid block of stone. "I just agreed to give money to a man I'm pretty certain is a felon. And I agreed to keep giving him money while letting him have contact with my child. It should be obvious why I did that."

"Tell me anyway." She took a deep breath to get her heart beating again, but the stubborn organ remained still in hope and fear.

Karl pulled his hands off her shoulders and placed them on her cheeks. For the first time she could remember since she had known him, his hands were warm. "I love you, Vivian."

Vivian opened her mouth to ask about his judgment of her near felony, then stopped. Loving her and her past were so intimately tied together for him that he couldn't say those words and still care that she'd nearly broken the law. To press him would be cruel and along the lines of crowing over a victory she didn't feel.

"It's my responsibility to keep our little family together, but that responsibility isn't a burden. It's a pleasure. It's a pleasure that I'll look forward to every day for the rest of my life." When he bent his head to kiss her, her heart started beating again, the blood it released warming her from head to toe.

Their kiss was short, but had the intimacy of two people who had finally tossed away all pretenses and were ready to open their hearts to each other. When Karl pulled away, Vivian reached up to put her hands on his cheeks. It was her turn to reassure him.

"It's my responsibility, too. There are two of us in this marriage." They were partners. No matter how unequally she'd come into it, their relationship would only work if they each carried an equal burden.

Karl smiled. "I love how you'll never let one of us take all the responsibility or credit for what's good or bad in our relationship. And I love your dedication to family, even if your family is sometimes your father. It's also me, my mother, my sisters and our child and you won't let us go, like I won't let you go."

"I love you, too."

Karl opened his arms and Vivian stepped into them. His embrace was warm and strong around her. He supported her, but neither held her up nor held her back. With her head resting against the cool cotton of his shirt and the smell of starch filling her nose, she wished every woman could be so lucky.

"Let's take your father out for dinner at Healthy Food. We can stuff him so full of pork, potatoes and cabbage that he won't be able to do anything other than sleep. Tomorrow we can follow him until he gets to the Iowa border, give him a grocery sack full of cash and you can get on with the rest of your life."

"With you. The rest of my life with you."

"I wouldn't have it any other way."

EPILOGUE

HEALTHY FOOD'S NEON Open sign was off, which didn't stop anyone from coming inside. Karl had given up making sure the people entering the restaurant were actually guests of the baby shower. With all the blue, pink and yellow streamers, the baby elephant decorations and the massive diaper-shaped cake on the counter blocking the register, most people who walked through the doorway sorted themselves. If the person walked in and didn't belong, they looked embarrassed and left. If they walked in and heard their name hollered in greeting by someone they knew, they stayed.

Karl was pretty sure the two college kids flirting with Phil's young and pretty cousin had walked in, run to the store for a baby shower present and returned without knowing another soul at the party. But the festivities had turned into a mix of block party, baby shower and wedding reception so Karl hadn't tried to kick them out. Plus, Phil's cousin looked as if she was enjoying the attention.

"You should go keep Vivian company," his mom said from behind him.

He didn't turn around to face her. "I'm enjoying watching her."

"You picked a good one," his mother said with a pat on his back. "I'm glad you didn't listen to me and my objections."

"My objections were the more troubling ones. I'm glad I didn't listen to those, either."

His mom chuckled, then hurried off to get something from the kitchen. More food, probably. The partygoers had healthy appetites and Karl hoped all that food didn't make them sick when the dancing started.

He turned his attention back to his wife, who was far too pregnant to do much more than waddle around from guest to guest. There was no way she was going to be able to dance after the polka band got set up—but she was enjoying herself. Her eyes were bright with joy and her face was gleaming with sweat because the air conditioning wasn't powerful enough for the crowds of people, but Karl still thought she looked perfect. Especially the small, contented smile she got on her face any time her eyes caught sight of the out-of-town guests.

Most baby shower/wedding receptions probably didn't happen when the woman was eight months pregnant, but it had been the only time Vivian's aunt Kitty, her two cousins and her friends from Vegas had all been able to attend. Karl hadn't intended to schedule the party around a time when her father could come, but apparently fate had wanted to make sure he remembered his promise to Vivian not to exclude her father from their lives.

Victor Yap's presence had delighted someone other than Vivian. Malcolm had abandoned his wife to the company of the Biadałas and was following Victor around the restaurant, practically sniffing after the man like a bloodhound on a trail. Whatever Malcolm was hoping to catch Victor in, Karl just hoped it didn't happen at the party. And he was thankful Malcolm was on grifter babysitting duty so he didn't have to be.

The concertina bellowed from the front of the room, scattering some unsuspecting partygoers and freeing up a path to the buffet for the people who hadn't yet eaten their fill. The concertina player was soon joined in the warm-up by two trumpets. When the clarinet and bass players started in, Tilly, Dan, Renia and Miles began to push aside tables and chairs for a dance floor. Karl looked back over at Phil's cousin and her two suitors. If they weren't game for polka, they'd soon find themselves short a date. Phil's cousin had been a popular dance partner at Phil's wedding, and the crowd at this party wasn't much different.

As Vivian's court of admirers started to forsake her for the dance floor, Karl left his observatory for his wife's side.

"Having fun?" he asked.

"Oh, this is delightful." Her cheeks were flushed a bright red as she looked up at him. "I wish I could dance, but my bowling ball of a belly would probably knock down all the guests."

He sat next to her, wrapping his arm around her when she leaned into him and feeling the warmth of her back against his chest as he continued his surveillance of the party. Miles and Renia were whirling about the dance floor, his sister with a small but delighted smile on her face. Tilly and Dan were feeding each other pierogies and laughing, his mother looking at his baby sister as if she'd researched marriage potions online and had spiked their food.

For the first time since he could remember, he wasn't thinking that the moment would be perfect if only Leon, his grandparents and his father were here; they were present in the smiles and laughter of his family members.

He gave Vivian a squeeze. "I'm sure we can think of an excuse to do this again."

"With my aunt and cousins? And father and Vegas friends?"

"We'll throw a baptismal party the likes of which Chicago has never seen." Vivian laughed. Karl kissed the crown of her head where she'd tucked it back against him. "You think I'm joking, but I'm serious. I'll be even more serious if I can come up with a time to have the party when your father won't be able to attend."

"This," Vivian said with a gesture to her father and then to her aunt, "is how I know you love me."

Karl looked from Victor on one side of the room to Kitty on the other. As happy as Vivian had been to have all her family here for her baby shower, they were not happy to see each other and were acting like magnets in opposition. Push one too close and the other jumped away. They hadn't yet exchanged even a single word. When it became obvious that Victor and Kitty were avoiding each other, Vivian had shrugged and declared it not her problem. "They can either behave like adults or go home. I'm too pregnant to care," she'd said.

"Wait, what do you mean *this* is how you know I love you? I gave your father fifty thousand dollars. You didn't know I loved you then?"

"*That* was for you." She turned her head to look up at him, her words barely projecting above the polka playing at the front of the restaurant. "You were throwing money at my father to make him go away. Honest people do that to him all the time—it's how he eats. What's more impressive is that you invited him back. And you did *that* for me."

* * * * *